HIGH TA[

JOANNA MAXWELL CANN[... daughter of] Charles Cannan, Dean o[...] Wedderburn, was born at [...] Oxford in 1896, and educated at Miss Batty's School for Don's daughters. Following a period at finishing school in Paris, she returned to England and, in 1918, married Harold James Pullein-Thompson, an infantry captain.

Her first novel, *The Misty Valley*, was published in 1922 and immediately established her as a popular writer. Other novels followed, including *The Simple Pass On* (1929), *High Table* (1931), and *Ithuriel's Hour* (1931), and though she later tried her hand at detective novels and pony books (she might be said to have invented the genre of pony books), her most accomplished fiction continued to provide a remarkable commentary on the social nuances, customs, and changes over half a century of English life.

After the Second World War her health deteriorated, and, in 1961, three weeks after finishing her thirty-eighth book, she died.

ANTHONY QUINTON was born in 1925 and educated at Stowe School and Christ Church, Oxford.

During the war he served in the RAF as a flying officer and navigator and in 1949 began his academic career by becoming a Fellow of All Souls, Oxford. Thereafter he was a Fellow of New College from 1955 to 1978, a Delegate of OUP from 1970 to 1976, and a member of the Arts Council from 1979 to 1981. Since 1985 he has been Chairman of the Board of the British Library.

His publications include *Political Philosophy* (1967), *The Nature of Things* (1973), *Utilitarian Ethics* (1973), *The Politics of Imperfection* (1978), *Francis Bacon* (1980), and *Thoughts and Thinkers* (1982).

In 1982 he became a life peer, and is at present President of Trinity College, Oxford, a post that he has occupied since 1978.

JOANNA CANNAN

High Table

<<<◇>>>

INTRODUCED BY
ANTHONY QUINTON

OXFORD UNIVERSITY PRESS
1987

Oxford University Press, Walton Street, Oxford OX2 6DP

Oxford New York Toronto
Delhi Bombay Calcutta Madras Karachi
Petaling Jaya Singapore Hong Kong Tokyo
Nairobi Dar es Salaam Cape Town
Melbourne Auckland

and associated companies in
Beirut Berlin Ibadan Nicosia

Oxford is a trade mark of Oxford University Press

First published by Ernest Benn 1931
First issued, with Anthony Quinton's Introduction,
as an Oxford University Press paperback 1987

British Library Cataloguing in Publication Data
Cannan, Joanna
High table.—(Twentieth-century classics)
I. Title II. Series
823'.912[F]   PR6005.A483
ISBN 0–19–282030–3

Printed in Great Britain by
The Guernsey Press Co. Ltd.
Guernsey, Channel Islands

INTRODUCTION

BY ANTHONY QUINTON

JOANNA CANNAN's *High Table* is an Oxford novel written by someone with the best qualifications possible without actually having studied or taught there. (In this respect she is even better equipped than Mrs Humphry Ward who first came to the place a few years before her marriage to a young don at Brasenose College in 1872, remaining until 1891 when her husband took a job at *The Times* and they moved to London). Joanna Cannan was the daughter of Charles Cannan, who had been Fellow and Dean of Trinity for twelve years at the time of her birth, on 27 May 1896. She went to school in Oxford, at 'Miss Batty's school for dons' daughters', and remained there, apart from a period of being 'finished' in Paris just before the Great War, until marriage in 1918 took her away, first, to Wimbledon and, later, to a farmhouse in the Chilterns. Her twenty-two years are more numerous than Mrs Humphry Ward's fourteen, and they filled a more impressionable part of her life. But it must be admitted that *Robert Elsmere* is a more substantial and considerable production than *High Table*. Gladstone, after all, reviewed it at some length, as did Walter Pater.

In a way Joanna Cannan was a product of the extensive mid-nineteenth-century reforms of Oxford which converted it from the ineffective and, on the whole, discreditably self-indulgent association of close college societies it had been in the eighteenth century into the increasingly earnest and respectable educational institution it has been ever since. Before the reforms few fellowships were awarded on merit; few fellows did any teaching; undergraduates were under no pressure to study; examinations were empty forms. The large buildings of the colleges were scantily occupied; the large incomes of the colleges were largely spent on providing incomes to largely non-resident fellows that were just sufficient to enable them to live without working.

The unwholesomely exciting nature of sex and religion have led historians of university reform to concentrate on the abolition of the rule of celibacy and of religious tests. Of equal importance is the fact that the reforms transformed university teaching into a profession, as admirably explained in A. J. Engel's *From Clergyman to Don*. Charles Cannan, with his wife and three daughters, his home at Magdalen Gate House and his active role as teacher and administrator, before he went off in 1898, when Joanna was two, to become the chief executive of the University Press, perfectly exemplified the transformation. It is characteristic that the Oxford Classical Texts, whose publication by the University Press he arranged, are, first and foremost, for purposes of instruction, despite the fact that they were also intended to embody the best and most up-to-date scholarship. It is worth mentioning, in view of the main interests of the central character of *High Table*, that Cannan's lectures on logic were original and uncoventional and that, when pressure of work ruled out all other reading, he would regularly settle down with Aristotle. His favourite vacation pursuit was mountaineering in Switzerland, in common with many of the more energetic academic spirits of his epoch. It was an interest Joanna shared with him.

High Table is comparatively unusual as an Oxford novel in seeing the place from the don's point of view. *Loss and Gain, Verdant Green, Tom Brown at Oxford, Zuleika Dobson, Sinister Street, Patchwork, Brideshead Revisited, Sixth Heaven,* the relevant bits of *Decline and Fall* and *A Question of Upbringing* all observe the place through the eyes of undergraduates, in whose field of vis-

ion dons are very much at the periphery: obscurely moti-
vated, slightly menacing figures in gowns. For most
novelists who have written about it, Oxford is part of the
essentially transitory background of a *bildungsroman,*
against which the formation of a youthful character can
take place, as it prepares itself for life in the real world
beyond. Even Robert Elsmere, in the novel named after
him, soon leaves the Oxonian world of Mr. Grey (in fact
T. H. Green, the leading new idealist philosopher) for
self-sacrificing work among the most miserable of the
poor.

The one kind of Oxford novel in which dons occupy the
centre of attention is the detective story: Masterman's
Oxford Tragedy, for example, Michael Innes's *Death at
the President's Lodging* (and many of his other books) and
pretty well the complete works of Edmund Crispin.
Oddly, Oxford has made no great mark in ghost stories,
unlike Cambridge with the tradition gloriously initiated
by M. R. James, apart from the sublime exception of J.
Meade Falkner's *Lost Stradivarius*.

But *High Table* is not really about the life of the new
professional, tutorial academics of Oxford. Only one of
those sitting at the article of college furniture in question
is closely examined: Theodore Fletcher, Scholar, Fellow
and eventually Warden of St. Mary's College. And the
book is more an investigation of his character than his circumstances. It is the peculiarities of that character that
make it seem natural for him to conceal himself from life,
love, action, emotion and risk behind the defensive
medieval fortifications of an Oxford college.

He is the solitary, oppressed product of a loveless marriage between a grim rural clergyman and his equally grim
wife. The fact that no critical point about Oxford as such
is implied by the book is emphasised by its action coming
to an end in 1919, while it was published in 1931. Much of
the book is concerned with the years between Theodore's

birth in the mid-1860s and his election to a Fellowship in 1886. The narrative then leaps to 1913 and the man-oeuvres by which he is used by the enemies of a particular candidate for the wardenship as the one Fellow sufficiently tame and inoffensive to keep him out.

In his early life the melancholy catalogue of Theodore's distinguishing weaknesses, the intrinsic nature he will never overcome, are set out. He is clumsy, paralysingly self-conscious, a coward. His more extroverted compan-ions at the squire's house are fully aware of all this. 'Some-times he heard them talking about him—discussing his clothes, or how thin his legs were, or why he bit his nails, or if he washed, or what made his hands so moist . . .' It is no surprise that such a person, to purify himself after his life's one great adventure, should lather himself in the bath with a frayed bath-glove.

One so ill-equipped for ordinary life inevitably falls back on books.

All round the room in the shelves stood the books, waiting for you, he thought, not criticising you, you needn't wonder or worry over what they were thinking, they didn't care if you lost races or cheated at games, they didn't whisper that you were short for your age or snigger at your spectacles.

The bleak condition in which he is placed is made clear by the particular books from which he derives solace: *Elementary Sketches of Moral Philosophy*, by the late Rev. Sydney Smith M.A.; *The Odyssey of Homer* trans-lated by Alexander Pope; *St Paul's Epistles to the Thes-salonians, Galatians and Romans* by Benjamin Jowett, and, as a king of apex of voluptuous self-indulgence, *The Rise of the Dutch Republic, A History* by John Lothrop Motley.

Joanna Cannan is not suggesting that all dons suffer from the kind of tormented introversion that afflicts Theodore. In the first place, of course, they have to be reasonably clever as well. 'He was extraordinarily clever, appearing more brilliant then that at any other phase of his career, for his accuracy, copper-plate memory and lack of intellectual imagination were admirably suited to the precise demands of school work'.

The man he is used to keep out is of a very different stamp, with 'his Rabelaisian humour, roars of laughter, six red-haired daughters, European reputation, mort- gaged home in Bagley Wood', the author of a novel 'one entire chapter of which was devoted to a description of a steeplechase'. The other candidate thought unlikely to avert the danger of this comparatively colourful figure is certainly on the dry side. But he is not a muff like Theo- dore. 'he was of a practical nature . . . But what many of the fellows feared in him was his passion for power; he'd sit on any committee—Hospital Committees, Political Committees, Bazaar and Fete Committees on which he was the only man—he'd champion any cause—Morris Dancing, Woman's Suffrage, the trace horse at the foot of Headington Hill—simply for the pleasure it gave him to control and direct.' Plainly he was no shrinking violet.

Although Theodore is almost exactly contemporane- ous with Joanna Cannan's father—they were born and became college fellows within a year or two of each other and Theodore's story ends in the year of Charles's death: 1919—they could hardly be more unlike. Charles was efficient, business-like, an accomplished mountaineer, the father of three girls. All he does is provide a few useful props for the dramatic presentation of his daughter's invention.

The intrigue which leads to Theodore's elevation is detailed and well-informed but its main service to the plot is to provide Theodore with another humiliation when he learns from the committee-addict just why he was chosen. Indeed his reaction to this comparatively harmless discov- ery is almost morbidly excessive. After all, he did get the job, and will continue to enjoy it long after the manner of his acquiring it has been forgotten, and the witness on whom he is relying is too personally involved to compel unswerving belief.

The same deficiences of character that destine Theodore to a particularly furtive style of academic life also impel him to a unique erotic transgression while on vacation as an undergraduate. The lending of such books as Bacon's *Essays* and the *Travels* of Marco Polo to a fairly plain, but nevertheless intellectually aspiring, young woman of lower social station lead, as such activities usually did in the fiction of the pre-modern age, to uncontrollable fumblings in the dark, inarticulate cries and sobbings and, after a few weeks, to terrifying news.

The girl departs, with a convenient yokel, to a Peggotty-like mode of life far away. Years later, in the middle of the First World War her agreeable son, who has been doing quite well in the drapery business, arrives at St. Mary's for a few months as part of the process of being commissioned. Theodore finds out who he is and becomes involved both with him and with the family of the auctioneer in Staverton Road who befriends the young man and one of whose daughters he marries. The developments of the plot from this point onwards are not too difficult to predict. But the account of the Logans, even if a little excrutiatingly class-conscious for the socially prudish, is perceptive and detailed in the way that Elizabeth Bowen's is of the Heccomb family in *The Death of Heart*, but less remorselessly condescending. Songs and foods and customs are vividly recorded over the fifteen year interval from 1916 to 1931.

High Table is only just an Oxford novel, in the non-geographical sense of that phrase. It is a retrospective romance about one of the sudden marriages of wartime attached to the study of an inadequate man, who does not do too badly in making a late effort to overcome his inadequacy. Joanna Cannan's own early experience supplied her with concrete materials of an academic, Oxonian sort to give specific realisation to the idea she had in mind. She was, as I said at the beginning, herself a product of mid-nineteenth-century academic reforms, to the extent that she could not have come into existence if they had not taken place. She is interestingly unaware of the recency with which the high tables of the Oxford she grew up in had come to be dominated by men who were university teachers by profession, family men, looking forward to some kind of pension. The time had not long gone by in which tuition was given by young clergy anxiously waiting for a college living to become available, allowing them to leave Oxford and marry.

Joanna Cannan makes her Theodore some kind of philosopher. His main, perhaps sole, publication is his *Short History of Logic*, published by the University Press in 1892. The early part of Theodore's career coincides with one of those intermittent periods of vitality which break out in the history of Oxford philosophy. There was one in the fourteenth century, made glorious by Duns Scotus and William of Ockham; another, smaller, but definitely perceptible one between 1945 and 1960. At the date of Theodore's birth the subject was in pretty low water. Its one distinguished exponent in the Oxford of the 1860s, Mansel, had gone to be Dean of St. Paul's. But in 1874 T. H. Green's introduction to the works of Hume inaugurated a period of great productiveness and excitement, as the members of his school followed his advice and rejected the authority of the reigning, metropolitan thinkers: Mill and Herbert Spencer. No echo of this excitement is to be heard in the pages of *High Table*. It persisted at least until the early years of the new century, to be followed by an ice age, kept arctic by the refrigerative minds of Cook, Wilson, Prichard and Joseph into the 1930s.

High Table is a retrospective novel, but it is not a historical novel. I do not believe that even his habitual nervousness in conversation would have led Theodore to say 'Archbishop Laud slept in my . . . er . . . bedroom in 1668', when that prelate had already been dead for twenty-three years at that date. And did dons drink brown sherry after dinner in 1916? Perhaps they did. Even to raise such questions is to confirm the judgement of Mrs Logan's elder daughter about dons: 'awful old kill-joys'.

HIGH TABLE

TO
CAROLA OMAN

CONTENTS

CHAPTER I

"I'VE DONE MY DUTY . . ."

IT is just a little tummy upset, says Dr. Harbutt, and
Mrs. Fletcher, meeting Lady Oliver outside the Post
Office and Miss Bird outside the General Stores,
described it as one of Theodore's tiresome little turns;
but in the afternoon she closed the pitch-pine shutters
of the dressing-room window across the view of the
bright, climbing pasture, and Theodore took off his
spectacles, laid down *Masterman Ready*, composed his
small body obediently among the crumbs from the
sponge fingers which he had eaten with his arrowroot,
and slept heavily until Kate brought in his tea.

Consequently, now night has come, he cannot sleep;
he has heard eight, nine, ten strokes quaver from the
church tower. The room in which he lies is unfamiliar to him—last night, when he first seemed
feverish, he was moved from his attic bedroom to his
father's dressing-room; not a chink of the light
which a full moon, travelling slowly towards Hampshire, diffuses over the Widdingfold pastures can
penetrate the well-fitting shutters: a basket chair,
invisible at the foot of his bed, gives forth suggestive
creaks. But he lies still; though he has heard his
mother come upstairs and hears her now, moving
about in the adjoining bedroom, shutting drawers,
pouring water, he does not call out that his mouth is
dry, that his eiderdown has fallen off or that his throat
feels funny, as Richard Oliver does twenty times in
an evening, says Kate, whose sister is nursery-maid

9

at the Hall. Theodore will not mount the grey pony which, once it's daylight, Sir Gilbert Oliver's heir gallops so blithely round the park, but he is not afraid of darkness, the unexplained creaking, nor what may lurk behind the doors of the huge oak wardrobe between the fireplace and the washhand-stand. He is not an imaginative child; and his creed is an enviable one; does not gentle Jesus, aureoled and efficient, watch over little boys who eat their crusts, say their prayers, learn their lessons and remember to feed their pets: and is not the Kingdom of Heaven of such as these? Richard forgets his rabbit; were it not for the under-gardener the poor dumb animal would have starved long before now: he slips his crusts into his pockets when Nurse isn't looking—he has shown Theodore exactly how—and after breakfast he throws them down the lavatory, and one day the pipe will get stopped up and there will be fever at the Hall: he will not say his prayers; he says, what's the good? He prayed for a ferret once and all he got was a box of crayons: he does not even try to remember what seven eights are; he says he doesn't care and that he knows an awful name which would just suit Miss Minns. It's no wonder, thinks Theodore, that Richard calls out when a curtain swings or a chair creaks in the handsome night-nursery at the Hall.

But Theodore is not thinking of Richard now. He hears the study door open and the bar on which the turkey red *portière* hangs give forth its peculiar groan: he hears his father call, " Lassie ! " and Lassie scrabble at the front door, and whine, and run out into the garden barking, run here and there, barking at the moon. Theodore is not fond of dogs; hot, animal, incalculable, they leap on him: he shrinks away: someone says, fancy being afraid of little doggies, such a great big boy ! But Lassie is different; she is ten years old, and stiff, and almost blind; except for this one wild rush into the garden for which she waits half the evening, not asleep, only dozing, in her basket under the pitch-pine staircase, she lies stretched out in the sunshine or by the fireside; she is obviously pitiful like sick children and the honest poor.

When Lassie has barked her way round the garden she comes in; there is no need for the Reverend Arnold Fletcher to raise his high, cultivated voice. Theodore hears her turn round and round in her basket, and he hears his father's footsteps coming up the stairs. He can picture his father, the grey hair, lofty brow, dry skin, thin lips and faded eyes that we should see, but not as we should see him, not an ageing clergy-man of middle height and poor physique whose brow, eye, lip proclaim the Pauline rather than the Christian, the theologian rather than the parish priest. He sees the supreme illusion of the necromantic generation which has begotten him; he sees a Father, immaculate, almighty, unquestionable. . . .

While Theodore is occupying the dressing-room, the Vicar of Widdingfold dresses himself in the spare bed-room across the landing, almost a desecration, it seems to Mrs. Fletcher, since the dear Bishop slept there and so enjoyed the view. When the spare-room door has closed, Theodore hears nothing but his own light breathing and an occasional bumping sound as his mother turns on her high brass bed. The picture of his father fades, for he has a clear conscience—once, when Miss Minns threatened to speak about his in-attention, his father's face was before his eyes all the night through. His young mind flits from one sub-ject to another—his stamp collection . . . the snails under the periwinkles on the rockery . . . his broken toe-nail which he must not pick—until he hears first the spare-room door and then his mother's door open

and shut; the swing of every door in the house and
the fall of every foot are quite different and distinguish-
able to the ear of the wakeful child. Then comes
another bump from the brass bedstead and the smell
of a blown-out candle reaches him; Father and Mother
are in bed; they will not lie awake as he is doing,
they will turn over on their sides and go to sleep as
he is always told to do. Docile Theodore turns his
head on the hot pillow and tightly shuts his large,
myopic eyes. He is thinking of his stamps again
—the Chinese one on the letter Father had from the
missionary is better than any Richard's got—when
a voice is raised in his mother's bedroom, a voice
which he thinks for a moment that he does not know.
He opens his eyes, turns his head and listens. The
voice is his mother's but strange to him, an uncontrolled torrent of words on a high, whining note, the
antithesis of her usually deliberate, firm and low-
toned utterance. To Theodore, as indeed to all her
neighbours, Margaret Fletcher, dark and sallow—
liverish, says Dr. Harbutt, and if he were consulted
would prescribe large quantities of calomel—has shown
a very quiet but very steadfast personality—a tower
of strength in the parish, says the Bishop: a damned
obstinate old she-devil, says rude Sir Gilbert at the
Hall. It has never occurred to Theodore to reflect
upon his own prompt obedience to her quietest word:
taught and tended by her, he has come and gone at
her bidding, small and subservient in the over-large
serge sailor suits which are her prudent choice. This
whining voice in the deep night can't be Mother's,
can't be the same voice that says, " Time to get up,
Theo," and, " Make haste with your porridge," and,
" Use your handkerchief," and, " What's that on the
side of your plate ? " and, " Bedtime, Theo," and,
" Remember your ears," and says it all so quietly as

to be almost inaudible, but only needs to say it once.
Theodore sits up in bed, leaning on his elbow, and he
hears a pause for breath and his father say, " Now,
Margaret, be charitable," and something about " our
only wealthy parishioners." Theodore has heard that
phrase before: he knows that his fortnight at the seaside depends on the mood in which Sir Gilbert Oliver
makes his Easter offering; but he doesn't understand
how the wealthy Olivers can need his mother's charity.
He puzzles over this while the voices in the next room
die down into some sort of agreement—" Very well,
since you wish it," says his mother, and mentions
duty; and of his father's answer he hears the one
word " sympathy." " It is impossible for me to
sympathise with such a woman. I wonder that you
should ask it," says his mother in loud, self-righteous
tones. " That side of life is, I'm glad to say, a closed
book to me. The respect and affection I feel for you,
Arnold, is as different from anything of that sort as
chalk from cheese. And I think I have done my duty
as a wife, although I have never pretended that I loved
you." She goes on talking, but Theodore doesn't
listen any longer. He lies down quickly and the
sudden, blank dreariness which has swamped his
mind, like cold seas breaking over, seems to run
through his veins, chilling his body until he shudders
violently. Yet what can it mean to him, that word,
love ? He loves his rabbit; he loves treacle pudding:
Kate is keeping company with jolly Jesse Lampeter
and Jesse loves her; God loves us all. How can this
solitary and in many respects backward child of ten
years old distinguish between half a dozen emotions
for which the niggardly medium of language gives him
but one word ? Until this moment he has never been
conscious of believing that his father and mother love
one another; but now he knows that he has always

believed it and that the belief has wrapped him round like a blanket, kindly and warm. Now he is out in the cold—suddenly out in a new world where fathers and mothers don't love one another, don't turn over and go to sleep, don't agree about something about the Olivers, don't do any of the things they pretended they did and you believed them; but lie awake wrangling in dreadful voices, no more immaculate, almighty, unquestionable, no more dependable than children are. " How did I get born, Miss Minns ? " " God sent you to your father and mother, Theodore, dear." " But why, Miss Minns ? " " Because they love one another," says Miss Minns, a thorough gentle-woman, who does not know herself, but has read a beautiful little book called *Love's Enlightenment* in which everything is so nicely put that when, after reading it, you think the matter over, you will find you have received no enlightenment at all. Now he is bereft of this heartening if vague explanation: he isn't the child of love but of duty—iron-grey duty which his father preaches so opportunely to his brute-dumb agricultural congregations between week and week of unresentful toil. Duty is a familiar word at the Rectory; it is Margaret Fletcher's duty to sit through golden afternoons at the bedsides of comatose octo-genarians: it is the Rector's duty to draw Sir Gilbert Oliver's unwilling attention to the morals of his game-keeper; it is Theodore's duty when he passes Rose Cottage to say a kind, cheerful word to Mrs. Maxon's idiot boy. Duty is always dreary, sometimes horrible; it is leaving the airy pastures for stifling sick-rooms; the jest for the sermon; going down the road towards Rose Cottage, wouldn't he give his knife, his stamp collection, his morocco prayer-book to be able to turn into the meadow and put the stout hedgerow between himself and the broad drivelling face in the cottage garden? Love is kind and pretty; his rabbit's fur against his cheek; Lady Oliver coming towards him in a pale mauve dress which smells of lilac and whispers " frou-frou " across the shining parquet at the Hall.

Theodore is going to remember this night as long as he remembers anything; deeply impressed on a child's sensitive brain cells, his parents' chance conversation will come back into his mind long after that unloving couple have gone the same indifferent way of the warm and the cold-hearted. But he is a child now: he does not lie brooding once the voices in the next room are still. His mind flits away to other subjects—will it be fine to-morrow? will he have bacon for breakfast? will there be time to show Richard his Chinese stamp before Miss Minns rustles into the schoolroom? The church clock strikes eleven; Saturn has dropped into the high woods of Hackhurst Downs; in the handsome night-nursery at the Hall Richard Oliver has been soundly slapped for calling out, and is at last asleep. And presently Theodore's thoughts grow hazy, the images before his mind's eyes are blurred; he turns over, a small sigh escapes his lips, and he sleeps too.

CHAPTER II

HAPPY DAYS

" Here comes the gift of God ! "

" Oh, blow ! "

" Bother it ! "

" Shut up ! He'll hear you," said Anne. Now that Theodore was getting nearer to the Council Chamber he could distinguish between the clear young voices floating down to him.

" I don't care if he does," said Richard.

" Do him good," said John Harbutt.

" Shut up," said Anne.

Theodore emerged at last from the green tangle of ground hazels and stood at the foot of the knoll on which, three summers ago, he had helped the Olivers and the Harbutts to build the Council Chamber. One of the highest points on Sir Gilbert Oliver's property, the knoll stands seven hundred feet above sea-level and looks northwards across the valley—before high summer muffles the woods and hedgerows you can see the Rectory chimneys, tall as they are, three hundred feet beneath you—to the chequered fields which climb to the woods of Ranmore and Netley; eastwards to Dorking, in those days a mere huddle of brown, domestic roofs under the bluff of Box Hill; westward down the widening valley to Gomshall and Shere; and southwards, much more humbly, into the woods that rise another two hundred feet to Leith Hill. It was not, however, for the beauty of its outlook that the children had made the knoll their head-quarters.

16

The Council Chamber was an unsteady erection of interlaced fir branches: four walls had been piled between the four pines which top the knoll and a roof of the same material was supported by poles filched from Sir Gilbert's timber yard and insecurely nailed to the gummy red pine boles. In the characters of Israelitish slaves, Anne, John, Cecilia and even " Baby " Harbutt had dragged the fir branches up the slope, directed by Richard, the Egyptian slavemaster, cracking a hunting whip borrowed from the gun-room at the Hall. Miss Minns' régime was already ended: Richard and Theodore were at different schools: their wholly circumstantial friendship was at an end. But poor little Theodore was " an only," said Lady Oliver in a pale mauve dress smelling of lilac and whispering "frou-frou" over the parquet at the Hall. And those dreadful spectacles on his poor little shiny nose ! she cried, and such elderly parents, and Church again on Sunday afternoon when Richard could be reading *Treasure Island* in the orchard her own, darling Richard must be kind. Her own, darling Richard, with a sulky mouth and a scowl between his handsome eyebrows, said, well, if the beastly kid came he must talk to the girls; and so Theodore, dressed up in an Eton suit, went to lunch at the Hall, and dragged fir branches all the hot summer afternoon until the sweat, pouring off his pale forehead, reduced his Eton collar to pulp. " He can come in the morning like the Harbutts, can't he, Richard ? " whispered Anne. " He's done lots of work and he'll make even numbers with Baby "; and Richard, caught in a good humour before his soaring walls of fir branches, said, " All right, as long as he doesn't come dressed up for Sunday school." Theodore limped home, all his pleasure in the invitation swamped by shame that he should be matched with Baby, the youngest Harbutt, an absurd toddler of half his own age. His parents, however, were delighted. Quiet as he was, his mother, an intellectual to her cold finger-tips, found his childish company almost unbearable on her morning excursions to the village and the shops, and she had no difficulty in convincing herself that he was as yet too young to derive any harm from the worldly atmosphere obtaining at the Hall. Her husband did not feel the same matutinal desire to be rid of Theodore, who was getting old enough to be sent about the place with messages and rarely forgot to tiptoe past the study door; but being, in spite of his faith—which was, after all, more in the Church of Christ than in the Galilean carpenter—a great respecter of persons, he was intensely gratified to find his son once more the daily playfellow of Sir Gilbert Oliver's heir. Neither the father nor the mother ever guessed at the hours of bitter misery which this desirable companionship caused their son. He was at school and presumably able to look after himself, for, with all his lack of physique, he was not bullied: he brought home glowing reports and every appearance of happiness. Richard and John did not bully him either, refraining probably for no more creditable reason than that they were afraid of Anne; it was because he was always the last to be picked for a side: because he was always paired off with Baby—Baby and Theodore can be the squaws, Baby and Theodore will do as passengers: because he was always last but one in races, last of all up trees; because he was small—a head smaller than Cecilia, who was a month his junior, and visitors, agonis- ingly guessing the children's ages, invariably judged him to be two if not three or four years younger than he was: because he was plain—pale with full, starting eyes behind thick lenses and a small, shiny nose choked with adenoids, and visitors would look at Richard

and John and murmur, "Splendid boys," and
then look at Theodore and say, "And who is
this little fellow?" in voices that any child on
earth could tell were schooled to be bright and
kind—because of all this, in the other boys' paradise
of hill and dale and holiday, the iron entered
his soul. At school he lived aloof from his fellows,
his eyes on his books. He was extraordinarily
clever, appearing more brilliant then than at any
other phase of his career, for his accuracy, copper-
plate memory and lack of intellectual imagination
were admirably suited to the precise demands of
school work. He was popular with his masters,
for he gave them no trouble and looked like
doing them credit, and the worship of the athlete
had not then reached its later disproportionate stage.
To the boys he was a "swot," but a successful
one as recurring prize-days showed them; and if,
on the playground, some light-hearted barbarian
should send his book flying with a dexterous high-
kick, he'd simply stoop and pick it up again, his
scholarly little mind not for an instant detaching
itself from the Dative of the Remoter Object or the
Cognate Accusative. But in the Hall woods he
carried no book, he was faced not with the calm and
facile mastery of the printed page but with Richard
Oliver and John Harbutt, active, strong and brutal,
their sole interest physical exertion, their sole ideal
physical courage, their conversation, when the girls
weren't there, like nothing so much as a plumbing
contractor's catalogue (and Theodore had been brought
up in a shame-stricken reticence and how could he
know—any more than their ignorant and horrified
Victorian mothers—that another year or two of it
would transform them into as clean-minded a couple
of boys as the country-side could boast?). "Up with

you ! " they said, and his trembling arms pulled him
insecurely among ominous fir branches which creaked
under his feet, scratched his dizzy forehead and dropped
dust into his eyes: " One, two, three, go ! " they shouted,
and he ran with bursting lungs, only to be beaten by
Baby Harbutt, now a stout girl of eight or nine:
" Jump ! " they cried, and he sprawled headlong and
oh, so funnily, at their feet. and sometimes he
heard them talking about him—discussing his clothes,
or how thin his legs were, or why he bit his nails, or if
he washed, or what made his hands so moist, or how
his biceps weren't a patch on Anne's although she
was only a girl. And now to-day they'd got a new
name for him, The Gift of God, and that was the
fault of his own mother. She'd had them to tea
yesterday in the shabby Rectory dining-room, of which
Theodore had felt suddenly and dreadfully ashamed ;
and, in spite of his scared protests, she'd given them
all the things that Richard most hated—madeira
cake and bread and butter—because they were whole-
some. Richard had remembered his manners though
the day was very hot and he had arrived in a giggling
mood. Unflinchingly he masticated bread and butter
and madeira cake while Mrs. Fletcher delivered
a discourse on the history of the parish church
which Anne and Cecilia punctuated with polite
little peristeronic sounds. Mrs. Fletcher disliked
Anne: she was a severe judge of human nature, and
she found it impossible to believe that so much charm
of manner came straight from the heart: she called
Anne sly. So she addressed herself chiefly to Cecilia,
who had a very plain manner, and presently she
began to talk about Saint Cecilia, and it was
then that she told the children that Theodore
had a very beautiful name because it meant " Gift
of God." Anne said, " Oh, Mrs. Fletcher, what

a sweet name for a little baby!" but Theodore was looking at Richard, and he saw one of Richard's large blue eyes close in a wink at John. Nothing had been said that evening while they chased round the Rectory garden and up and down among the mildly surprised heifers which were pastured on the Rector's glebe land, but then Richard, so casual in many ways, had the most strict and elaborate notions about the laws of guestship; and Theodore knew that, and had lain awake anticipating what he heard now. But it had not occurred to him to prepare a protest; he had only felt misery and dread; and he clenched his weak fists not for battle but for endurance as he made his way up the slope.

" Good morning, little Gift," said John.

" ' Where did you come from, Baby dear?' " asked Richard, for once remembering something he had learned from Miss Minns.

Anne turned on her brother a pair of baleful eyes as blue and beautiful as his own.

" You're not funny, you're only blasphemous," she told him, and asked Theodore, " Have you seen Cecil and Baby?"

" No, I haven't," said Theodore, who believed what his mother said about Anne; and Richard said to John, " I'll race you down to meet them: you go by your secret path and I'll go by mine." John rose without a word from his couch of pine-needles and Anne said, " One, two, three, go!" and off they went. Why can't they ever go anywhere without running, and why can't they ever run without racing? Theodore wondered as he sat down in one of his characteristic cramped positions. He could never spread himself out on the ground like the others could: when they lay on their stomachs with their faces in the grass and the sun shining down into their bodies, happy little animals near to earth, he'd sit bolt upright; he didn't like leaves in his hair, the smell of the summer earth, the tickle of an ant or a spider across his hand.

Anne waited until the crashing and slithering sounds of Richard and John descending their secret paths were no longer to be heard, and then she said, " I can't think why you let those boys treat you as they do."

The words were no sooner out of her mouth than Theodore felt himself damply hot all over and horribly embarrassed. He'd spent hours of lonely misery over just this matter, but he would never have dreamed of speaking of it; he couldn't speak of it any more than he could beg his mother not to wear the sage-green djibbah which the Olivers and the Harbutts laughed at, or ask his father to increase his pocket-money. The fault was chiefly his mother's. " That is something one does not talk about," she had answered his awkward questions: " That will do," had been her response to his infantile caresses: arguing that it was best to be firm from the beginning, she had crushed shy, foolish requests once and for all with sledge-hammer phrases like, " How can you ask such a thing ? " and, " How silly ! " and, " Certainly not ! " To hear Anne speak out what he had bottled up for years made him feel as though she had said something indecent, but what can you expect of her ? he thought, remembering an evening on the terrace at the Hall, the white pseudo-Italian house with its absurd pillars, the fountains playing, Anne coming home from a picnic and rushing up to Lady Oliver, a whirlwind of curls and embracing arms and kisses, crying, " Oh, you darling Mummie, how I love you ! " " Quite an hysterica outburst," had been Mrs. Fletcher's comment, and though Theodore hadn't known what an hysterical outburst was, he had felt the same disapproval that he had recognised in her voice for the horrid scene. He looked at Anne with dislike now, and muttered, " How do you mean ? "

" I mean the way they tease you and laugh at you. You shouldn't have it. I wouldn't. They're quite sporting; they'd be all right if you'd only stand up to them."

" How could I ? "

" Next time they make fun of you, give Richard one on the nose that he'll remember—not John, because he's taller, you couldn't reach. Don't say anything, but take him by surprise, and he'll be ready to fall flat with astonishment, anyway."

" How can I ? "

" Of course you can."

" I can't. I can't fight because of my spectacles. The boys at school aren't allowed to hit me because of them. It's dangerous. A person might be blinded for ever."

" Well, take them off before you hit Richard."

" How can I ? I couldn't see to hit him."

" Oh, bother it ! " Anne felt irritated; his sight couldn't be as bad as all that, she considered; he'd broken his spectacles once and had been able to walk about without running his head into walls or trees. She shot him an exasperated glance; but she had come to pity earlier than most children and at the sight of the cramped little figure in its ill-fitting garments her anger melted. " Hard lines—about the specs," she added, and after a moment's thought, " I'll speak to John about it and tell him it's jolly mean to rag you when you can't hit him because of his not being able to hit you." She had been brought up among boys and was past-mistress of their tortuous code.

" I wish you wouldn't," said Theodore. He didn't

know that when Anne and John were grown up they were going to marry each other and live in Dorking in one of the newly built dolls'-house villas on the Westcott Road which Anne thought so much more attractive than the Hall; so that if John didn't want to do exactly what she asked him, she had only to toss her curls and say, " All right, then I won't marry you," to bring him to heel. She didn't tell Theodore that; she said, " Well, we'll see," and shut her rose-bud mouth, leaving him horribly uncertain and hating her. For who but her Creator could tell what this sly and hysterical creature would say to John, and who could tell what John, broad and towering, would, in his turn, say to Theodore ? He was glad—though Anne said, " Bother ! "—when he saw that, with Cecil and Baby, Mrs. Harbutt and Lady Oliver, stalked with noisy stealth by Richard and John in the undergrowth, were making their way up the slope: that would stop Anne's mouth for a little. He stood up beside Anne as the ladies came nearer, and Mrs. Harbutt, who knew what boys were—boys like John, that is, not boys like Theodore —called out, " Surrender in the name of the King ! " in the merry voice that issued so appropriately from her round, comfortable throat; and pointed her parasol. She was a plump and motherly woman of indifferent education and deplorable taste: she loved fringes and canaries and sick-nursing and a good gossip, and Vine House was a heaven of comfort and amiability. Though her own daughters were plain and stocky, destined, it seemed, from birth to become the plucky wives of Indian Army subalterns, she looked at Anne with genuine admiration and affection, and then at Theodore with the expression of a housewifely woman who sees something that she longs to scrub.

" Let us sit down in the shade for a moment, Emily dear," said indolent Lady Oliver.

" And see the dear children at play," replied that unaffected soul. " I can't watch them too often. These are their happiest days."

The ladies billowed down on the shady side of the Council Chamber, smoothed their polonaises, patted their chignons, touched their moist, pink cheeks with cambric handkerchiefs, one very fine and delicately scented with a lilac perfume from Paris, the other coarse, touchingly embroidered with an " E " by Cecilia's inexpert hand, strongly scented with eau-de-Cologne from the large bottle—quite a feature in the Harbutts' simple family life—which the Doctor had so faithfully and thoughtfully brought back from the jaunt to dear romantic Germany which he had made *en garçon* some few years ago.

The children agreed to play Hide and Seek, and John and Richard picked up sides. " That poor little oddity's always left to the end. Does he feel it, I wonder ? " whispered Emily Harbutt. " I'm sure one hopes not," said Lady Oliver, and watched Theodore with so much pity in her tender brown eyes that he knew at once he had been the subject of the matrons' whispering; they're saying how short I am for my age, he thought wretchedly, as he moved off to hide. " One, two, three, four . . ." Richard and Cecilia began glibly counting. I'll get home first, thought Theodore, and then see what they say. There was a strict rule governing Hide and Seek on the knoll which forbade anyone to hide near the summit; but John and Anne had already run down the slope and disappeared into the hazels and Theodore's necessity knew no law. He tiptoed round the Council Chamber and hid himself in a heap of brush-wood which the children had collected for repairing their roof and walls. It wasn't the first time he had cheated at games; once or twice he had moved a croquet ball with his foot when no one was looking; sometimes he'd peeped through his fingers to see where the others were hiding; yesterday in a race he had found that Baby was beating him and he had fallen down on purpose and afterwards pointed out to everybody that Baby wouldn't have beaten him if he hadn't fallen down. And it's not my fault, he thought, trembling with excitement among the brushwood. It's theirs for being so beastly and bullying. And they're wicked too; they swear and make jokes about sacred subjects and giggle in church—why should I keep their rules? "Ninety-eight, ninety-nine, a hundred. Coming!" called the high, clear voices, and Richard shot past the pile of brushwood and crashed into the hazels. "You go down towards the cowfield and scout along the fence, Baby," directed Cecilia. "I'll go towards the Park." Theodore gave them two minutes timed by the traditional method of repeating, "One chimpanzee, two chimpanzees," and then he crept out of his hiding-place and ran round to the front of the Council Chamber, shouting, "Home!" Lady Oliver clapped her hands. "Theodore's first!" she cried. "What a clever boy," said beaming Mrs. Harbutt. "Bravo, dear!" Theodore gave a smug little smile and sat down.

Then there was a commotion in the wood. John emerged from the hazels and, pursued by Richard, fled madly up the slope. Cecilia came running across the knoll in an attempt to cut him off from the summit, but he dodged her and reached "home," hurling himself down on his mother. Meanwhile Anne, who ran like a fawn, had taken advantage of Cecilia's deflection and was found to be sitting demurely at the door of the Council Chamber. All John's side was " home."

Richard said, " Where did you hide, Theodore ? "

Theodore pointed vaguely behind him and said, " Just down there."

" You must have been in a jolly good place, then," said Richard, not ungenerously.

As he spoke, Baby, stout and hot, came running through the pines. She was a big child for her age and her plump indefinite face was later to fine down to a statuesque loveliness. Just now it was dirty and angry: Baby was losing her first teeth in a very unbecoming fashion and, as she ran, from an almost toothless mouth came the indignant lisp, " It's not fair, it's not fair."

" What's not fair, Baby ? " said John.

She pointed a thick forefinger. " *He* wasn't. He hid in the woodstack. I saw him. It's against the rules. It isn't fair."

" Of course it isn't. Beastly cheat," said Cecilia.

" Little rotter," said Richard.

" Dirty swine," said John.

" Send him to Coventry," said Cecilia.

" Give him a good licking," said Richard.

" Lay him out," said John.

" Boys, boys," said Lady Oliver.

" Perhaps Baby saw wrong. *Did* you hide in the woodstack, Theodore ? " said calm Anne.

" No, I didn't."

" You did, you did," shrieked Baby, jumping up and down.

" Well, if you did, Theodore," said Mrs. Harbutt, " I must say I think it was very wrong of you. And instead of adding untruths, you had much better own up to it." But so versed was she in the long and difficult art of domestic diplomacy that before a mouth opened she had got to her feet and was saying, " I haven't my watch with me, but I feel sure it is luncheon-time." " Very likely," said Lady Oliver, who was helpless to deal with the situation but had too much social sense ever to miss her cue. " Come, chicks." And with a few words about the look of the weather the ladies, each accompanied by her children, set off in the respective direction of the village and the Hall.

Theodore walked down the wood among the hazels and across the clearing, purple now with loosestrife and murmurous with insects, to a stile in the thorn hedge over which he climbed. There was a tight lump in his throat which ached unbearably and his difficult tears—he could never howl lustily like the Olivers and the Harbutts—misted his spectacles. Old Joe Forest, hedging and ditching along the high road, gave him good-day, but he couldn't answer, and the old man uttered into the nettles a severe comparison between Parson's boy and young Squire. Theodore trotted blindly upon the road until he came to the white , five-barred gate and the kissing-gate beside it, which give access to the roads leading to the church and the rectory. Here he stopped to dash the moisture from his eyes and glasses with his fingers—a process which left him a sorry spectacle, for they were damp with perspiration and grimed with the black, dusty dirt of the conifers—and to attempt to read the hour by the church clock. By a trick, which short-sighted children learn, of screw-ing up his eyes behind his spectacles, he could just make out that it was barely noon—Mrs. Harbutt, he thought, had been sadly mistaken when she had reckoned that it was luncheon-time. There was nothing to do, however, but to go home, and if any-

one asked him how he came to be home so early, he
must say, "Because the others went home," and, "I
don't know," if he was asked why. "And please
God, don't let them tell Mother I hid in the woodstack," he whispered, but he knew that God didn't
listen to wicked boys.

The road to the Rectory winds down through the
glebe-land pastures, and they were gay with all
manner of wild-flowers—cornflowers, poppies, ladies'
slippers, clover and buttercups. Mrs. Fletcher was
æsthetic enough to detest the bright bedding-out of
geranium, calceolaria and lobelia which was the
alpha and omega of the horticultural artistry of the
period, and had learned to prefer grottoes, dells and
cavernous shrubberies; but no one had ever shown
the wild-flowers to Theodore, and they did not comfort him now. He slipped through the drive gate
and crept round the tennis lawn, a dark, nervous
little figure in the prosperous noon. From the back
of the house came very faintly the tinkle of china,
the slam of dust-bin lid, the continuous, heavy
splash of water running into a pail; but the garden
and the front rooms were deserted, and with a slight
lifting of his sad spirits, he walked into the hall. The
study door was open. After the heat and brightness
of the fields and garden, the room looked dim and
cool: after the many sweet smells of the sun on
leaf and blade and petal, cloistered, lifeless was the
single smell of leather bindings: at the window the
long leaves of the laurels made a screen against summer
and the world. Instinctively he entered. All round
the room in the shelves stood the books, waiting for
you, he thought, not criticising you, you needn't
wonder or worry over what they were thinking, they
didn't care if you lost races or cheated at games,
they didn't whisper that you were short for your

age or snigger at your spectacles; quiet and brown and learned, no mouths to grin, no hands to jostle, they waited for you, and you only had to open them and they'd each a world to give you, not a hot, hurrying, jeering world full of races you couldn't win and balls you couldn't catch and trees you couldn't bear to climb, but the cool, slow, smooth world of the mind presented, black and white and dispassionate, on the calm printed pages. He knelt on a chair which stood by one of the bookcases, brought his eyes level with the titles, rubbed his fingers along the bindings. *Elementary Sketches of Moral Philosophy*, by the late Rev. Sydney Smith, M.A.; *The Odyssey of Homer*, translated by Alexander Pope; *St. Paul's Epistles to the Thessalonians, Galatians and Romans*, by Benjamin Jowett—the words themselves meant little enough to him, but they touched him as place-names touch the exile: here, not out in the world of doing things, and getting hurt, and being laughed at, was his mind's home. His bitten finger-tips travelled across the titles, rested on the first of three faded leather volumes, *The Rise of the Dutch Republic, A History*, by John Lothroy Motley. He pulled the book from the shelf and, still kneeling, opened it. . . .

CHAPTER III

FELLOW SUFFERERS

RICHARD OLIVER grew into a handsome undistinguished young man whose pleasant circumstances called out no more from him than a charming social considerateness; he was liked by everyone, but adored by governesses, poor relations, spinsters and plain débutantes. His mother was disappointed. She was not an intellectual woman, but she was talented. She played her Steinway piano with a light, sensitive touch, sang in a small, true voice, spoke French and Italian very fluently and with a perfect accent, sketched prettily both in water-colour and pastel. And though she had married a man without a thought or desire beyond his own march fences, she had expected, as such women do, to have a brilliant son, and had enlivened many a lovely, tedious summer afternoon at Widdingfold with a vision of Richard's maiden speech in Parliament, the first step to a career modelled on that of the younger Pitt. Richard, however, had mocked gently, amiably and obstinately at the idea of himself in Parliament and on leaving Eton had passed very low on the list into Sandhurst, destined for the Guards. Not long afterwards, the news of Theodore's Oxford scholarship filtered to the Hall. "You always laughed at him, but now he's turning out better than any of you," said Lady Oliver, who was losing her looks and her lovers nowadays, and was usually spoiling for a scene of some sort by dinnertime. Richard nodded cheerfully and filled his mouth with strawberries and cream, but his father took up the strain. "That boy'll get himself educated for about one-tenth of what I've spent on you and be able to keep himself at the end of it." "He'll need to, poor fellow," said Richard. "Every holiday he looks a bit more of a freak." "He can't help his looks," said Sir Gilbert. "No," said Richard, "but he can help his ties." "Deeds matter more than ties," said Lady Oliver. "Oh, if I were a man . . ." said high-spirited Anne.

Anne made her début before Theodore went up to Oxford, but, although Sir Gilbert took a house in London every season and Anne might dance herself silly with sleepiness all through May and June, she often cajoled him into giving a small dance for her at the Hall. There, among her partners—for he always came very early and she had a perverse way of saving her favours for ugly, indigent or unpopular men— was the young Oxford scholar in split gloves and a bulging shirt-front, holding his partners at arms' length and yet contriving to step on their feet as he shuffled round the room to the seductive strains of a Hungarian Band. He detested girls, their chatter, their gushing effusiveness, their lack of education, their futile accomplishments, their quick, shallow, illogical minds, but most of all—one supposes from fear—their dressed-up bodies. Anne was a vain doll, he thought; and what drove John Harbutt crazy with a love that he was beginning to understand was hopeless, repelled Theodore; the sweet charm of her highly sexed nature enhanced by every frill, every rosebud of her elaborate toilettes, horribly embarrassed him: he avoided the glances of her bright eyes and the touch of her little hands, would turn his head away from the rose perfume which she exhaled. If he ever married—and certainly the idea of an intellectual

companionship appealed to him—his wife would be
a very different woman to Anne Oliver, a woman not
unlike his mother, flat-chested, tight-lipped, angular,
thickly apparelled, no lovely difference to scare him.
But for all that, he cared desperately, miserably, what
Anne and her friends thought of him, wondered about
it, worried over it, was alert for mocking voices or
amused glances as he stood, hour upon hour, against
the wall of the ballroom, his head making a grease
mark on the *rose du Barri* brocade. " That poor boy
of the dear Rector's . . . so clever . . . can't someone find him a partner ? " whispered the dowagers
behind their fans, and Theodore marked their glances
and the tiaras nodding together. But when girls
were introduced to him, they were usually able to tell
him, without a glance at the programmes on their
wrists, that they hadn't even a problematical extra
to offer him, while the humblest wall-flower would
scurry through the door, preferring a self-conscious
quarter of an hour under the supercilious eye of the
maid in the ladies' cloak-room to a dance with him.
Sometimes shame would drive him out to pace the
shrubberies or to the refreshment room to drink glass
after detestable glass of lemonade.

" If I were as young as you, my boy . . ." said the
Rector, and Margaret Fletcher quoted Emerson in
support of invitations from the Hall. And Theodore
couldn't say, " I'm sorry if you're disappointed in me,
but I hate and loathe every moment that I spend at
these dances. I can't dance: girls say, ' Let's sit
out,' before I've got half-way round the room; and
I can't talk, much less take girls behind screens and
kiss them as Richard does. I'm a scholar, and there's
an end of it. Let me shut myself up with my books
until I can go back to Oxford." He said, " Very well,
Mother," and sat down at the writing-table in his old

schoolroom, and accepted another evening of torture, in his fine, academic hand.

It was at the beginning of the summer vacation of the year eighteen hundred and eighty-five, that he first consciously set eyes on Hester Adams. He must have seen her as a child, before her mother left the village, but he had a poor memory for faces, and when, after several moments of nervous hesitation, he pulled up the governess cart just outside Dorking and offered a lift to Mrs. Maxon, whom he could always recognise because the face of her idiot child in the cottage garden made the Westcott Road horrible to him even now, he had no idea that it was the pallid girl walking with her who had been the subject of conversation at the Rectory supper-table the night before. " I was sorry not to see Adams' girl in church this morning," the Rector had said as he had helped himself to beetroot; and his wife, passing the mustard, had replied, " I looked for her too. I think someone should speak to Adams "; and, having trouble with her teeth, she had vigorously sliced her grey and yellow fid of beef into tiny squares. " The man is impossible, Margaret." " The girl's position is impossible, Arnold." " Adams is Sir Gilbert's tenant," the Rector had remembered more brightly. " Perhaps he can be prevailed upon to speak." Mrs. Maxon, a coarse-minded, sanctimonious woman who, by dint of running down everyone in the village until only she herself seemed without sin, had for twenty years imposed on Margaret Fletcher, climbed adroitly into the governess cart and called to the girl who was hesitating in the roadway. " Come along, dearie. Mr. Theodore means to take you too." Theodore was no more at his ease with the village people than with anyone else; with the slightest excuse he would have let Mrs. Maxon walk her six miles home; he said nothing, but fumbled with the reins until the girl had got in and sat down opposite him; then he clicked up the pony. He was a shocking driver, but poor Tom, an old brown gelding unskilfully bred by the Dorking confectioner, had had his once tender mouth jerked at and pulled on for the last fifteen years by Margaret Fletcher, and Theodore's clumsy hands meant little to him now. At his own pace, which was an exceedingly slow one, he trotted on.

Mrs. Maxon rearranged Theodore's grocery parcels and said that it was a fine morning. She was right. The sky above them was cloudless and of June's clear blue; from the fields came the cheerful sounds of haymaking; faint and faëry in the hills the cuckoos called; wild roses ran in the hedgerows. That meant nothing to Theodore. He was not a nature lover. Suns might set, shadows fly: he shut the window, decided to take his umbrella. His eyes saw the roses, his ears heard the creak of the hay carts and the shouts of the brown-throated labourers, but neither eye nor ear flashed back its lovely message. While Richard Oliver would have chatted naturally and pleasantly about the weather and the crops and the Mothers' Outing, Theodore was racking his brilliant brain for something to say.

Mrs. Maxon, meeting with no response, fell silent too. She thought, Mr. Theodore's too proud to have a word with anybody, but who's he when all's said and done? Then she began to wonder: what does that old skinflint at the Rectory do with his clothes when they're finished with? They'd fit our Joe a treat if they came our way. . . .

And Hester Adams, her anæmic lips compressed in a discontented line, was wishing herself back in Manchester.

Worrying, scheming, wishing, old Tom happier

than any of them, they jogged on down the valley
until they came to Rose Cottage, picturesque and
fetid among its lavender and hollyhocks. Theodore,
suddenly possessed by a nervous terror that he'd
been mistaken and this wasn't Mrs. Maxon but a
woman from Holmbury-St.-Mary who faintly resembled her, drew up tentatively outside the cottage
and saw to his relief that she was collecting her parcels,
obviously intending to alight. But the girl didn't
move. She sat silent until Mrs. Maxon, uncomely
against her floral background, called out, " Good
day, Mr. Theodore ! Good day, Hester ! " when she
answered " Good morning ! "—the first words he had
heard her speak—in a quick, thin voice. He shook
the reins on Tom's back and drove on, horribly embarrassed. He was the Rector's son : he had lived
all his life in the village : he was evidently expected
to know where this girl lived and he had not the least
idea.

Who could she be ? Starting at Rose Cottage he
began a mental census of his father's parishioners,
but he broke down long before he had reached the
Goat and Compasses. Then he took a sidelong glance
at her features and experienced the awkwardness of
meeting the unsmiling glance of her grey eyes. That
forced him into speech. He said, " Er . . . where
would you like to be driven ? " and " Tck, tck," to
the pony, so that he might look away.

Hester blushed faintly and had to say, " The Goat
and Compasses, please," but she added, as though
she were giving an excuse, " I'm Hester Adams."
Theodore said, " Of course, of course," and again
" Tck, tck," But Hester wanted to explain. She
said, " I can't get used to saying that I live here. I
still want to say, ' Ninety-six Commercial Street ' ;
that's where I lived with Mother in Manchester."

Her voice was utterly different to the broad, slow, affable voices of the country-side: it was sharp and mincing and nervous; it inspired Theodore with a certain confidence, and after a moment he jerked out, " This must be a change after Manchester."

She gave a light, bitter laugh. " It is. The country . . . and the people too. Mother and I lived with Grandfather. He was a great reader and Mother was a school-teacher. . . . Now Father expects me to help serve his customers."

" Surely not ! " Theodore had never entered the bar of the Goat and Compasses; in summer, when the ground-glass window was open, he had seen, in passing, broad red necks and lounging shoulders, smelt the fumes of beer, heard the loud laughs of the bemused and innocent labourers at their ease. No wine or spirits were drunk at the Rectory, but the Rector would take a glass of port when he dined at Vine House or brown sherry at the Hall; and at Oxford, from the scholars' table, Theodore had seen at High Table, among the men he most revered, the incomparable wines of his college flow. He had no cause against Bacchus when the god sat at High Table expounding, confuting philosophies, but could it be the same god whose loud laugh floated from the tap-room window with the smell of sweat and beer ?

Hester nodded. " And some of these men can't read or write. Isn't it shocking ? They're like animals. They just eat and drink and sleep when they're not working. Like your pony. They wouldn't go to night-schools if there *were* any, or try to improve theirselves."

Theodore found himself talking, " You see, what they *are* taught is wrong. There's a sort of traditional conspiracy between Church and State, between the squire and the parish priest. The squire doesn't want them educated; he wants them to work in his fields for eighteen shillings a week all their lives, so the priest tells them that they must do their duty in the state unto which it has pleased God to call them."

" Mother was an atheist," said Hester aggressively; and looked at Theodore, expecting some shocked rejoinder from the parson's son. But he nodded, looking between the ears of his pony, and she was surprised, for she knew that he was at Oxford, studying theology, and that like his father—only much more of a scholar, said the village—he would be a parson one day.

" A lot of people up that way are atheists," she said in a more conciliatory tone. " It's because living in a city sharpens your wits up, I suppose. But Father's always on at me to go to church. He says it never did no one any harm. And you can't reason with people here. They're like cows. Whatever you say to them don't make no difference. I expect I shall come to church next Sunday." She glanced Theodore's way. Along the hot, yellow road the Goat and Compasses was in sight now, and she wanted to make sure that she would see this young man again. It was not a matter of sex but of nostalgia. Her school-marm mother had brought her up to value the mind and ignore the body, and, as she loathed the lusty, brute-stupid sons of earth pouring earth's vintage down their brown throats in her father's bar, so she admired this pale scholar, even to the nervous inefficiency of his manner and his insignificant physique. His long white hands, fumbling on the reins, enough to spoil the mouth and the temper of any pony, didn't irritate her; they argued refinement —the men in the bar had broad red paws with grimed and broken nails, rough and heavy to touch you, if they were gentle with beasts. His narrow chest and stooping shoulders bespoke the open book; his spectacles, the worn eyes of a reader. In the rude, warm, sensual life of the vigorous and fruitful valley, she had suffered a mental home-sickness for her girlhood's desiccated creeds.

" The Rector will be pleased," muttered Theodore. He couldn't say more than that, for the subject of religion and his intention to enter the Church had lately become a problem of the solution of which he wellnigh despaired. He had lost his faith. Knowledge, his lack of imagination, distrust of emotion, small necessity for beauty or comfort, and slight human affections, had made a sceptic of him, though he still respected and upheld the teachings of St. Paul. His parents had never ceased to take for granted his faith and his choice of a profession—he was not to know that his father sometimes doubted how one so sensitive and unpractical could succeed as a parish priest: they constantly referred in terms of joy and hope to his future—when Theodore's ordained . . . when Theodore preaches . . . when Theodore's a bishop—and it sometimes seemed to him that he would never summon the courage and brutality to undeceive them, that he must spend his life in just such a village as Widdingfold, setting to rights, in the light of a creed he didn't believe in, the embarrassing affairs of men and women whose minds he didn't understand and whose faces he couldn't tell apart. He couldn't say, as she expected him to say, " Yes, do come to church," but he was conscious of a rising interest in this other young creature whose tastes and difficulties seemed to echo, faintly, his own. He was naturally generous, but shyness and his mind's preoccupations made his acts of generosity infrequent and mostly inappropriate. He hesitated a moment, weighed up any amount of trivial, fantastic pros and cons before he blurted out, " I could lend you some books."

Hester's grey eyes shone.

" Oh, I couldn't thank you enough ! "

" I'll bring them up this afternoon. I shall be passing—going up to play lawn tennis at the Hall."

" I shall be so grateful. And you'll tell me exactly what to read ? "

Unconsciously she struck the one right note. He felt the pedant's desire to impart his knowledge— that function of the mind. He said, " Very well," and jerked at Tom's mouth in an attempt to draw up at the door of the Goat and Compasses. The old horse paid no heed but turned right-handed into the road leading to the Rectory, and came to a standstill a few yards down the slope, surmising that Theodore wished to shut the gate.

" I can get out just as well here," said Hester, and her pale lips turned up in the ghost of a charming smile. " Thank you for the ride. I don't know how I should have managed those six miles." As she spoke, she picked up her parcels and ineptly accomplished the awkward descent from the pony cart.

Theodore had opened his mouth to say, " Good morning, Miss Adams," when Tom started off quite briskly in the direction of food and water. Hauling on the reins—he'd been warned that the old pony might stumble downhill—and bungling with the handle of the door, Theodore clattered down between the pastures, past the mosquito-haunted ponds, past the gate of the drive, into the stable yard under the chestnuts. Jim, the odd man, came out with a frown and took the pony, and Theodore carried the grocery parcels into the kitchen by the back door. He was unpopular with the servants: like the villagers they misunderstood his shyness and called him " proud."

The cook and the housemaid were in the kitchen, but he hadn't a word for them; he placed his parcels on the kitchen table and walked into the hall.

It wanted a quarter to one, the hall clock told him; he would have time to choose the books for the poor girl at the Goat and Compasses before luncheon. He was a true bibliophile and the task delighted him: he turned into the old schoolroom. This tiny room had been done up for him quite recently; on all the suitable wall space book-shelves had been erected: his mother had indulged her taste for sage-green serge in choosing the window curtains and the *portière*: the carpet was a useful dark blue: the woodwork was painted brown. Above the fireplace hung the only picture in the room—a large, clear photograph of the Acropolis.

With hands which had become curiously effective, Theodore pulled out his darlings: *The Travels of Marco Polo*, Bacon's *Advancement of Learning*, *Essays of Elia* and More's *Utopia* seemed to him at once a catholic and a suitable choice. He placed the books ready in a neat pile at the corner of the writing-table and was about to leave the room when his mother entered.

"Rearranging your library?" she asked him, with a note of approval in her low, firm voice, for it was really very gratifying to have a son who stayed at home and put his books in order while other young men were out and about, spending their parents' money on horses or on girls.

Theodore stood for a moment without speaking. He wanted to say, "Oh, no. I was looking out some books for Adams' daughter. I gave her a lift in the pony cart this morning. She's a superior kind of girl and she's had some sort of education; and she's hungry for books, and that's an appetite I can under-

stand." But he couldn't say it because he knew that
if he did he would colour up and stammer, and his
mother might think that the books were merely an
excuse for a vulgar flirtation with a village girl. Why
he should blush and stammer he didn't know; he had
lent his books before: *Pilgrim's Progress* to a little
girl who had lain dying of meningitis, Green's *Short
History of the English People* to the dropsical ex-post-
man, *Chums* to the gardener's boy when he had fallen
out of a tree and broken his leg. And both his father
and mother had applauded his thought for others,
and, since Theodore did not shine at sick-beds, Margaret Fletcher herself had delivered the books to the
sufferers. It was true that Hester Adams wasn't ill;
but the Rector and his wife would be the first people
to encourage in anyone the desire to read. Theodore
could find no reason for his embarrassment, yet he
could not conquer it, and when it became imperative
that he should speak he said, " Yes, Mother," and
added, " My new Herodotus has crowded up my
classical shelves," " Your library is growing," said
Margaret Fletcher, looking about her and seeing very
little with her foolish intellectual hazel eyes. " And
there are all your books at Oxford too . . ."

Luncheon at the Rectory was a good solid meal—
Irish stew, to-day, followed by a roly-poly pudding,
though there was a glut of fruit in the garden—and
Margaret Fletcher always rested after it, attributing
this necessity not to an overloaded digestion but to
the natural fragility of her sex. The Rector ambled
away into his study where he would cover up his face
with his pocket-handkerchief and sleep too; and it
was quite easy for Theodore to escape question as
he walked out of the house with his books under his
arm. Earlier in the day he had not looked forward
with pleasure to the afternoon; he was a very poor

lawn-tennis player and his game showed no sign of improvement, although (simply because he could be invited on the spur of the moment) he was often asked to make up a four with Anne, Richard and Cecilia, all fashionably crazy on the game. But now, walking up between the pastures, he felt a pleased excitement; he forgot that his striped flannel trousers, having shrunk in their last washing, revealed, rather oddly, five or six inches of his black woollen socks, and that the last time he had played Cecilia had suddenly burst out that she'd go mad if he served any more double faults. He was thinking, I'll tell her to read the Essays first . . . and then Bacon . . .

But when he reached the gate into the high road, a new problem occurred to him. He was uncertain at which of the several entrances into the Goat and Compasses he should present himself. The taproom door was on the left of the building; the porch, which led into a narrow hall, in the centre, while on the right was a garden gate opening on the lawn. The front door scared him: suppose he knocked and Adams' burly figure appeared? He wandered across the road to the garden gate, and to his relief he caught sight of Hester seated on a bench which was built round the trunk of a walnut tree. He could not see her face, for her head was bent over some mending, but at the click of the latch she looked up and, recognising him, dashed a dark stocking off her arm with unhousewifely haste. He noticed that she was bareheaded now, but could not have told you that her hair was a light brown and luxuriant, or that it was arranged like his mother's and almost as untidily, with a centre parting and a heavy knotted plait.

"I've brought the books," he said, pushing them forward. "I don't know your interests, so I've brought a choice. It will be easier when you've told

me which you've liked." The feel of the volumes in
his hand gave him the self-confidence of the artisan
gripping his tools, and he added with authority, " Read
the Essays first. They're shallow, of course, just
comments, journalism *de luxe*, someone called them,
but they're beautifully written—the prose is a joy for
ever. And then read *The Advancement of Learning*.
And Marco Polo's interesting—the travels of a Vene-
tian in the thirteenth century. More's *Utopia* I feel
sure your grandfather's read."

" He read it aloud to us, one winter, in the evenings,
just to Mother and me. I'd like to dip into it again.
Oh, thank you, Mr. Fletcher," she went on as she
received the books from him. " I do appreciate your
kindness. You don't know what it means."

" Oh, but I do, I do." He wrung his hands. " I
understand perfectly," he brought out. " I've felt
that intellectual isolation too."

She gave her faint smile. " We're fellow sufferers,
then . . ." Perhaps she wondered if he'd think that
too familiar—people down here in Surrey knew their
places; some of the older women still curtsied to Lady
Oliver and the Squire—for she changed her tone to a
brisk, cheerful one. " I'll take the books indoors,
Mr. Fletcher. I'll be very careful with them."

" And you'll tell me which you prefer some time,
won't you? and then I can lend you others. And
perhaps I could tell you a little about the authors,
that is, if you would not find me too prolix? " He
hesitated, shifting his weight from one foot to another,
and then, abruptly, he said, " Good afternoon," and
left her.

And Hester Adams carried the immortality of
Charles Lamb, Thomas More, Francis Bacon and
Marco Polo into the little sitting-room which her
father had given her for her own. I'm not pretty like

Polly Greenaway, she thought, as she crossed the lawn, and no young man would ever throw himself into the river Mole because of me, like Bill Garstin did because of Susy Twigg; but I'm clever, and a scholar from Oxford lends me books. Beauty fades—the old, desperate thought—but you can go on being clever to the end of your life and long after you're old and ugly people go on admiring you for that. She let the books tumble on the horse-hair couch by the window while she glanced at her reflection in the overmantel mirror. I wish my hair was fluffy like Susy's hair, she thought.

CHAPTER IV

I'M DIFFERENT

OF course Plato is right—friendship between a man and a woman is possible, discovered Theodore: not to fellows like John and Richard, I daresay; but I'm different. If there were the least sentiment or vulgarity in my friendship with Hester, I'd never have gone on with it; anything of that sort with a girl of one's own class is bad enough. But when two intellectual and spiritually minded people, both in mental exile, meet together, and one can help the other, surely it is incumbent on him to do so—we're like two fellow countrymen meeting in a foreign land. The girl's starved. She's very creditably crying out for knowledge—the bread of the mind. I can't pretend to the love of knowledge and ignore her cry just from fear that ignorant or vulgar minds might misunderstand. Thus admirably justified, Theodore came and went between the Rectory and the Goat and Compasses, the volumes under his arm a sort of ethical passport endorsed by such exalted names as Samuel Johnson, William Wordsworth, John Milton and Thomas Browne.

And Hester, reclining on the horse-hair sofa, yawning her head off, hopelessly stuck at line fifty-three in the first book of *Paradise Lost*, decided: Mother wouldn't have made no objections, whatever Father with his nasty thoughts may say. (He'd said, "Dang it! Books or no books, scholard or no scholard, I won't 'ave 'im 'angin' round 'ere. And I'm serprised

46

at you, 'Ester, that I am, after the devil's fuss you
kicked up over Sam Twigg's bit o' fun in the bar!")
Mother would have been only too glad to know that
I'd got the chance to go on improving my mind instead
of turning into a common barmaid which is what
Father 'ud like, and didn't the Reverend Thompson
used to lend her books and talk them over afterwards
just like Mr. Fletcher does with me? *But his doom
Reserved him to more wrath; for now the thought Both
of lost happiness and lasting pain Torment him*, she
read, thinking, of course, if it were Polly or Susy, it
wouldn't do, but I'm different. Love-making's horrid
—leaning on stiles or sprawling in the hay, dumb as
animals, not interchanging ideas, and ugh! their red
faces and beery breath! I shall never marry if it
means anything like that, or like Sam Twigg's "bit
o' fun" as Father calls it; and at the thought of Sam
Twigg she could feel the little hairs at the back of her
neck rise and a thin, shuddery thrill run down her
spine.

Samuel Twigg, brother of fluffy-haired Susy, was
horseman at the Hall farm. An industrious and
energetic worker, patient and clever with his beasts,
in the society of his fellow-men he was irritable, conten-
tious and over-ready with his fists; up and down the
valley from Dorking to Gomshall he bore a reputation for wildness; he was out of favour at the Rectory
though indulgently considered at the Hall. His
appearance had furthered his reputation. Of medium
height and classic proportions, with a swaggering gait,
brown skin, eyes like sloes, white teeth in a laughing
mouth and vigorous, blue-black hair, he gave an
impression of recklessness and insolence not altogether
unpleasing—you'd have trusted him with your purse,
though not with your daughter; you'd have been
glad to have a dozen like him waiting to go over the top

with you, though you wouldn't have engaged him as your chauffeur. Now, after half a dozen more or less discreditable amatory escapades, Sam Twigg had made up his mind to settle down, and, guided no doubt by Nature, earliest and most powerful Eugenist, had fixed his obstinate fancy on the last girl in the world for him, said the village, pale and innocent Hester Adams, wilting with refinement behind her father's bar. His first efforts to ingratiate himself with Hester had been crude and impudent, for he had no reason to doubt his success—the long empty summer evenings; nothing else to do; the days and the seasons like the cud the red cow's chewing over; the moon coming up, white, silver, golden above the elms; the scents of haytime; Nature, her one aim in mind, urging, staging, mixing her aphrodisiac of shape and scent and sound, had made it easy—given eyes like sloes and a reputation for recklessness which extended from Dorking to Gomshall—to overrule the poor, dry, little Sunday-school principles of Moll and Peg. He had boasted of his knowledge of women, this rustic Lothario, but when Hester met his advances by turning paler yet, shrinking back, saying nothing, he felt the ground slip beneath his feet, he felt young and helpless for the first time since he had pulled himself up by the handle of the clothes-basket and swaggered across the wash-house floor. He had kept quiet for a little, carried his pint tankard over to the oak seat in the window, and Hester had disliked, no less than his impudence, the leer—she called it—of his sloe-black eyes. Then, one Sunday evening, while the church bells were playing *Now the Day is Over* and the faithful, in twos and threes like cattle at milking time, passed through the kissing gate, his short patience ran out. This waiting, the deadly dullness of these continent evenings were getting him no forrader—might as well chance her melting at a kiss. His action had been misunderstood both by Hester, who had considered it an insult, and her father, who, entering on his daughter's muffled shriek, not so careless a chaperon as Margaret Fletcher would have it, had laughed a great, vulgar laugh indicating that boys would be boys and where's the harm in a bit o' fun? There the matter stayed.

Hester did not confide in Theodore: that she could be desired by so disreputable a fellow must surely cause her to decline in the fastidious estimation of the Rector's son. To Theodore himself, Twigg, like Forrester or Heritage, or Garstin, was a name vaguely connected with the cachinnatory groups on the green on Sunday evening which he would pass rapidly with averted glance where Richard would call out, " Well, Sam, how's the new mare shaping? " or, " Hullo, Ted! how's your father's sciatica? " and Ted and Sam would stop grinning and answer him man to man.

It was on a Sunday afternoon at the beginning of August that the licensee of the Goat and Compasses said, " Dang it! Books or no books, scholard or no scholard, I won't 'ave 'im 'angin' round 'ere! " and, as it chanced, Theodore, driving into Dorking on Monday morning for the groceries and craning his neck over the hedge to see if he might timeously substitute *Paradise Regained* for *Paradise Lost*, peered straight and earnestly into the broad red face of Adams, who was attending to his bees. " Tck, tck! Gee up, Tom! " cried Theodore, scarlet with embarrassment, but his nervous voice conveyed nothing to the pony; he jogged on; and Theodore, not daring to look back, felt a hard blue stare between his shoulder-blades until he had rounded the bend of the road. On his return journey he was no luckier; he met his mother, who, having at last responded to Mrs. Maxon's

hints about his cast-off clothing, had walked down to
Rose Cottage with a large parcel and was glad to be
driven home. In the early afternoon he passed the
inn for the third time, but now Adams was sitting in
the porch, smoking a pipe with Jimmy Marks, the
carrier; and Theodore stayed on the Rectory side of
the road as he walked by. All through the long,
disastrous afternoon, *Paradise Regained* weighed heavy
in the pocket of his jacket. "No wonder you look
such an odd shape if you stuff great books into your
pocket," said frank Cecilia. There was quite a large
party assembled at the Hall; while their parents
walked in the gardens or talked under the cedars, the
young people were to play lawn tennis; Lord Abinger's
lively daughters were there and the Vicar of Hart-
bury's supercilious soldier sons. Theodore played
badly, even for him. As usual, the worst racket had
been dealt out to him: the sun was scorchingly hot
and the heat of his brow misted his spectacles: he had
omitted to bring a handkerchief and could only smear
the lenses with his fingers. In the course of a losing
game, one of his elastic garters broke, leaving his black
woollen sock to wrinkle itself down over his brown
canvas shoe; and Violet Abinger, who had dissolved
into a fit of giggles over the incident, gave way to sup-
pressed shakings and gurglings whenever the frayed
black strip, lying up near the service line, caught her
eye. Her partner, infected but ashamed, explained
incoherently, eyes watering, voice breaking, that something very funny had happened in the wagonette.
"Do tell us," begged Cecilia, but Theodore knew very
well what had caused their merriment; he walked
away, allowing them the opportunity to confide the
exquisite joke to Cecilia, pretending to look for balls
in the rhododendrons, angry, humiliated and alone.
When the set was over and he put on his jacket, the

book against his thigh felt comforting; through the flippant chatter round the tea-table, John Milton spoke to Theodore.

But Anne said, "A penny for your thoughts!"— that hateful, arch phrase—and Violet Abinger, who had recovered her self-control and was regretting her bad manners, sat down beside him and asked him if he went to many dances and if he didn't think *Myosotis* too divine? Theodore said, "No," and "Yes"; made phrases in his mind—isn't it a fine day? how green the grass looks!—and rejected them; found one that would do—are you going abroad this winter? —waited to utter it; waited so long that the opportunity passed; spoke in desperation just as Violet Abinger turned her head to speak to someone else; was tortured with shame because he'd spoken and she'd paid no attention, and everyone at the table must have noticed it.

"How are you going to play after tea?" asked Lady Oliver.

"Miss Abinger and I will take anyone on!" "John, shall you and I challenge them?" "Let's continue our unbeaten partnership, Miss Harbutt." "We'll give them a beating, shall we, Richard?" For Theodore it was like the old boyish days when "picking up" had clouded the holiday mornings. He stared at his shoes and waited; only to hear the plain Miss Abinger declare that she would prefer not to play. "I'll look for that ball," he muttered, and went off to flip the evergreens in his old refuge, the shrubbery.

Several of the guests, Theodore among them, had been invited to stay to supper; Theodore had longed to excuse himself, but what excuse, asked his father, can be offered to so small a community? Out on the bright lawn, bungling his shots, failing time after time to get a racquet he didn't know how to hold to

a ball he couldn't see, hot, leg-weary, ashamed of
himself, and ridiculed for his pains, he'd felt unhappy
enough; but supper in the long, white dining-room,
everybody very merry and friendly, laughter rippling
round the table, only himself silent, obliged to force
his laughter—this was the climax of the miserable day.
When the women left the room—backward glances, a
whisper, perhaps, for all but him—no one moved into
the chairs beside him; he sat fingering his wine-glass,
too modest to join in the discussion of· Mr. Gladstone
at the Squire's end of the table, incapable of contri-
buting to the round of funny stories at Richard's end.
Presently the cadence of *Venetia*, floating in through
the open windows, brought the younger men to their
feet—Sir Gilbert, the doctor, and Lord Abinger's heir
were deep in the Irish question and passed the marsala
for the third time. Theodore knew not whether to
go or stay. He rose and sat down again. Sir Gilbert,
anxious to be quit of the dismal figure, broke off in
the middle of a sentence to suggest: " They'll be
dancing in the drawing-room, Theodore. That'll
amuse you better than our dull politics." Theodore
said, " Oh, thank you, sir, thank you," and hurried
out in time to have the drawing-room door shut in
his face by Richard. " Oh, I say, I'm sorry," said
Richard. " I didn't know you were behind me. I
thought you'd stopped to talk politics with the
guv'nor "; and he waltzed away across the shining
parquet, enviable, light-hearted and young.

Theodore took a hasty glance around him. The
floor at the end of the room where he stood had been
cleared for dancing; everyone was sitting at the opposite
end where the piano was; to reach them, he must
cross the floor. Although the August dusk was blue
at the windows, the lamps had not yet been lit: he
needed stronger glasses (but had not liked to put his

parents to the expense of a visit to the oculist): and
he could not be sure that there was a chair vacant for
him—supposing I get down there, he thought, and I
still can't see one, and I have to fumble round among
all those people? Best to stay, he decided, and he sat
down on an ottoman which had been pushed against
the wall and secluded by a Japanese screen and a fine
spreading palm.

"Under the spreading chestnut tree, Theodore?"
called merry Anne from young Vere Abinger's arms;
the other dancers spared him no more than fleeting
glances, into which his mood read pity and contempt,
as they whirled laughing by. *The laughter of fools
is like the crackling of thorns under a pot,* he quoted to
himself, but the sour sage could not comfort him to-night.
He was twenty-one: it was summer: he had drunk a
glass and a half of champagne and two glasses of
marsala: they were playing *Venetia*; and although
he had no ear for music, couldn't tell that it wasn't
Estudentina or *Le Premier Baiser,* the saccharine
rhythms stirred, in those depths of his mind that are
outside the reasonable brain's control, an immense
vague longing to be understood. The same longing
had taken Richard out into the shrubbery with the
prettiest Miss Abinger, had placed his confident young
arm round her eighteen-inch waist and his mouth on
hers; but Theodore was far from realising that such
a silly little emotional thrill was the precise answer to
his laudable intellectual need. Oh, to be out of this
great noisy room, he longed, away from these brainless
fools who despise me because I can't join in their folly,
can't chatter, shuffle my feet, hit balls over nets, laugh
at nothing; oh, to find one soul in the world to whom
I need not pretend anything, with whom I could be
myself! Youth and summer, music and alcohol
offered him the same suggestion as Richard had acted

on, but worded it more discreetly: he didn't think, as Richard had thought, what a red mouth! If I can get the little devil into the garden I'm damned if I won't kiss it; he thought, I've more in common with Hester Adams than with any of these dressed-up ninnies: I'll leave early and take *Paradise Regained* and hear what she thinks of Milton on my way home.

Lady Oliver brought her little white hands down on the final chord of *Venetia*, and rose at once, and came across the room to Theodore. "If they want me to go on playing, will you come and turn my music over for me?" she said sweetly. "John's been doing it, but I'm sure he wants to dance." Theodore's thought was, good heavens, how shall I know when to turn over? I shan't be able to tell when she gets to the bottom of a page, and even if she makes a sign to me, the pages will stick together and I shall bungle it: but he didn't say that. He said, "I can't. I must be going." "Oh, but you're not going so early, surely, Theodore?" He shuffled his feet while he sought for words. "Yes, yes," he brought out. "I must say good night." "Good night then," said his hostess, thinking of all the charming young men who had pined to turn over her music, quite a crowd of them sometimes, glaring at each other, manœuvring to get nearer to the piano, while this boorish creature wouldn't do it, even though she had asked him to. Vain little beast, she thought, just because he's clever and a personage, I suppose, at that stuffy old Oxford, he thinks he's too good for any of us; and she gave him the tips of her fingers and a cold glance.

It was dark in the avenue. Tense young voices were whispering in the shrubberies; the lilt of *Myosotis* followed him down into the dim fields. They won't ask me again, he thought; between tea and coming

away I never spoke a word except just at the end to
Lady Oliver; and where the vain man that Iris Oliver
considered him would have felt a splendid isolation,
he felt lonely, wretched and a failure. I've only three
more terms at Oxford, he brooded dismally; then, as
a curate, I shall have to go out among people: preach
to them, call on them, sit beside their sick-beds, console
them, upbraid them, old men with senile minds who'll
scarcely answer you, young men with coarse minds
that you shrink from following, unmarried mothers,
naughty boys, drunkards . . . I can't, I can't!
Leave me in peace with my books! He put his hand
into his jacket pocket, drew out *Paradise Regained* and
opened the gate into the garden of the Goat and
Compass.

It was eleven o'clock. Lady Oliver had said, " Oh,
but you're not going so early ! " and, in his vague way,
he supposed that it was early and expected to find
Hester at the window of her sitting-room if not on the
bench under the walnut tree. As soon as he entered
the garden he saw that there was no light in the sitting-
room and that the window was closed. He walked
across the lawn and tapped on the panes.

For a moment he heard no answering sound. There
was a murmur of voices from the taproom, a croon
and flutter from the hen roosts behind the house.
Then, above him, a sash was lifted and a voice,
thin, nervous, and mincing, whispered down, " Who's
there ? "

" It is I."

" Mr. Fletcher ? "

He stepped back, and could see above the tangle of
the jasmine the outline of her head with the hair
flowing.

" Perhaps I'm too late," he whispered. " But I've a
book here for you. I've been carrying it about all day."

" Very well. I'll come down," said Hester.

He stepped back to the window, and in a moment
or two could see a light moving into the room behind
the lace curtains. Then the window parted and
Hester stood before him, a candle in her hand. Her
long, straight hair flowed over her shoulders; the
hastily donned cloak which she clutched round her
thin figure revealed the neck and the hem of her
white cotton night-gown; in the soft candlelight her
indefinite face was beautiful, romantic the lines of her
draperies and hair. Except for his mother, and Cook
on the night when the boiler burst, Theodore had never
seen a woman with her hair down or her figure un-
corseted; but he was thinking of John Milton—was
Bagehot right? Had Milton, so far from justifying
the ways of God to man, merely " loaded the common
theology with a new encumbrance " ?—and he noticed
neither Hester's hair nor her apparel as he stepped past
her into the room.

" I'm afraid I'm late," he began again in his high
voice, " but, as I said, I've been carrying this book
round all day. And I've had a most wretchedly un-
profitable afternoon at a tennis party. I felt I must
exchange ideas with some intelligent person before I
went home."

Hester, setting the candle down on the gimcrack
piano, smiled. I'm not the sort of girl who'd sit and
talk to a young man in her night-gown at eleven o'clock,
she thought, but Mr. Fletcher's different. Time and
clothes and the like don't mean anything to him.
But I wish I'd got on my embroidered one—the
marguerites would just show at the neck where the
cloak won't come together—or at any rate the one with
the yellow ribbon run through. . . .

" Sit down," said Theodore. " The light's very
bad, but I think I can find my favourite lines."

He opened the book, peered into it as he turned the pages, and presently began to read. Hester, sitting on the couch beside him with every appearance of attention, found herself soothed into sleepiness by the rise and fall of the sonorous rhythms: her thoughts wandered cosily into speculations as to what Susy and Polly with their nasty minds would think. . . .

Theodore shut the book and said, "I could go on reading for ever. It's such a rest to come into contact with a mind like Milton's after spending the afternoon with nineteenth-century young ladies at the Hall. Is it a paradox that the society of fools is far more difficult and exhausting than the society of wise men?"

"It's what you'd expect," said Hester. "After all, ploughing a bad piece of land is much more difficult and exhausting than ploughing a good piece." After she had spoken, she regretted that her analogy had so smacked of common earth, but Theodore said, "How true! You see so clearly!" and the day having been a cheerless one—hour after hour of sunshine on dumb trees and empty meadows, nothing but blame from her father because she'd broken a couple of glasses and the cork in a bottle of Booth's gin —she felt overwhelming gratitude to this odd creature for his heartening words. "Why are you so kind to me, Mr. Fletcher?" she asked impulsively. "Everyone else says I'm clumsy or stupid or why can't I enjoy a bit of fun." He opened his mouth to answer, but she said, "Hush! Listen!" and sprang to her feet and across the room to blow out the candle. "It's Father going up to bed. He'd see the light under the door," she whispered near Theodore's ear, and not even then did he realise that he was committing an indiscretion, that it was night,

and that he was in the parlour of an alehouse with a
girl. He waited until the tramp of hob-nailed boots
had faded across the house and then answered, as
though there had been no interruption, " People
think me awkward and clumsy too, and I can't enjoy
lawn tennis or dancing. . . ." Which of these two
young and unhappy creatures made the first movement? Theodore never knew. But now they were
clinging together like miserable children, blotting out
the bitter day in sympathetic arms. Their first embrace ended—chiefly to draw breath, his face being
pressed against her shoulder—there came the need
for speech. He sought words, an explanation, and
became aware, suddenly, shockingly, that he, Theodore, the Rector's son, the senior scholar of St.
Mary's, who'd never thought of, never talked of
girls, shying away from the subject should his com-
panion lead up to it, quitting the group when the
talk got ribald, was here in the dark with a girl whose
hair was flowing over her shoulders, whose warm
body, just now pressed against his, was unlaced,
unclothed but for the thickness of a calico gown.
" I must go, I must go," he muttered, yet his awkward
hands felt in the dark for her, felt and found her
thin young shoulders, drew back into his arms her
thrilling, different body. She did not resist. Innocence had led them beyond the brittle false modesty
which was all they had learned of sex from their
parents and from their age: the flesh which they had
ignored, coming to all the greater strength for want of
its normal safety valves—kisses in shrubberies, ribald
stories over heady second glasses—had turned the
tables and was master now. Neither spoke: for here
was nothing which the body could not itself express,
nothing of the spirit to struggle into words. Theodore's spectacles pressed into his face as his mouth

fastened on Hester's; though it was a second nature to him to care for them, he pulled them off and flung them on the ground. Not gently, or diffidently, but on the full tide of passion he took her, her scholar from Oxford, narrow-chested, with stooping shoulders that bespoke the open book, the worn eyes of a reader, and refined, white hands. . . .

CHAPTER V

MORNING

"Your bath, Mr. Theodore."

"Thank you, thank you, Lizzie," said Theodore's voice, while his mind groped its hard way back from sleep's delicious groves. Morning! he thought. *Morning in the Bowl of Night had flung the Stone that puts the Stars to Flight*, as that intolerable old Sophist has it; and then he thought, it's Tuesday, thank goodness, no driving into Dorking with a shopping list and no wretched lawn tennis; I'll be able to do some work; surely no one will object to that with my schools only three terms away. Then he looked at the window and was sorry that it wasn't raining: his father would invite him to Wordsworthian walks—come, Theodore, a pleasant walk across the pastures to Farmer Gray's will sweep away those cobwebs! Theodore was in danger of slipping back to sleep when the calm old voice of the church clock chimed out, telling him that Lizzie had been late in calling him as usual, and that it was already eight o'clock. He was not consistently punctual: engrossed in a book, he'd forget to notice the time, wouldn't hear the gong though it boomed fit to deafen him or his mother's voice though it grew sharp. But he desired to be punctual; as soon as he had consulted his watch or heard his mother he would fuss quite disproportionately, almost burst his lungs sprinting in from the garden, risk a broken neck hurling himself downstairs. When he heard the

clock strike all his agreeable sleepiness left him. He
flung back the bedclothes, jerked himself into a
sitting position. Then, with full consciousness: my
God! he thought, was it a dream I had of Hester and
myself last night?

He knew it wasn't; but he put his face down on
his knees, buried it in the crumpled sheet, and said
aloud, " It didn't happen. It didn't happen. It
couldn't have happened. It was a ghastly dream."
He wanted to believe that so much that he almost
succeeded; retrospectively, the events of the night
before, so far from possessing the sharpness you'd
have expected, seemed nebulous, dreamlike. . . .
He lifted his head and stretched out his hand to the
bedside table for his spectacles—impossible to think
clearly with the room so vague and smudgy about
him—and, when he'd got the wires round his ears
and was trying to flick something off one of the lenses,
he remembered, I cracked that last night when . . .
The thought was submerged in bodily discomfort.
He felt sick at it. But I must get up, he worried;
I shall be late for prayers and breakfast too, if I don't
hurry; and he scrambled out of bed, divested himself of his home-made flannel night-shirt and sat
gingerly down in the hip-bath which the maid had
set out on a large red and white bath-mat in the
middle of the room. He soaped himself hastily,
beginning with his feet, wearing his spectacles till
he came to his face; and the everyday procedure
in the room familiar from childhood, the view of
Littlehampton over the mantelpiece, *The Light of
the World* over the washhand-stand, his night-shirt
on the floor, morning at the window, everything as
usual, again almost reassured him: these lathered
thighs, this hand in the frayed bath-glove—it was
fantastic to contend that only last night they had

caressed a woman's body. I'm myself, thought
Theodore, it did not occur to him, vain-gloriously;
I've never thought about . . . that sort of thing, nor
talked about it, nor wanted it, at most I've dreaded
it when I've looked forward to the intellectual companionship that marriage might be. It's madness
to think that I should seduce a girl. I'm not a
seducer, thought Theodore, drying his face, putting
on his spectacles; the whole thing was a ghastly
dream. If it were true, he thought suddenly, as-
suming with his garments a more practical outlook,
if it were true it would be an awful thing . . . the
Rector's son . . . after all that Father has preached
and done in the parish, I could never look him in the
face again. But if it were true—an awful thing like
that—how could it all seem so vague and dreamlike
and far away? I shouldn't feel, as I do, that it's
made no difference . . . everything wouldn't seem
just as usual . . . I shouldn't look the same . . .
So his harassed mind revolved its insane hope while,
at the pit of his stomach, a purely physical feeling
bore witness that the awful, the incredible thing
had happened and that life wasn't now, as it had
been, a quiet, obvious affair of straight way and
primrose path, but a furious, treacherous chaos to
which you woke one morning and found that a seducer
of village maidens wasn't a wicked, lustful man with
flashing eyes and black whiskers and a London tailor
. . . but yourself.

The gong boomed. Theodore pulled a comb through
his stubborn hair, knotted a tie haphazard, struggled
into his coat and hurried downstairs. The dining-
room door was shut. He could hear his father
praying for the conversion of the Jews: " *Gather
into the fold, O Lord, Thine ancient people, Israel.*"
He hated to enter the room once prayers had begun

and the servants were kneeling, their pink print
dresses flowing out behind them like slopped blanc-
mange. I'll wait, he thought, and walked across
the hall to the sunny front door where Frisk, banished from prayers since he'd taken advantage of
the Gospel of the Monday before Easter to gnaw the
ham, was sitting on his haunches, scanning the prospect
for cats. Theodore said, "Good dog, Frisk," for
Frisk did not like him, and would come sniffing round
his trousers: but the conciliatory voice conveyed
nothing to the terrier: he did not even cock an ear.
For a moment or two Theodore stood, feeling the
incongruity of his load of trouble in the early morning
freshness; then he remembered: last time I waited
outside, Father said, better late than never; and
hurrying back to the dining-room door, he opened
it, and came face to face with Cook, who was leading
out the small but solemn procession. Simultaneously
Theodore and Cook recoiled; simultaneously they
advanced again. Fate's an inept tragedian; her
"cheerfulness keeps breaking through"; but Theodore was too young to know that: it did not strike
him as funny that, on this tragic morning and pious
threshold, he should clownishly gavotte with Cook.

At last—so long it seemed—the awkward incident
was over, and he was in the room. "Good morning,
dear," said his mother, as his cheek brushed hers;
"Good morning, my boy," said the Rector, sitting
down at the head of the table, hoping it wasn't bacon
again, wondering what could be done to improve
the attendance at Communion. "Help the bacon,
Arnold," said Mrs. Fletcher as Lizzie set a dish before him; and he removed the lid and served large
slices of gammon which had been dished up in good
time and were already congealing on squares of flaccid
toast. "Thank you, Father," said Theodore, cutting

off the rind, thinking, if they knew! They must never know, he thought; but appalling possibilities occurred to him—village gossip creeping nearer and nearer: Hester crying on the doorstep: Adams raging in his father's study—I'd sooner commit suicide than face it, he thought, masticating mouthfuls of bacon that he neither tasted nor knew that he swallowed. "You're not looking well, dear," observed his mother, and the Rector said, "Late hours! Late hours! I'm going to visit poor old Heritage this morning, Theodore. You had better walk with me." Theodore shuddered. To walk up the pasture in full view of the windows of the Goat and Compasses and along the high road beside the garden hedge, perhaps to meet her—it was impossible; no power on earth could make him go. "I'd like to work," he muttered. "You must consider your health," said his mother, and the Rector, "*Mens sana in corpore sano.*" Theodore gulped down his tea and left the room.

He took his books into the garden, hiding himself, like a schoolboy, in the summer-house. But he could not read. Regret and shame tortured him, but stronger than either was fear—the crude fear of being found out. If only he could guess at Hester's mind, count on her silence! But you can't count on human nature, he'd discovered, since last night he'd counted on her being different to other girls, himself to other men. Would she confess to her father or confide in some other woman? Would she assume from last night's madness that he desired to embark on a liaison? Was she insulted or ashamed? Did she desire reparation or, like himself, to forget . . . to forget. . . . There was one way of ending that suspense—to see her. But he couldn't do that. His will could never force his shrinking body up the

familiar road to face his disaster. He could only
wait. . . .

The morning wore through. He heard his father
call him, saw the crown of his black clerical hat bob
above the beech hedge as he walked that way and
this; but he bent his head over his notebook, scribbled
nonsense, and made no reply. "I looked for you
before I set out for Long Leas," said the Rector at
luncheon. "Where were you, Theodore?" "I took
some work into the garden, Father. Logic. I wanted
to run through my lecture notes." "You didn't
hear me call?" "No." The Rector's eyebrows
twitched. Always morally alert, he'd scented a lie.

"You didn't hear me?"

"No, Father."

"Curious! I called repeatedly. Frisk was with
me, jumping up at me and barking, dear old fellow,
in his noisy way. Were you so deep in your premisses
that you actually heard nothing?"

"I heard Frisk barking," allowed Theodore. "But
he's always barking."

"Then I must say," said the Rector acidly, "I'm
surprised that you didn't hear me."

Theodore was silent. He stared dejectedly at
his plate. A glance passed between his parents as
he refused stewed prunes.

"What's the matter with the boy?" asked the
Rector that evening as he rested in his worn arm-
chair while his helpmeet prepared the study for the
Confirmation Class. "There's something on his mind.
He didn't mean to walk with me this morning. He
lied deliberately."

"He looks ill. I was sorry he refused the prunes."

"His stomach would not affect his truthfulness,"
said the idealist. "He is harassed, worried. Thank
God we can rule out the two most frequent sources

of trouble—debts and—if you'll excuse me, Margaret
—women. Theodore has never given me a moment's
anxiety on either score. I believe that I've read his
heart aright. He is worrying over his future, his
choice of profession. He knows how deeply we have
hoped that he would enter the Church. And he does
not feel called. . . ."

"Oh, Arnold, how disappointing! I've always
looked forward . . ." Yes; at the end of the crying
and the whining and the maddening questions and
the tiresome little ailments and the washing and
the darning and the economising that her son's childhood had been to this unmotherly woman, there had
waited for her, sustaining her, like an object of interest
at the end of a boring walk, a vision of the godly young
clergyman whose spiritual and temporal circum-
stance should win her the reward which her naïve
religion had led her to expect—the envy of her neighbours and the approval of her God.

"It is a deep grief to me too. But we cannot all
serve Him in the same way." The Rector shouldered
his cross with gusto. No cross, no crown.

"What do you intend, Arnold?"

"I will speak to him. I wish he showed a greater
frankness."

"Modern children do not confide in their parents.
One hears that everywhere. And Theodore is reserved even with his contemporaries."

"I'll insist that he walks with me to-morrow. In
simple, rural surroundings, it is easier to broach a
difficult subject. . . ." "Don't get engrossed in
your work to-day, my boy," he said at breakfast
next morning. "I particularly want you with me.
I shall be going down to the Railway Cottages as
soon as I've seen Garstin about the pegs in the vestry."
Theodore did not mind going down to the Railway

Cottages; they stood on the other side of the valley. He said, " Certainly, Father. I'll wait in the house for you."

When the Rector had finally decided that four pegs in a row would be more efficacious than six in two rows, they set off down the path through the woods together, the hopeless strangers that father and son usually are. The Rector hummed and hawed: asked questions about Theodore's tastes and recreations; and gradually his nervousness communicated itself to Theodore; he remembered other walks when his father had hummed and hawed and asked questions as a prelude to horribly embarrassing warnings against the dangers of public school life, or biological enlightenments, or tests of faith; and he knew that his father had something embarrassing to say. God in Heaven! Can he have heard anything ? Not the whole—his manner's too kind—but enough, perhaps, to involve me in an explanation; and with a throbbing heart and moist brow he began to talk rapidly, feverishly, to question his father, in his turn, on such subjects as the direction of the wind and the names of the trees. The Rector answered at random, but when Theodore mentioned the fine elms at Oxford, he interposed with some adroitness, " Oxford ! Ah, yes ! By the by, I want to talk to you about your future there." Theodore experienced such a feeling of relief that the green woods swam before his eyes. He closed them, saying in a queer voice, " Yes, Father ? " and when the Rector repeated the gist of the conversation to his wife, he told her, " I could see by the poor boy's manner when I opened the subject that I was right."

" We acted a little unwisely, I think," began the Rector, " in taking your future career for granted at so early a stage of your development "; and he went on to relate to Theodore his own difficulties as a curate. " It is not the question of your faith which troubles me," said the Rector, " but the question of your ministry: not your dealings with God, but your dealings with man." His voice went on. A week ago, yesterday even, Theodore must have felt surprise and joy: his father was relieving him of a task he'd lacked the courage or the brutality to accomplish. But to-day his trouble had swamped everything; the past only meant, how could I ? the future, shall I be found out ? He answered dully, " Yes, Father," and, " No, Father," and, " I see." " We'll talk more of this on the walk back," said the Rector, at the Railway Cottages. " Think it over while you wait for me." Theodore sat down on the grass at the wayside. He could look across the high, ripe cornfields to the woods and the hills; in the middle distance stood a farm, brown and homely, eloquent of earth's bounty: it was a pleasant place for a young man to sit and dream of summers to come. But Theodore couldn't see beyond his misery. His mind revolved a circle of appalling possibilities. He saw himself disgraced, disowned, homeless, a suicide. " What is your own idea ? " asked the Rector on the way back; but Theodore's dearest desire was nothing to him now. " I'll think it over," he muttered. " Wisely said," approved the Rector. " Talk it over at Oxford with your tutor and your friends." Oxford ! Surely belonged to some previous existence, some other planet, the peace of mind that he remembered at the name !

The fearful days went by. Theodore slept badly; moods of remorse and self-loathing followed the nervous apprehension of the daylight hours, when a ring at the door-bell would set his heart thumping so that it shook his body, the suggestion of a walk

into the village would rack his brain for stammered
excuses. But gradually, as the days passed and
nothing happened, his fears grew less. If the girl
meant to denounce him, she would have done so
already; to confide her secret she would have flown
straight to a feminine bosom. He found that he
could forget his remorse, as he had not been able
to forget his fear, in his work. Unknown to his
parents, he read far into the night.

August gave place to September. Brown corn,
pale oats and sturdy barley lay in sheaves now;
barn doors stood open; wagons creaked along the
lanes in the golden early sunsets; harvest hymns,
vigorous and gaudy, echoed in the ascetic Perpen-
dicular arches of the church. One Sunday, after
morning service, Theodore, walking into the Rectory
behind his mother, was stopped by Lizzie, who held
a book out to him. " A young person left this for
you, Mr. Theodore," she said.

" What is it, Theodore ? " asked Margaret Fletcher.

Theodore said, " It's *Paradise Lost*. I lent it ";
and stumbled past her into his dark little room.
He'd seen at once that the smooth gilded pages were
parted; he opened the book and a small lilac envelope
fell into his hands. Feeling sick, hands fumbling,
knees shaking, he waited until he heard his mother's
footsteps on the stairs; then he tore open the envelope. *I must see you. Please come into the fir*
wood behind our garden this afternoon, Hester had
written in a round, girlish hand. With almost a
savage gesture, Theodore crumpled letter and envelope into a ball and stuffed it in his pocket. What
does she want with me ? he wondered wretchedly,
obeying the summons of the gong, walking into the
dining-room, sitting down, unfolding his clean dinner-
napkin, agreeing that the attendance had been un-

usually satisfactory this morning. If she wants
to upbraid me, he thought, saying, " Only one slice,
please, Father," I must bear it. She can't hate
me more than I hate myself. And if she wants
money, I must get it somehow. But I won't have
anything more to do with her; love's horrible: it
carries you away and makes a beast of you: in spite
of your education and training, you behave no better
than a farm hand. If that's what she wants and
I can't manage to tell her, I'll have to write afterwards, but I must go this afternoon or she might
come here again. Supposing Mother had had one
of her sick headaches, and hadn't gone to church,
and had seen her . . . Supposing the note had
dropped out when I took the book from Lizzie . . .
Supposing . . . " No more, thank you, Father,"
he said. " No, thank you, really. No more."

He arrived first in the fir wood, the dark outline of
which makes so effective a background, declares
a later generation, avid for beauty, to the russet
roof of the fifteenth-century building; he had wanted
to get out of the house before his father started off
for the children's service or stolid young couples from
the farms and the village began their dumb per-
ambulations of the lanes. After the hot sunshine
of the pastures and the high road, the shady wood
was pleasant; Theodore could see over the laden
boughs of the orchard—the little red harvest apples
had all been gathered, but brambling seedlings grew
yellow among the yellowing leaves—the long roofs
of the inn and the patched outhouses; doves, perched
on the gables, cooed soothingly; mingled with the
smell of the conifers, there came to his nostrils the
smell of a garden bonfire, autumnal and calm. But
the scene brought him no solace. Mind and body
alike were sick with apprehension. Only a greater

dread kept him standing thère, shifting from one
foot to another, picking the skin at the side of his
thumb-nail, when he saw the gate into the orchard
open and Hester's figure approaching under the boughs.

He didn't call to her. She gathered the skirts of
her pink print dress together and stepped through
the tumble-down wire fence which separated the
orchard from the fir wood. Then she looked about
her, shielding her eyes with her hand, for she wore
no bonnet, and presently noticed him. He looked
away from her—at his feet, into the wood, anywhere
—as she came towards him. When she was quite
close to him, she said, " Good afternoon."

Theodore said, " Good afternoon. I got your letter
. . . and I came. . . ."

She said, " I didn't want to trouble you. I'd never
have bothered you, or gone out of my way to see
you. But something awful's happened and "—her voice
grew aggressive—" it's your fault as much as mine."

" What's happened ? " Fear's stronger than shame,
and his eyes, large and startled like a hare's behind
his thick lenses, met hers at last. " What's happened ?
Does someone know ? "

" Who's to know ? " said Hester, " without you've
told them. It's not likely I'd go round the village
telling that. But they'll know soon enough."

" Why should they ? You don't realise what it
would mean. . . ."

" Not realise it ? I've thought of nothing else
ever since. Every night I've lain awake thinking of
it, and I've wakened up thinking of it every morning."
Her voice rose. To his horror he saw tears come
in her eyes.

" Well, why should anyone know ? " he said
roughly. " It's bad enough knowing ourselves, at
least it is for me. I'm sorry . . . I'd do anything.

When I came into your room I hadn't a thought of it . . . I didn't know it was like that."

"And didn't you know what sometimes happens afterwards? Haven't you heard of girls having babies?" The tears dropped from her lashes and straggled down her cheeks.

Theodore's hands went out to grip a branch of a fir tree. He felt like falling. A baby . . . I'll be a father . . . the father of an illegitimate child . . . His white lips uttered a wordless sound.

"Oh, I was mad," cried Hester, beating her hands together. "Mad to have anything to do with you. Say something! For goodness' sake, say something! Don't stand there!"

"How can I say anything," groaned Theodore. "I've never thought of it. Other people . . . village people . . . but not me . . ."

"What's the difference?" asked Hester, suddenly calm. "What's the difference, when all's said and done? Except that you don't seem able to face it. What shall we do?"

"What can we do? It's dreadful. . . ."

"If it's dreadful, we must do something. . . ."

"Oh, don't keep on repeating that!" he almost screamed. "I don't know what to do! Father's the Rector. . . ."

"And Father's the publican."

"It's quite different. Don't you see . . .? I can't stay here if it gets known."

"I've got to. Unless Father turns me out."

"Well, I'll help you . . . with money . . . somehow . . ."

"I don't want your money," said Hester, staring at him.

"I'm sorry," he said miserably. "I didn't mean to offend you. But I can't do anything else."

"That's where it comes—the difference between you and the 'village people.'"

"What do you mean?"

"The village boys make . . . honest women of the girls they get into trouble."

Silence fell. As though the world were a pleasant place to live in, the golden September sunshine lingered on the orchard; as though life were simple and happy, the doves cooed.

"I can't marry you, if that's what you mean," Theodore burst out vehemently. "I can't. Don't you see that I can't? I've not left Oxford yet. My parents wouldn't allow it. They'd think I was mad if I suggested it. It'll be years and years before I can afford to marry—besides, I think it's horrible. I've finished with all that."

"I don't want to marry you," said Hester. "I haven't finished with 'all that' as you call it, but I've finished with the likes of you." She dashed her hand across her eyes. Her voice had lost its genteel accent; uncontrolled, it rose and fell: in spite of her fairness, you'd have known her for Adams' daughter. "I'd sooner look out for myself, thank you," she said. "You may be a wonderful scholar, but leave you alone with a girl and you're no better than the rest; and when it comes to taking the consequences of what you've done, you're like a maggoty apple, rotten to the core. 'I can't do this. . . . How can I do that . . .? Oh, it's dreadful . . .' That's all your wonderful education has taught you. No, thank you, Mr. Fletcher, I don't want nothing from you. There are those I've been fool enough to look down on who'll stand by me."

"You're wrong. You don't understand. It wasn't my fault."

"It's never no one's fault. But that doesn't prevent it happening. Good-bye, Mr. Fletcher. I dare-say you'll be a very famous man one day," she added spitefully, " but I hope my baby won't take after you, all the same."

She turned to go. He stepped forward. " If I can help you . . ."

" You can't. You! You couldn't help anyone," she said, and left him, walking away into the fir wood, not a disconsolate figure but a shrewish one, a young virago, elbows out, head in air. For a moment he stood staring after her, thinking, can that be the girl I thought would understand me? to whom I read Milton? human nature is as treacherous and horrible as its love. But she means to keep silent about me, he thought, walking rapidly from the hateful scene; and, whatever her motive is, thank God, thank God. That side of life will be a closed book to me henceforward, he resolved. The harm's done, but I'll try to forget it . . . try to forget that I'm a seducer and the father of a bastard . . . I can't forget it . . . I can't . . . cried his tortured mind. He passed out of the wood by a stile into the lane which leads up to Friday Street; in the shade of the hedgerow two lovers, a beery young man in stiff broadcloth, and a perspiring girl, who looked like bursting from her faded cotton dress and button boots, were standing, their bodies pressed together in a vigorous embrace. They did not move apart, though Theodore had to pass them; and, as he did so, he felt the colour rise in his cheeks. Horrible . . . he thought, horrible . . . and Hester's shrill words reminded him: " Leave you alone with a girl and you're no better than the rest . . ."

CHAPTER VI

SOME COMFORT

" THE Oxford train ? Number three platform, sir,"
said the porter, and called out, " You've half an
hour to spare ! " But the young gent was already
legging it down the platform as though he'd old Nick
behind him ; he looks a trifle barmy, thought the
porter; studies too much, that's the long and the
short of it, I daresay.

Theodore hated railway travelling; hated asking
where the trains went from: sometimes the porters
didn't hear you or wouldn't hear you (especially
on the London and South-Western): sometimes
(especially on the Great Western where they were
so fatherly) they shouted, like this man, something
after you that you couldn't hear. And you missed
the one who'd got your luggage on a truck, lost sight
of him before you'd told him where to label it to:
there was a written label on the gladstone bag and
two on the book-box, and three, one at each end and
one in the middle, on the trunk: *T. Fletcher*, *Passenger
to Oxford*; so perhaps he'd know: on the other hand
he might be uncertain and leave the whole lot in
the booking-hall. And the engine was puffing out
steam and looked like going; he had thought that
he had half an hour, but he couldn't catch sight of
a clock anywhere, and his watch was very likely
wrong. He sprinted down the platform, and collided
with his own luggage. Instantly a new problem presented itself. Would twopence, threepence or fourpence

content the man? Twopence was what he merited,
but perhaps he'd scowl at that—scowl and mutter.
It would have to be fourpence.

Theodore chose a compartment already occupied
by an elderly clergyman, travelling with two young
boys: he did not want to travel with his contemporaries and overhear impressive accounts of visits
to the Rhineland or the number of grouse slaughtered
on Lord B.'s Scottish moor; still less did he desire
to travel with acquaintances and be questioned about
his own vacation. " Your luggage is in the front,
sir," said the porter at the window, and Theodore,
tearing his purse from his pocket together with a
handkerchief, a penknife and a spare luggage label,
stumbled over the feet of the clergyman to hand the
man sixpence. Would he be as fortunate in getting
a porter at Oxford? he wondered, as he opened his
little black handbag and took out a volume of Tacitus.

The crowd of young men fast assembling on the
platform at Paddington on the last day of the Long
Vacation of the Year of Grace, eighteen hundred
and eighty-five, differed less from the crowd which
assembles there in these Octobers than our ardent
modernists would have us to suppose. The types
were more pronounced, perhaps; the horsy man
from Christ Church was horsier: the burly athlete
from Brasenose more brawny: the Magdalen æsthete
living more nearly " up to his blue china ": Verdant
Green more innocent: and the fashion for heavy
moustaches gave the young faces an older, graver
look: but behind the modes and manners of the
age was the heart of youth, turbulent and frightened,
unchanged since poor, heroic Greece. Speeding down
the Thames valley, Theodore kept his nose in his
book, but, as the train slowed down in the Hinksey
water meadows and crept into the station between

the cemetery and gasometers, he looked up and saw
the silhouettes of the towers, a dark, calm grey against
a wet, primrose sky. It was then that he realised
that he was not the first young man to bring a load
of trouble back to his Alma Mater: in all these years,
he discovered, there must have been many who did
as I did—worse, perhaps—and found out that life
was quite different to what they had imagined—a
terrible force that gripped and tortured you, not
" a little holding, lent for a mighty labour "—and
love quite different—no admirable, intellectual con-
summation, but a mere rude function of the body—
and they themselves quite different—seducers and
cowards (he'd thought of that), not the mild, familiar
I. And they came back, thought Theodore (later;
for now he had to pack his book into his bag, and
look out to see which side the platform would be,
and press towards the door to be ready to call a porter,
and identify his luggage, and find his ticket, and get
a tip ready, and go out into the damp, riverside atmosphere which seemed to wrap itself round him body
and mind); they came back and found, after all
they'd suffered, everything the same—the calm grey
towers, their heads in the wise heavens, important
young men, getting Blues, getting Double Firsts, no
more to them than part of the centuries-long whisper
of footsteps down there in the street; the giants
of a generation passing by, leaving no impression,
only a few peacocks' feathers in a college dust-bin,
the *genius loci* undisturbed. Life's terrible, thought
Theodore, crossing Carfax in his hansom; it's a hot,
animal thing that claws at you and drags you down
and then screams at you because you've fallen; in
the physical and spiritual world, as we know it, knowledge is the only thing that's wholly admirable, the
only thing that we can safely trust. To feel, he

thought, passing All Saints' and the pigeons busy
round the empty cab rank, to feel is scarcely more of
an activity than to be. But to know! The curve
of the street, clean-cut and colourless; stone; the
sharp spires; seemed to him the antithesis of the
agonising muddle he'd turned his back on: he summed
it up in the fine word, " austerity." And to the
intellect there's no beauty except in austerity, he
thought; the rose, the sunset, appeal to the emotions, produce horrible sensual stuff like Swinburne's.
He shuddered.

The hansom came to stop outside the gates of St.
Mary's. He got out; paid the cabby; his luggage
was carried in. " Good afternoon, Mr. Fletcher,"
said the college porter, who would know him for the
rest of his life, greet him by his name when it was
silent on the lips of his dearest friends. Theodore
said, " Good day, good day, Jordan." Although he
was struck dumb with shyness if he must exchange
a few words with the villagers of Widdingfold, he
could be perfectly genial with the porter or with his
scout. The college servants, he'd realised, weren't
surprised whatever you did or said or wore or were:
walk into the lodge clean or dirty, drunk or sober,
mad or sane, on your hands or on your feet, it wouldn't
occur to them to criticise you: like the towers, they
saw nothing in you; you were just the young gentlemen passing by . . .

Theodore walked across the quadrangle and the
noise of the street—clip-clop of horses' hoofs, roll of
wheels, jingle of hansoms, clanging of trams—died
away. Instead, he heard the familiar sounds of
college: Homeric laughter from groups gathered
here and there; clear young voices bawling greetings
as heads and shoulders leaned from mullioned
windows; footsteps in a hurry on stone staircases;

a bell tolling over by New College. No one hailed him, but several men nodded to him as he walked on through the dim cloisters into the garden quad. He'd the same rooms this year as last, the second pair on Staircase A, very coveted on account of their size, panelling—here was work by Grinling Gibbons —and view. Theodore hurried up Staircase A, and threw open the heavy oak door. His room was waiting for him, the Turkey-red sofa he'd taken over from a previous occupant, the deep wicker arm-chair from Minty's, the window seat and the cedar at the window, the fireplace that presently would send its light to flicker on his leather bindings, the kettle that boiled the water for his tea, the big table at which he worked —Oh, hours serene and blissful, I have you back again! Theodore walks to the window, looks down into the grave, green garden, wanders round the room till he comes to his bookcase, stands there, reading the titles till his hand creeps up . . . There's scarcely a sound to be heard in these rooms which look on the garden; seventeenth-century building, straight and true, muffles even the joyous arrival of Mr. Edward Mainwaring, Captain of the Boat Club, President of the Wine Club, in whose rooms, below Theodore's, the Grinling Gibbons cherubs are coiffed with policemen's helmets and hung with notices forbidding bad language or gambling in the Bar. When they bring up the book-box, thinks Theodore, fingering *Formal Logic*, I'll rearrange this bay. I'll have Herodotus here; Tacitus there; and move Plutarch into the other bay. . . . The streak of primrose above the pinnacles of the chapel has broadened; a late shaft of sunlight, warm on the stone mullions, enters the room; very gravely and sweetly Magdalen tells the hour. " Oxford . . ." Theodore utters; " Oxford . . ." and now he sees beyond the misery that has engulfed him, beyond the trick life's paid him, to a future when these last weeks will fade into a sorrowful memory, faint as comes to his window now the sound of the traffic on the London road. This shall be my life, thinks Theodore, and, like other young men, sees visions—quiet college rooms; lamplight on the wise page; summer walks round Christ Church Meadows; calls at Blackwell's; talk, reasoned and learned, in the dignity of Senior Common Rooms —" *Vitam vitalem,*" his sage encourages him, " in the feast and not in the throng, in the light and not in the heat "; I'll learn . . . and teach so that my knowledge may live after me . . . I'll write— Fletcher on The Nature of Error, Plato's Republic translated into English with Analyses and Introductions, by Theodore Fletcher, M.A. And perhaps one day, I'll be Warden . . . Look! there's the Warden of St. Mary's. . . . He's the next Vice-Chancellor. . . .

Theodore lost no time in making his decision known to his father. On the first Sunday in term he wrote: *To reopen a subject which we discussed during the vacation, my return here has convinced me of the wisdom of your suggestion; I should like to remain at Oxford, and feel that, without undue optimism, I can hope for, nay, almost count on a Fellowship.* From both his parents he received encouraging letters. Immersed in his studies, his mind travelled farther and farther down " the dusty corridors of learning," farther and farther from a golden September afternoon and the cool of fir branches and a shrill voice upbraiding him. Only towards the end of term, when it became necessary to write the date of his arrival to his mother, did it occur to him that his Christmas vacation must be made hideous by the dread of meeting Hester or of hearing her discussed. He would have given anything to join a reading party in Wales or Cumberland, but no such suggestion was made to him and he had to return home. He was quickly reassured. At dinner, on the very evening of his arrival, his mother told him, " Your dear Father had such a busy autumn. First of all there was a succession of marriages, beginning with the Adams girl and ending with Anne Oliver . . ." " Whom did she marry ? " asked Theodore, bending down to examine a minute black speck in his Scotch broth, for he knew that his face was scarlet. " Still the same old dreamer! " cried his mother. " Don't you remember, I sent you a newspaper account of the wedding ? " " I didn't mean Anne," mumbled Theodore, " I meant Adams' girl." " What did you say, dear ? " " I didn't mean Anne, but Adams' girl," he repeated, scarcely louder. " Rather an unsatisfactory fellow, I'm afraid," said Margaret Fletcher. " A man you wouldn't know, who worked at the Hall Farm." " He rejoiced in the euphonious name of Twigg," put in the Rector. " Sam Twigg. His parents have lived for years in that tumble-down place beyond the Railway Cottages. After his marriage, he left the village and went to a farm, so his mother tells me, somewhere in Kent. *Not* a great loss to this parish." " Well, that seemed to start quite an epidemic of weddings," said Margaret Fletcher. " And then, later in the year, when the cold weather came, we lost a great many of our old people." " A very sad time," said the Rector. Their voices went on. I'm safe, thought Theodore. It's over. It was hell, but it's past and gone now. I needn't worry . . . lie awake . . . avoid the village. And though he was never to forget the shame and misery he'd felt that summer, though fits of remorse were still to keep his candle alight and his book open in his attic bedroom at

Widdingfold, it did not occur to him to wonder how
Hester had come to marry the "unsatisfactory fellow,"
nor what she had told him concerning the unborn
child which later would bear his name. Theodore
was young, devoid of imagination, and ignorant of
life. If you had said to him, across the Rectory
dinner-table: "Isn't it a mean piece of villainy to
palm your child off on another man as his own?"
he would have exclaimed, "Dreadful, dreadful!
What a shocking thing to do!" But so impossible
it was for him to imagine himself a father, much
less the father of a child to be born six months hence,
on a farm in Kent, to a man and wife named Twigg,
that this aspect of the affair never crossed his mind;
his sorrow was that he'd fallen to the level of the
brute creation that he despised. But other men
have been brutes, he was able to see now; and brutes
and heroes have gone pell-mell into oblivion—not even
a personal oblivion, but the oblivion of their civilisation—Crete, Egypt, Sparta had their disillusioned
boys. It hasn't wrecked my life, thought Theodore;
it has just closed that side of life to me; and, with
a good appetite, he began to eat his soup.

CHAPTER VII

WHAT'S TRUE?

SCARCELY a year later, Theodore was elected to a Fellowship at St. Mary's. In a letter which he wrote to his father, announcing his success, he remarked, *I feel an added delight in the fact that I need not transfer to another college the affection I feel for my own.*

He was, in truth, relieved to find that this break in his life meant no more than an excursion from the second pair of rooms of Staircase A, in the Garden Quad, to the third pair of rooms on Staircase B, in the New Buildings: he'd miss the cedar, but look into St. Mary's famous elms; the same lawns would lie about him; the same walls surround him; above all, he'd be among men whom he already knew.

His first evening in the Senior Common Room hadn't been so terrible. His tutor, Edward Coleridge, with whom he was really more intimate than with any of his contemporaries, had been full of praise for his Double First; the Warden, so old and wrinkled and oddly dressed that guides, showing American tourists round the colleges, would point him out as he walked towards them, his small head stuck out on the end of a long, stringy neck like a tortoise's, his blurred blue eyes seeming to regard the Infinite (the Americans said, " Gee, I guess he's learned," and were mistaken, for he was a very poor scholar but a very astute business man and doubled the income accruing from the college estates during his Wardenship), addressed him by name (he'd usually make a show of not knowing you, though he knew the name of every man in college down to curly-headed freshmen he'd look through as though they were glass windows); Christopher Haughton, the only don whom Theodore really disliked, had bicycled back to his home in Bagley Wood—he was married and seldom dined in college; Mr. Jeeves, Dr. Quears and Professor Hooker had nodded affably to him; Mr. Weldon, Reader in Chemical Physiology, had buttonholed him, like the Ancient Mariner, to outline his insane dream of a laboratory in the Park. To have faced the Balliol Common Room, shadowed by Jowett, silent and severe, or the high and chilly dignity of Christ Church under Dean Liddell, would have terrified Theodore into physical discomfort; he loved his college because it protected him: its walls were arms which enfolded his too-sensitive mind.

And there, inside those walls life came easily to him. Oddly enough, the lecture-room did not daunt him. His lectures were dull, erudite and sound to the dry core; he read them, making not the least attempt to capture or hold the interest of his audience; the fact that he was delivering an informative and precise lecture satisfied him; he scarcely ever glanced at the bright heads before him and certainly never noticed how, shortly after the beginning of his lectures, a third of his audience would leave the room, crawling out, on hands and knees, under cover of their more studious fellows.

Undisturbed, then, by any emotion whatsoever, he saw, but scarcely noticed, the contemplative days slip into weeks, into terms, into years. His greatest pleasure was probably the feeling of utter contentment induced by an excellent dinner and a couple of glasses of the college brown sherry (the brown of calf

bindings it was, yet golden with the deep, deep gold
of southern eves; dry as Reason it was, yet warm
as Life; it was like silk in the mouth, a song in the
throat, and sunshine in the belly; and, when the
war came, it poured down the gullets of temporary
officers, who couldn't have shut their eyes and distinguished it from invalids' port); his greatest pain
was the sight of a stranger in the Common Room or
a suggestion that any further concession should be
made to the women's colleges. In eighteen hundred
and ninety-two his first book, *A Short History of Logic*,
was published, at a loss which he didn't care to estimate, by the Oxford University Press. The excitement of seeing his name for the first time in print;
of inscribing a dedication to the Warden, Fellows
and Scholars of St. Mary's College, Oxford; of re-
ceiving congratulatory letters from his parents and
a grunt of approval from the Warden; of walking
down Queen's Lane behind two Balliol dons who were
agreeing that the chapter on the Peripatetics was
arrant nonsense; made a sort of stir that he didn't
really appreciate; in fact, on catching sight of the
volume in Mr. Blackwell's window, one November
evening, lying there for all the University to see, he
scurried back to college, wishing that, like Professor
Hooker, he'd kept his knowledge illegibly pencilled
in innumerable penny notebooks under his bed. However, in a day or two, the volume had gone from Mr.
Blackwell's window; conversation in Hall was of
nothing but the fall of the Government; the towers
dreamed on. A couple of years later, he did not
hesitate to undertake another work, and this was also
published by the University Press.

In war and rumour of war, the sturdy century
ended. Looking back, Theodore saw that the cloistered years were solid, like a wedge, between him

and the disaster of his early manhood—for several moments he could not recall the young woman's name. Time, he decided, is the greatest force we know; and his scholar's bird's-eye view showed him Time, a mighty wave, rolling over, flattening into smooth sand the ant-heap activities of the human race. He'd been a catholic reader once, but now humanity's long expostulation seemed to him puerile, ineffective; literature was a baby crying, a tiny, irritating wail, in a corner of his mind. He became more and more absorbed in his own subject; and a habit of silence grew on him: it didn't interest him to talk on general matters, and his social relationship made no such call on him; to his bird's-eye view it didn't matter whether a twentieth-century Oxford don said " Good morning," on one of the century's thirty-six thousand and five hundred mornings, or held his tongue. It didn't matter either that his hat was out of fashion or his coat shiny at the seams— fashions had changed many times since the Ionian Chiton was no longer modish, and many suits had been worn threadbare. He developed a curious hurrying gait as though he were always trying to get back to St. Mary's as soon as possible; he looked at his feet as he walked and would step off the pavement without a glance at the road. Oxford cyclists grew accustomed to him, and when motor traffic began to flow through the city, he paid it the scant compliment of raising his hand to check it, still without looking up, as he crossed the road. He'd caught the spirit of the University: he " chose to await . . . ignored clamours of the moment and the market ": the petrol engine might revolutionise social and commercial life: he dreamed on.

Meanwhile, beyond the long green ridges of Cumnor and Elsfield and Whytham, the new century brought new manners. "What are we coming to?" sighed the Vicar of Widdingfold on his death-bed in the room where Theodore had lain awake and heard his parents talking, in just such a midnight—the moon travelling into Hampshire; Saturn dropped into the woods of Hackhurst Downs—thirty years before. "Your father has been worrying himself over the modern tendency towards scepticism," explained Doctor Harbutt's successor. "Since his mind began to fail, he's kept on repeating, 'What are we coming to?' over and over again. Very trying for those about him." "Now that your father's gone, I shall be able to travel and see something," said Margaret Fletcher, with an avid light in her faded, hazel eyes. Theodore did not find fault with her indifference; he was too relieved to find that he need not comfort her. During his father's last hours, he had been worried by visions of tears on his shoulder; over and over again as he had watched his mother move about the sick-room, he had wondered what he should do or say. He wouldn't be able to bring himself to caress her: she was his mother, but he scarcely knew her—living in the same house, the morning and evening kiss, can make greater strangers than any separation. He'd have to struggle into speech, find words he didn't mean, for his own thoughts would be far from comforting—there's no life after death; immortality's a fairy tale to any reasoning man. But, as things were, his task was limited to selecting a Latin epitaph and looking out trains to the Continent. The Rector was buried in the churchyard where he had so constantly officiated: his wife travelled to Rome, where, a few months later, she died from the effects of a mosquito bite: Theodore returned to Oxford. The new century bustled into its 'teens.

These were days before the Royal Commission had
laid an efficient, ineffective hand on the conduct of
University affairs. The Warden of St. Mary's was
a very old man, a very sick old man, but he had no
intention of retiring from his position until Death
called, in the proper manner, at the Warden's Lodgings. Since nineteen hundred he'd appeared in public
so seldom that flippant undergraduates had circulated
a rumour to the effect that there was no Warden—he
had died and his butler, the august Parker, who bore
so close and indiscreet a resemblance to the then
Chancellor, had thrown his body, by night, into the
Cherwell, and was carrying on in his stead.

In the year nineteen hundred and thirteen, however, the tale was more or less discredited, for doctors'
broughams drew up outside the Warden's Lodgings,
Parker was seen to emerge from the dim entrance
hall and to affix daily bulletins on the door: presently
you read that the Warden was a little weaker, and,
on a drear November evening, that he had passed
peacefully away. The chapel bell tolled dismally.
In the Common Room in Oxford, his possible suc-
cessors were discussed. There were two obvious
candidates: Professor Haughton and Dr. Quears.
Haughton was an Irishman: his Rabelaisian humour,
roars of laughter, six red-haired daughters, European
reputation, mortgaged home in Bagley Wood, com-
bined with the fact that he'd written a novel, one
entire chapter of which was devoted to a description
of a steeplechase, put him entirely out of the running
with men of Theodore's type; but there were younger
Fellows who sat at his feet, echoed his laughter, recorded his epigrams, followed him to Brittany in the
Long Vacation: he could be sure of a certain amount
of solid and enthusiastic support.

Quears, both mentally and physically, was his

complete antithesis, a small man with pink cheeks, neat snow-white hair and beard, blue eyes, a girlish mouth—seeing him, you'd think of Christmas joys . . . crackers and holly . . . surely those plump fingers were designed to convey half-sovereigns to favourite great-nephews, chocolate creams to laughing baby girls! You'd be wrong. Gregory Edward Quears, D.C.L., had no great-nephews and never gave half-sovereigns away. He was clever and disagreeable—his was the most bitter tongue in Oxford at that time. He was unmarried—that was better than having a red head poking out of every window of the Warden's Lodgings—and he was of a practical nature; he'd keep an eye on the Bursar and carry on the late Warden's profitable conduct of the college estates, whereas Haughton didn't know a freehold from a leasehold. But what many of the Fellows feared in him was his passion for power: he'd sit on any Committee—Hospital Committees, Political Committees, Bazaar and Fête Committees on which he was the only man—he'd champion any cause— Morris Dancing, Woman's Suffrage, the trace horse at the foot of Headington Hill—simply for the pleasure it gave him to control and direct. "Quears would make a lot of innovations," said Professor Seaton, stepping out round Addison's Walk with Dr. Blore. "He likes doing things. He's always doing things." "He's certainly energetic," said Blore. "Energy isn't what's wanted from the Head of a House," said Seaton. "The late Warden was, to my mind, ideal." "I'd prefer Quears to Haughton, though," said the other. "Haughton's distinguished, no doubt, but imagine those roars of laughter and dirty jokes coming from the head of the table! And that meretricious Bohemianism! You wouldn't be able to tell the Common Room from the Café Royal! And then, his female women! I'd support anyone to keep Haughton out."

"You won't keep Haughton out by putting up Quears," said Seaton. "He's made too many enemies with that tongue of his. D'you remember what he said about Hamilton's *Life of Cicero*? Someone repeated it to Hamilton, and, though Hamilton doesn't like Haughton, he'd sooner see him elected than Quears. And Hamilton's the sort of fellow who'll go round pulling wires. You'll have to get a stronger candidate than Quears to keep out Haughton."

"Then we shall have to bring in someone from out-side."

"We don't want to do that. That would mean innovations, if you like! Rows of new lavatories and hot baths for the undergraduates—we've seen *that* happen in other colleges. Besides, who *is* there?"

"There's Sir Hadley Jevons at Cambridge and Martineau at Durham University."

"Pah!" said the Professor. "Jevons is a charla-tan and Martineau is a scientist. I've a better suggestion to make. What about Fletcher?"

"Fletcher? I never thought of him."

"One doesn't, except when he's got a cold in his head and he sniffs in that horrible way in Hall. But he's quite a sound scholar."

"Sound? Yes, but scarcely distinguished, and he can't say ' Bo !' to a goose."

"Isn't that as well? We don't want an iron hand in the college any more than a new broom."

"Ha, ha! You're right there. But . . . I don't know, I've always thought him a smug."

"He *is* a smug. I wouldn't suggest him but that I'm afraid of Haughton, and I know that we shan't keep Haughton out with Quears. Quears' enemies

would go solid for Haughton, whereas Fletcher's got
no enemies. He's no friends either, but the whole
of the anti-Haughton fraction would vote for him."

" Hamilton would."

" Yes. We'd have to sound him early . . . let
him think it was his own idea . . ."

Theodore was elected Warden of St. Mary's at the
beginning of the Easter term of nineteen hundred
and fourteen. No member of the University was
more surprised than he; he had dreamed of the
Wardenship, but as one dreams of heaven or of unlikely legacies. The plain fact staggered him. " I'm
Warden, I'm Warden," he muttered as he hurried
through the city, looking at his feet, stepping off the
pavement without a glance at the road, holding up
his hand to check the traffic; but it was days before
he really believed what he told himself and didn't
expect to find, on his return to college, that it was
all a delusion and that he was still Mr. Fletcher with
rooms on Staircase D. He explained it to himself:
all these years, the Fellows have had a much higher
opinion of me than I ever suspected. I've under-
rated both my abilities and my popularity. At
last, self-respect came to him; I've reached the
summit of my ambitions, which is more than most
men do, he argued; and that, not through believing
in myself but because other men believe in me, because
they value me before Haughton, with his international
reputation, or Quears, that fine scholar. And men
whom I've never set eyes on must have backed me
too. I thought that no one outside Oxford had ever
heard of me, but I was wrong. Scurrying about the
streets, he did his shopping. The furniture from the
Rectory at Widdingfold had been warehoused after
his father's death, and this he sent for and arranged,
with timid and severe taste, about the stately rooms;

but he bought mezzotints of portraits of such eminent persons as William Pitt the Younger; the Reverend E. Cogan; Richardus Fox, Episcopus Winton; and Sir Joshua Reynolds, Knight. He also bought Persian rugs, dim and decorous, and a large quantity of cut wine-glasses and decanters. Perhaps I'll entertain a little, he thought, saying, " Send it all round to me at St. Mary's. Yes, to the Warden's Lodgings." If my colleagues think enough of me to elect me, it's not unreasonable to suppose that they'd be glad to come. " I'd like to see a dinner service, too," he suggested. " Crown Derby, perhaps." He saw the rich gleam.

It was not until the end of term that his eyes were unkindly opened. In spite of his new self-assurance, he'd found Collections trying—he felt sure that the Dean had criticised his mildness and shaken his head over college discipline. That worried Theodore; and, at a Fellows' Meeting, he erred in the opposite direction: from sheer nervousness he was overbearing and abrupt. In the most hasty and unconsidered manner, he squashed a really sensible proposal from Dr. Quears. At the time Quears' pink cheeks deepened to rose colour and his neat beard trembled, but he remained silent. That evening, however, he seated himself next to Theodore in the Senior Common Room. " I hear that Haughton's thinking of selling his house," he observed pleasantly, as he lifted a glass of old brandy to his small red mouth. " Really ? " replied Theodore. " That should not be difficult if we continue the present exodus in the Boar's Hill direction." " I imagine it was a blow to him that he wasn't elected," said Quears, smacking his lips. Theodore thought the remark in execrable taste: he hated gossip. But he didn't want to be disagreeable to Quears, so he decided to change the subject. While

he was thinking of something to say, Quears went
on: "He thought he'd only have me to contend
with. He didn't guess that certain far-sighted gentlemen would produce a candidate expressly for the
purpose of keeping him out." He said something
else, but Theodore wasn't listening. So that was it;
he was telling himself. I wasn't elected because the
Fellows had a higher opinion of me than I ever suspected. I was elected by Haughton's enemies to
keep him out. "Certain far-sighted gentlemen" saw
that Quears wouldn't get enough support, so they
found a candidate who hadn't any enemies, and then
they went round—he looked at Hamilton, the wire-
puller—and got support for me . . . "If you don't
back up Fletcher, you'll have Haughton as your
Warden . . ." I was just a pawn in their game. He
looked down the long, mahogany table—exquisite
wood, exquisite glass, exquisite wine—and, in that
moment, hated the men among whom he lived his
life; hadn't they talked him over, written tactful
letters about him, walked down the Broad and the
High, down Queen's Lane and the Turl, out to Headington and Hinksey, saying, "He's a smug, but he's
harmless": "He's not much good, but he's manage-
able": "We don't really want him, but we *must*
keep Haughton out!" So piercing was the bitterness
of the discovery that he feared lest his face should
betray him. He excused himself, and rose, and
scurried out, past the portrait of the first Warden—
a great scholar, he; no mere pawn—out into the
cloisters and across the quadrangle. It was a fine,
spring night; the sky was full of stars, surely not
to be explained at the Radcliffe Observatory, but
strewn there, haphazard, by some lavish and poetic
hand. From an undergraduate's window in Founder's
Buildings floated the cadence of *The Chocolate Soldier*.

The floods were out, and the wet, river smell pervaded
the town. Theodore noticed nothing. He took a
key from his pocket, opened the door of the Warden's
Lodgings, and switched on the light. St. Mary's is
a wealthy college and lodges her Warden well. The
hall, in which Theodore stood, is richly panelled;
a double oak staircase leads up to a gallery; on his
right was his big, dim library, on his left an ante-
room and a dining-room; above the library was his
drawing-room; his bedroom—Archbishop Laud had
slept there—looked out on his own garden, an acre
of lawn, shadowed by immemorial trees. Now, in
his vast house, nothing stirred. It was all his—
simply because some of the Fellows had wanted to
keep Haughton out. He went into the library and
sat down, a poor, ungainly figure, his legs stuck out
this way and that, his fingers in his straggly brown
moustache, under the mezzotint of the Reverend
E. Cogan. To keep Haughton out . . . to keep
Haughton out . . . his hurt mind reiterated. Not
because of my *History of Logic*, nor my lectures, nor
my love of the college, but simply to keep Haughton
out. And now there's nothing to come, nothing to
hope for. I've got years and years before me; years
and years of being Warden and keeping Haughton
out; and all of it to be spent with these men who've
used me, who put me in this place when they had to
find someone for it, because they thought, we'll be
able to manage Fletcher; he's as weak as water;
he'll be wax in our hands. I shouldn't have been,
thought Theodore, if I'd gone on thinking that they
had a high opinion of me, but now I know what they
think, how can I assert myself? He pictured, with
horror, Fellows' Meetings—Quears getting satirical;
Hamilton fresh from wire-pulling; the Dean sneering
at his leniency; the Bursar at his unworldliness;

himself equivocating, silly with nervousness, insanely hoping to please everyone, ending by pleasing no one, not even himself. And then he saw himself coming back across the quadrangle, harried and humiliated, back to his fine house that his predecessors had lived in because they were loved and honoured; he, because another man had enemies. I've reached the summit of my ambition, and this is all it means to me; others attain their heights with colours flying; I with my tail between my legs. " Warden of St. Mary's . . . Warden of St. Mary's . . ." he mutters, picking the skin at the side of his thumb-nail, staring before him with eyes that don't see his library; and he is suddenly out in the cold, out in a new world where fathers and mothers don't love one another; where you're not yourself, but, in spite of your education and training, no less of an animal than a brute-stupid farm hand; where it isn't splendid and honourable to be Warden of St. Mary's. What's true in life? he wonders; not love, not yourself, not success . . .

CHAPTER VIII

LENNIE

*He was looking straight at our hiding-place.   I felt
my blood curdle in my veins.   Hardly I dared to breathe.
He came nearer and nearer. . . .*

"Lennie !   Lennie ! "

*Then at last I caught a glimpse of his face.   In the
gambling hell at Frisco I had not been mistaken.   I
saw once more the evil yellow countenance and leering
eyes of . . .*

"Lennie !   Lennie ! "

"Yes, Mum !   What is it ? "

"Lennie, see to Albert.   He's hollering his head off
in the back garden."

"Oh, bust 'im ! "

"Go on, Lennie, there's a good boy."

Lennard Twigg got up from the floor where he
had been lying on his stomach, and carefully dog-
eared the page which he was reading. He slipped
out through the kitchen door, and at once tasted
the salt of the sea on his lips. Above the roar of
the waves on the shingle, he could hear his younger
brother's lusty howl of "Len ! Len ! Len ! " He
ran down the path by the side of the tea-house.
There was Albert, flat on the ground. He put his
thin arms round the stout child's body and hauled
him into a standing position. "Tumbled down
again, have you, ducky ? " he asked in the bright
tone you'd hear from a well-trained nurse or a
leisured mother. "There, there ! Don't cry, now.

Come indoors and brother'll wash it for you in the
sink."

Lennard and Albert, the eldest and the youngest
of Hester's five children, went into the house together,
and Hester met them at the door. " Hurt himself ? "
she asked Lennie. " What, only grazed his knee ?
We thought you was killed, Albert, from the noise
you made." She picked up the little boy, carried him
across the room, sat him on the draining board and
dabbed at his knee with a dishcloth. Lennard
searched in his pockets and produced a piece of toffee
with some scraps of paper sticking to it and a few
hairs. He popped this in Albert's mouth and returned
to *Chums*. Hester got Albert out his Sunday puzzle,
poor little fellow, and then she took the lids off the
big saucepans which were boiling gently on two oil-
stoves, and, overwhelming the smell of oil and warmth
and dishcloths, the smell of boiling shell-fish filled the
room. Lennie sniffed languidly. He didn't care for
whelks. He liked sweeties, especially Margate Rock.

When Samuel Twigg had died in Ramsgate
Infirmary as a result of rather a gallant attempt to
stop a runaway horse, Hester had found herself in
possession of a hundred pounds of insurance money
in addition to the thirty pounds a year which had
come to her at her father's death. Ten years with
Sam Twigg on a Kentish farm had changed her from
an anæmic, contemptuous girl into a healthy, common, motherly woman, who alluded to her early
strivings after culture as " my airs and graces what
Sam soon knocked out of me." To tell the truth,
Hester had always been her father's daughter, but
environment, repression and a tendency to anæmia
in adolescence had made her a docile victim of her
mother's militant primness. All through her girlhood,
in the censorious atmosphere of free-thinking, she had

heard the pleasures and consolations of an earthly life
condemned: she had been taught to despise love,
sport, beer, charity, religion: to sit in a sunless house
in Manchester, reading the works of John Stuart Mill,
keeping yourself to yourself, beholden to no one, was
to feel chaste, intellectual, ascetic, independent, coldly
reasonable—in fact, superior. Theodore's short-
comings had opened her eyes (she felt) to the practical
value of culture . . . "You may be a wonderful
scholar, but leave you alone with a girl and you're no
better than the rest . . ." Once she had realised that,
she had admitted to herself that his books had bored
her : there's more important things than book-
learning, she'd tell her little girls, and indeed at Myrtle
Cottage it seemed so, what with beds to make, and
clothes to wash, and water to draw, and fowls to feed,
and dinner to get, and floors to scrub, and children to
scold, and baby to nurse, and, on the top of it all,
things you could have done without, like whooping-
cough, and the jam working, and Lennie to go to the
Infirmary for his adenoids, and a rat getting the chicks,
and the cat kittening. Hester's mind had grown
kindly and narrow; her voice slow and reassuring;
her arms stout and strong; her thin shoulders comfortable for poor, bumped heads. A typical country
woman, you'd have said, thinking of a small useful
cow; but she wasn't that. When Sam Twigg, who,
like many violent men, had made an excellent husband, had closed his sloe-black eyes in Ramsgate
Infirmary, Hester, refusing to buy a bit of decent black
for the children or to take in the Vicarage washing
cheaper than it could be done at the laundry, had
expended all her money on a ramshackle bungalow
built on the pebble ridge to the west of Whitstable,
along which a road runs between particularly desolate
marshland and the sea. The bungalow was badly

built; it warped; peeled; and crumbled; but it
was roomy. In the front, looking out across to
Sheppey and the East coast, was a double bedroom
distempered in pink, a single bedroom distempered
in blue, and a sitting-room distempered in red, which,
in summer, Hester had no difficulty in letting to
London working-class couples on holiday. Out of the
kitchen opened two other bedrooms where she and
the children slept. In the garden was a good-sized
hut where cyclists and Whitstable holiday-makers
might eat fish-teas and purchase postcards and ginger-
beer and bars of chocolate. " A hand-to-mouth sort
of business," sniffed the Vicar, whose washing Hester
had rejected; but it wasn't. The cyclists not only
bought their teas; they bought bags of shell-fish;
and they saw the rooms and thought them homely,
yet refined, and if they liked a bit of quiet or no
remarks passed, then they'd ask Hester straight off
for the refusal of the rooms next year. And the children
were getting handy, Hester could remind herself, in
dispiriting small hours when the sea spray was flying
over the roof of the bungalow, and the wind came
sweeping over Europe, howling round the outhouses
as if, all the way from Asia, it had had Hester's bungalow in mind. The three little girls were like their
father. They had sloe-black eyes and quarrelsome,
affectionate natures. There had been little need, she
saw now, to warn them against the inadequacies of
book-learning. They waited very sweetly on the
lodgers, could wash up, make their own beds, and set
the table for tea. It was Lennie, however, whom she
called her right hand. Fair and fragile-looking,
subject to colds in his head and atrocious chilblains,
Lennard was known to his schoolfellows as " Sissy,"
and derided for his girlish appearance and dislike of
games. He did not, however, mind very much: his

teachers were kind to him because he was so quiet, neat and obedient; and he, for his part, was always anxious to get home, where there were more interesting things to do than playing hop-scotch in an east wind or wrestling with smelly boys from the village—distempering the lodgers' rooms, for instance, or rearranging the postcard stand (the cyclists, muddle it up terribly, pulling the cards out one after another and replacing *The Pier, Herne Bay*, on top of *Faversham High Street*) or painting notices, *Teas*; *Cyclists' Rest*; *Ladies*, with an elegant, directing hand emerging from a frilly feminine cuff, and *Gentlemen*, with a larger hand and severely masculine cuff. Lennie got to know about bicycles too; he helped to repair them and was given tips, twopence and threepence, by the cyclists. His sisters and Albert adored him; all of them, except Edna, the eldest, he had pushed in the go-cart about the lanes round Myrtle Cottage; ever since they could remember he had picked them up when they had fallen down, stuffed sweets in their mouths, wiped their noses with their pinafores. Somehow he came by a mouth-organ, and then, in the winter evenings, he'd entertain them, playing tunes he had heard when the school treat had taken him to Margate —*Good-bye, Dolly, I must Leave You, The Absent Minded Beggar* and *Bluebell*, over and over again in the kitchen that smelled of oil and shell-fish and warmth and dishcloths, with the wind howling round the outhouses, and Hester thanking goodness that she could sit down for a minute, and the sloe-eyed little sisters cuddled up together by the fire. Lennie liked music—that sort of music—and he liked Margate, the shops and the people and the trams and the dancing waves and the boats bobbing in the harbour. "Lennie," said Hester, "likes a bit of life."

And when the time came for Lennard to leave school,

she acted with wisdom and unselfishness. She would have been glad enough to keep him at home to help her, for the hard years had taken toll of her body: she suffered mildly but incessantly from varicose veins and corns. And he would have been glad enough to stay. He had no stomach for adventure. He didn't want to go away and be lonely, perhaps, and miserably uncomfortable. He liked to be at home where everything was bright and familiar and happy, and he could stay indoors by the fire when he had one of his colds. But when his mother told him that she had found him a place at Vallis's, the Margate haberdasher, as shop boy, he received the news very amiably, and travelled away, docile and forlorn, one October morning, on the Margate Express, his few possessions in a wicker basket at his side. For three years he hauled the shop shutters and the sun-blinds up and down, cleaned the plate-glass windows, shook the door-mats, polished the brass surrounds, delivered and collected parcels, so politely and obediently, though his chilblains might itch unbearably and his head feel as though it were stuffed with wet cotton-wool, that, when he was just seventeen, young Mr. Vallis sent for him and offered him the position of junior assistant at the silk counter. " The boy, Twigg, has no push," contended young Mr. Vallis, " but he looks refined." Lennard had no " push," it is true, but he had ambitions. He wanted a bike, for instance, a snappy-looking Raleigh, very glossy, with low handlebars; and he wanted—terribly badly—a gramophone with a big red horn; and he wanted coloured handkerchiefs, and a pair of brown Oxford shoes, and a gun-metal cigarette-case, and a wrist-watch, and socks with clox. Such things filled his blond head as it bent earnestly over satins, tussores and japs; and his yearnings gave his blue eyes a sort of wistful mildness, which attracted to his end of the counter timid women, who were afraid of being bullied by less spiritual-looking assistants into spending more than they could afford. In consequence, his commission at the end of the month often equalled that of his seniors; but he made no enemies. He hated unpleasantness, and, however just his cause, at the least sign of it would give way. " Lennie can't say ' Bo ' to a goose," complained Edna. " He should have been a girl. I wouldn't care to have a young man like that, would you, Beattie ? Mild as mutton ? " " And a lucky thing for you too," said Hester sharply. " There's precious few boys who'd bring home the money Lennie does and keep so little for themselves." " Men are all soft nowadays," sighed romantic Beattie. " Whatever on earth would happen if there was a German invasion, I don't know. . . ."

Until he was one-and-twenty, Lennard stayed at the silk counter. A small rise in his salary gave him his coloured handkerchiefs and his socks with clox and his brown Oxford shoes; but the snappy-looking bike was as far off as ever, and now his ambitions reached beyond it, to a motor-bike and a hornless gramophone, and a silver cigarette-case and a best girl—this last, after sunset, when the place wasn't looking quite as it did in plain daylight, and impossible things seemed possible, and the German band was playing selections from *The Merry Widow* on the pier. If wishes were horses, then beggars would ride, thought Lennard, who considered that there was a lot of truth in these old adages; and in the horrible little basement bedroom, which he shared with two other assistants, he sat down and wrote an answer to an advertisement that he had noticed in the *Drapers' Record*. *I am twenty-two years of age and of good address, and I am well introduced in this district*, wrote Lennard, applying for Messrs. Pugh & Roadnight's position of traveller

for south-eastern districts at a commencing salary of
one pound a week and a commission of two and a half
per cent. . . .

Lennard had always thought that it must be a fine
thing to be a traveller. Standing behind his counter,
he would watch them come in of a morning, spruce
and urbane in bowler hats and light overcoats, pitching
cigarettes into the gutter before they sauntered in
through the swing-doors. They hadn't spent the
night in a basement bedroom under the shop with
Spokes, who snored, and Curtis, who ground his
teeth; breakfasted with the same old crowd in the
basement dining-room; come upstairs to stand along-
side Curtis, with Spokes just opposite in the habby.
They lived among shifting scenes and changing faces.
They'd come in speedy trains, through the fresh
morning landscape, from rooms in London or the
commercial hotel at Canterbury: when they'd seen
Tremliss, the silk buyer, and been up to Smart's, and
perhaps Cable's, at Cliftonville, speedy trains would
bear them hence to Broadstairs, Ramsgate, Dover,
Folkestone, Hastings. . . . Evening would find them
sauntering into coffee-rooms, pressing bells for waiters,
ordering at will. Sometimes, he noticed, they looked
depressed, standing by the velvets, waiting and
waiting; but I shouldn't mind waiting, thought
Lennard, standing there in a bowler hat and a light
overcoat, with nothing to do. And then, when people
asked me what I was, instead of having to say, " I'm
in the silk department at Vallis's," and know that
they were thinking, like Edna, that it's soppy for a
man to stand behind a counter and measure out silk
and say, " And the next thing, please ? " I'd be able
to say, " I travel for Pugh & Roadnight, the London
firm," and they'd think, well, he travels about all over
the place and knows what's what. Lennard went up

to London to be interviewed by Messrs. Pugh & Roadnight, and was selected from among half a dozen
applicants—no footsore army of energetic ex-officers,
accustomed to organise, able to handle men, or pukka
sahibs, willing to go anywhere and do anything, sprang
to life at a hint of employment in those Arcadian days.
Hester's lean years were, so she believed, over. Lennard promised a lavish increase in the amount of
money he sent home to her; Edna, who helped with
the teas and the lodgers, was engaged to a prosperous
young farmer, and Daisy, the youngest sister, was old
enough to step into her place; Beattie worked in
Tankerton Post Office; Albert would be leaving school
in a few months, and had been promised the job of
making himself useful in a garage.

And what had it all been worth? thought Hester,
sitting by the kitchen fire, in a lop-sided arm-chair,
tired to death, resting her poor feet on another chair
and rubbing camphor ice on her chapped hands. My
hair's grey, she thought, and I've lost all the looks I
ever had, and my figure too—and what hands to go
anywhere with! and my legs are a sight, and don't
they ache ! And all for what ? she demanded looking
back into her past, seeing it rich with incident, like
an old tapestry, rich and dim and romantic as only a
full, hard life can be. Just as you can stand in a room
and look at a tapestry, picking out this and that, so
she could pick out, at will, wedding day or holiday, a
feast or a funeral, an illness, a quarrel, a birth or a
bridal night. Yes, I've lived, she thought; I've had
all the things that stories are made of, and poetry,
and pictures too. But when I go, my past will go
with me. I've not, as you might say, made my mark
on the world. But haven't I ? she thought, with a
sudden lifting of her sober mood. What about Lennie
and Edna and Beattie and Daisy and Albert, them

and all the things they'll do? I'll have to go, and goodness knows where and goodness knows why, but my blood will go on living on earth in them; you won't be able to say I'm done for, any more than you can say the tree's done for when this year's apples are off. If I'd lived as some do, hoarding up—not money, I mean, but things like your strength and your looks and your refinement—then I might have said it wasn't worth it, all the fuss and worry, and then just to die. But there's Lennie; I've lost my nice ways of speaking, but listen to him! and I've lost my looks, but look at Edna! And Lennie will get on, and he'll marry some nice girl and have a dear little house, near London, with bow windows and a lawn, and his children will go to a High School; and Edna will have some little girls as pretty as ever she was; and then there's Beattie, so clever and full of ideas, understanding politics and all the rest of it; and Daisy, going to be as pretty as Edna; and Albert and his engines. And if all that isn't worth the rough and the smooth of these years, and what looks I had, and my airs and graces—well, I don't know what is, thought Hester, rubbing the camphor ice well into the worst crack of all.

Edna married her farmer, and went to live in a big farmhouse, set in rolling cornland, between Herne Bay and Birchington, where she had servant girls for all the rough work, and a pony and jingle of her own. Hester's grandchildren made prompt and regular appearances: sturdy, sloe-eyed children; Sam's blood crying aloud. Beattie conducted what she called a platonic friendship with a well-educated young Whitstable tradesman, who showered gifts on her and proposed to her at frequent intervals. Daisy scorned numerous admirers, having found her ideal when she went to stay in London and Lennie took her to the

dress-circle to see Lewis Waller in *Monsieur Beaucaire*.
Albert got a couple of rises, and Lennie in a bowler
hat and a light overcoat, pitching his cigarette into
the gutter, sauntering in through the swing-doors,
waiting and waiting among the velvets until his feet
ached and his heart ached and he wished he were one
of those lucky devils behind the counter, was one of
Pugh & Roadnight's smartest travellers.   So matters
stood in nineteen hundred and fourteen.

And when the war came—why, he didn't bother
his head—docile Lennie, just back in London, after
a fortnight's holiday, to find nothing on earth doing,
what with its being August and then this war, presented himself at a recruiting office on his first sight
of a poster stating that his King and Country Needed
Him.   *Just a line to tell you I joined up this morning,*
Mother, he wrote to Hester on a picture postcard of
the Albert Memorial.   *Should like to have a slap at*
Kaiser Bill, Your loving son, Len.   In spite of colds
in his head, early rising, coarse food, squad drill, route
marches, vaccination and army boots, he enjoyed his
weeks of training; he liked living in a crowd; he was
a " good mixer "—evenings in commercial hotels, chats
in third-class railway carriages, and a tolerance that
was almost a weakness had made him that; he liked
a good laugh, and singing—*Who's Your Lady Friend?*
You're My Baby, Who Were You With Last Night?—
he liked noise and bustle and " a bit of life."   He was
drafted early out to Flanders.   Like many funda-
mentally pacific persons, he made an excellent
twentieth-century soldier: not winter in the Salient
nor the might of the German Empire could spoil his
enjoyment of a good laugh.   Patriotism, duty, sacrifice—such words as inspired the Gallic warrior—meant
nothing to his light, English heart.   He was going
through to Berlin with the boys and he wasn't down-

hearted—that was what Lennie thought when he
thought seriously about the war. The fear of death
or of mutilation troubled him very little after his first
twenty-four hours in front-line trenches; he accepted
the admirable philosophy of the music hall—*What's
the use of worrying? It never was worth while*, he sang,
while the Commander-in-Chief's despatches reported
The Second Battle of Ypres. At Christmas in nineteen hundred and fifteen, he came home on leave a
sergeant, and less than a year later, he was recommended for a commission. He was pleased, and he
wasn't. It must be fine to be an officer when it was a
matter of sitting in a roomy dug-out, plastered with
pictures torn from the *Bystander* and *La Vie Paris-
ienne*, drinking double whiskies and censoring letters,
but not so fine to be first over the parapet or on the
mat if anything went wrong. However, he was to
be sent to a Cadet Battalion, and that, it appeared,
meant at least three months in England—three months
of sheets and tablecloths and cinemas and shops and
shows and gramophones and one-steps and the girls.
On a very lovely September morning—pearly mists
wreathing the hideous desolation of the Salient, Jerry
quiet (but not for long, said Rumour); larks singing
as soon as you got out of the trenches and the sun
began to struggle through—Lennie said " Cheerio ! "
to the boys and, " Mind you don't go through to Berlin
till I get out again ! " He had to report to his regimental depot at Canterbury, and there he learned
that, after ninety-six hours' leave, he was to proceed
to St. Mary's College, Oxford. " Well, Mother !
Oxford College for me ! " cried Lennie, bursting into
the kitchen that smelled of warmth and dishcloths,
but no longer of oil and shellfish, for no cyclists came
to the bungalow now.

CHAPTER IX

"I HAVE A CHILD"

THEODORE was no alarmist. When people predicted a war with Germany, he would pooh-pooh them. "The idea emanates from the busy brain of the ha'penny press," he would state contemptuously. "It is untenable by anyone who realises how closely the intelligentsia of the two countries are associated. Scholarship, literature, art, know no frontiers"; and he would think of mild, spectacled, scientific Dr. Grimm and mild, spectacled philosophic Professor Eckermann, who had stayed with him during Commemoration when they had received honorary degrees; and of how absurd it was to imagine himself their enemy, wanting bayonets to be stuck into their inoffensive bodies and bullets shot through their admirable brains. "We have reached a stage of civilisation in which a European war is unthinkable," said Theodore, sitting at High Table, sipping *bisque homard* from a Queen Anne spoon. "Setting aside the question of human life, I cannot imagine our German friends training guns on the Bodleian." "I can," said Haughton. "What's civilisation but a muslin blind?" "Without stopping to define civilisation," said Theodore, who loathed Haughton's picturesque and fallacious fancies, "I think we may say that the Germans are the most civilised nation in Europe. With the possible exception of the Swiss, they are surely foremost in co-operation and mutual aid . . ." "No," said Haughton, "ants are."

Theodore was at Grasmere when war was declared. Every year he spent some part of the Long Vacation staying with his erstwhile tutor, Edward Coleridge, now a man of over eighty, who had retired, with a poor relation for housekeeper, to a small, solitary house under Silver How. This annual excursion provided him with a change of air, but not of atmosphere. A fine library spread itself over the little house, even into the bathroom; coloured prints, depicting Oxford buildings and Oxfordshire scenery, hung wherever it had been found quite impossible to erect a bookcase. The sitting-room was furnished like a college sitting-room, with a sofa facing the fireplace, two arm-chairs on either side, and a large, solid table directly behind the sofa; a reproduction of the portrait of the late Warden of St. Mary's hung over the mantelpiece; sitting there on the sofa, the kettle singing on the fire, the kettle-holder at your hand, the poor relation banished to her bedroom, the Lakeland mist obscuring the view across the water to the fells, you might have been sitting in rooms in the Fellows' Building at St. Mary's. Theodore realised that, thanked heaven for it, and, when he had nothing else to worry over, worried over the question of where he should spend his vacation when death called for Edward Coleridge at the home from home under Silver How.

The first days of the war did not move Theodore very deeply. Edward Coleridge had held the same views as himself and allowed him to blame the Prussians for the singularly uncivilised behaviour of his admired Germany : he imagined that before the beginning of the October term, the thing would be satisfactorily fought out by the Expeditionary Force. A crumpled postcard from France from a young don of his college, who had been called up with the Special Reserve, shook him a little; " I hope that we shall have Jones back before term starts," he said, but Jones was in the Casualty List next day. The Bursar wrote about college servants, reservists who had been called up; and distracted parents to say that their sons had enlisted or applied for commissions. Theodore hurried back to Oxford, through the length of a country alive with soldiers, his world falling more and more into bits about him since scholarship, literature, art, were nothing, and men were blowing each other's bodies to pieces, fighting like savages, jabbing, slashing, piercing (as though Mill had never reasoned, or Heine sung), soulless, heartless and bloodthirsty, no better than animals, over there in France. " Oxford," said Theodore, changing at Bletchley. " Oxford." The word was shelter in the hurricane, a rock in the whirlpool. Her walls would be arms about him, her towers dream on . . .

And until the beginning of term, he did find a little comfort; for it was Vacation, and the streets were always a little queer then with Extensionists and Americans. Not until he dined again in Hall would he really believe that Jones, brilliant and benevolent, was rotting somewhere between Mons and Frameries, and that Dr. Quears, who had lingered too confidently with charming friends at the University of Bonn, was learning " the meaning of captivity " in an internment camp in freezing Prussia. Battalions swinging in over Magdalen Bridge, Army lorries grinding up the High, newsboys shouting, " Fierce Fighting on the Aisne ! " and " Fall of Antwerp ! " and " Heavy Casualties at Wipers ! " were distressing enough; but he could withdraw from them, hurrying through the front quad—the noise dying away behind him—into the cloisters, quiet and dim, never sunlight so mellow as the autumn sunlight coming in through the arches, where the red Virginia creeper was dropping its leaves, slowly, softly, on the suave, old grass. He thought, here; Oxford waits . . . "ignoring clamours " . . . not blaming . . . not praising . . . and, when it's all over, they'll come back to her. Crete, Egypt, Sparta had their wars. But, when he was forced to see the vacant places at High Table; the half-empty hall; boys, who should have been bicycling up Iffley road in sweaters and shorts to play foot-ball or jogging down Rose Lane to the river, going off in khaki to drill in the Parks; presently the Schools a base hospital; " Godley's Own " marching down Holywell; above all when it became his duty to scan the Casualty Lists and record the fate of St. Mary's men, he began to realise that they wouldn't come back, that, in these dreadful days, the bright heads he'd read his lectures over, the decorous faces he'd admonished, the Hellenic limbs he'd applauded from the barge, were luckier than most if they got shovelled underground. He hadn't been like the late Warden, who could fit name and record to every face in college; he'd mixed them up—mistaking a double Blue for the winner of the Newdigate, the Varsity cox for a freshman—all the worse because he was afraid of doing so, knowing that they laughed at him, imitated his nervous manner, told the story of how he had said, " I don't know you, I don't know you," and scurried away from an undergraduate who had ventured to approach him in the Turl. Individually they had meant nothing to him; good and bad, dark and fair, athlete and scholar, laughing, swear-ing, idling, working, loving life, eating their hearts out, they had passed by, just a stream of youth flowing through the city: but collectively they had meant everything to him and he had been power-less to help them—St. Mary's couldn't shut her lovely gates against this war. Savage, incredible, monstrous, it had forced its way in across the quad, through the cloisters, to empty Founder's Buildings, to empty the Hall. The gramophones were silent now, and the bicycle bells, and the long murmur of youth setting the world to rights, and the cheers from the river and from the football grounds; strange and agonising names—La Bassée, Ypres, Givenchy, Passchendaele—rang in the streets and in his ears; yet beautiful as a dream, Magdalen rose to the stars and Theodore still sat at High Table eating from Queen Anne silver, still sipped brown sherry, stately, in the Senior Common Room. We're not waiting, he discovered, one evening in Hall, the place much more than half empty now, only a handful of physical defectives at the scholars' table. We're not waiting. We're left behind. Oxford's no use in this war any more than scholarship or litera-ture; a heap of earth out there that a man can take cover behind is of more use than the loveliest of our buildings; in spite of my position and attainments, the most doltish yokel of eighteen, who can march and jab with a bayonet, is of more use than I. Did the others at the table realise that, he wondered, and, if so, how did they support it—this ghastly feeling that your world had been nothing all along but an illusion, that everything you had lived for had been useless, impotent all the time? He strained his ears listening to the conversation. " I had a letter from my eldest boy last night," said Hamilton; and Haughton, " My daughter tells me they had a new convoy in to-day." Boles sat silent; but Crawley was making a map of some sort of salient with his knife and fork and a pepper pot, and arguing over it with the Dean—Crawley's daughter had recently married a staff officer. " That's what my son-in-law told me," said Crawley, and Hamilton was saying,

" Billy's been recommended for the D.S.O." Well, thought Theodore, that's what keeps them going. They've got children. They may be ghosts themselves, inhabiting this place that's a shell, but their flesh goes to fight, it's their blood that's spilt. They've handed on the torch of life, he thought, true classicist; when I die, and Boles, that'll be the end of us, but they've got immortality: their blood will race, their hair blow in the wind, their voices speak long after they're in Holywell Cemetery. I've been a fool, he thought, getting up, proceeding to the Common Room: I've loved books and worshipped knowledge, and all the books in the world and all the knowledge haven't stopped this war. I've sat here in Oxford, sat at High Table, " in the light and not in the heat, in the feast and not in the throng "; I've hated the coarseness of ordinary life and the coarseness of ordinary emotions, and I've lost my immortality. He passed under the portrait of the first Warden, a great scholar, a great divine, but a celibate, and dust now; and took his seat, the present Warden, not so great a scholar, and a bachelor, and he'd be dust, too. " What do you think of the news to-night, Warden ? " asked Hamilton, peeling an apple. " There's nothing new, is there ? " said Theodore. " There's a push expected, and ' all quiet on the Western front ' usually means that the Boche is blowing up for something," said Hamilton, adding, " You're fortunate." " Fortunate ? Why ? " " No one out there—to worry over." " Of course, of course," said Theodore; and, as he spoke, the wedge that the years were fell away: he was back in a fir wood, the September sky blue above an orchard, doves cooing on a red roof, and a girl screaming at him— incredible things. But I have a child, I have a child, thought Theodore.

CHAPTER X

"I'M HUNGRY"

In the spring of nineteen hundred and sixteen, St. Mary's hall was full again. "The concerted noise of them is different," discovered Haughton, and for once Theodore agreed with him; the noise was louder, gruffer, less continuous: there was more laughter. These cadets, most of them home for three months of cinemas and shops and shows and gramophones and one-steps and the girls, three months without night patrols, mud, duckboards, bully beef, vermin, had no ambition to set the world to rights. There was more laughter at the High Table, too. The officers of the cadet battalion dined here with the dons and drank brown sherry with them in the Senior Common Room; gravely the Fellows listened to talk of George Robey and Gwendolen Brogden and Murray's and the "Cri." "It's humanising," said Theodore, "it's humanising," and Hamilton stared at him. What was the matter with the Warden that he wanted to be humanised? Theodore noticed the stare. Hamilton, with his three sons, thinks I'm a dry old ghost with my world in ashes and no stake in the future, he told himself, and remembered the other's words, "You're fortunate. No one out there—to worry over." He'd be surprised if he knew, thought Theodore quite commonly, and caught himself wishing that Hamilton did know. When Hamilton's boy was awarded the D.S.O. Theodore thought, perhaps *he's* been decorated too: when the news of fighting came, he thought, perhaps *he* was

114

there—never for a moment did he doubt that his child
had been a boy. He hadn't enough imagination to
picture his son, and was shy of thinking of him by any
name. Perhaps *he's* out on patrol to-night, he would
think, lying in bed in the solemn room overlooking
his garden; and the heartbreak he had felt for youth
as a whole, he felt now for this vague young
figure in khaki to whom he had given life and—
God knows why, he cried now—refused his name.
Was I mad? he wondered at such times, looking back
over his life, seeing things, too late, in proportion;
what on earth would it have mattered if my parents
had made themselves disagreeable and the village
had gossiped, compared to the fact that the torch
hadn't burnt out in my hand? When one's young,
he reflected, and brought up, as I was brought up,
to value culture, which isn't an activity but simply
a drawing-back from life, how the small things
loom—the girl was a different class; I hadn't got
my degree; people would have guessed that there
was a baby coming—and how vague the big things seem
—Nature's got one purpose; life's to be lived, nobly,
if you can, but not evaded; our immortality is here
on earth. He looked still farther back. Why didn't
my parents teach me what mattered? he asked.
They were of the age that I am now when I
was a boy of ten; and, almost at the beginning
of his recollections, as such things are, he heard
his mother's voice, high and uncontrolled: " I
have done my duty as a wife although I have
never pretended that I loved you." Child of unloving parents, the meagre fruit of duty, what
wonder that he had not seen the world as other
people see it, as a place in which to love and laugh and
walk bravely and take what comes? It wasn't altogether my fault that I behaved like a coward and a

fool, Hester, he apologised. I was young and feeble
of will and they misled me. The body's a brute and
the spirit's an angel, they taught me, and the world
went to pieces when I found I was everything I despised.
If I had married her, he thought, and how strange
that sounded ! if I had married her, I shouldn't
have been Warden of St. Mary's. I couldn't have
stayed at Oxford. I should have had to find some
other employment. She would have dragged me
down; down from the High Table, he thought
ironically, to the heroic level of these ordinary
men.

Such was his outlook at the time when Colonel
Kennedy was pronounced fit for active service, and
Colonel Sir Richard Oliver, a Guardsman, recovering from an arm wound received at the second battle
of Ypres, arrived at St. Mary's to take command of
the battalion. Richard Oliver had hardened into a
handsome, well-mannered, well-dressed man of round
about fifty, forty-five, you would have guessed, and
surely ten years younger than the Warden of St. Mary's.
Then you would have said, a man of the world, and
thought of big-game hunting and double whiskies
and Ranelagh and the Royal Enclosure, and in spite
of the charm of manner which his school and his own
unaffected heart had taught him, you would very likely
have dismissed him as a type that any intelligent person
must contemn. That would have been a pity. It was
a small world that Richard knew so well, and an in-
consistent one—the world that pampers the horse
and hunts the fox, drives grouse and contributes lavishly
to the S.P.C.A., opposes democracy and lives up to a
merciless tradition of service to the state. The small-
ness of his world was very evident in his conversation.
He would go purple with choler at a mention of Ramsay
MacDonald, conscientious objectors or wire: he

was intolerant, prejudiced and ignorant, but he had the virtues of his type too. He was so brave that everyone, except his own officers, said he must be drunk: he was truthful and charitable and unselfish and optimistic. When, at his father's death, he had inherited Widdingfold Hall and a hundred thousand pounds, forsaking his circumspect flirtations, he had married the quietest of Lord Abinger's daughters, bringing to his marriage more friendship than sentiment; and his wife, at a sacrifice of four seasons' riding to hounds, had presented him with three lovely daughters and finally with his heir. Richard's only terror was that the war would last until Clement was eighteen; and Clement's only terror was that it would not.

When Richard came to St. Mary's, he knew that he was going to meet Theodore, but Theodore had not paid any real attention to the name of the new commanding officer, nor did he recognise, in the splendid soldier, who strolled in through the porter's lodge one autumn morning, the small boy who had been smacked so often for calling out in the night nursery at the Hall. Emerging from the Warden's Lodgings, Theodore scurried innocently across the quad to meet his future and his past. " Well, Fletcher, this is a funny sort of meeting after all these years ! Do you remember me ? " said Richard, who was much too simple-minded—some people said, too self-assured— to be shy. Theodore, who had been looking at his feet, looked up through his thick glasses. " I'm afraid I don't," he muttered, madly searching his memory. About five-and-forty or less . . . he'd have been up in the later half of the nineties . . . looks more like a rowing man than anything, but they all look like soldiers nowadays. " Who is it ? Who is it ? " he asked in a frenzy of embarrassment. " Oliver. Richard

Oliver." "Of course, of course," said Theodore. "One forgets. One forgets. How are you?" They stood there in the quad, talking, a queer pair to a stranger's eye.

Richard thought Theodore a funny old stick, and God, what a life! but his heart's in the right place, he discovered, talking about the war over the walnuts and the brown sherry that was silk in the mouth and a song in the throat and sunshine in the belly— "That goes down nicely, by Gad, it does," Richard would say. He wrote home that Theodore looked like nothing on this green earth, but was of the same stuff as the Fellows who melted down the college plate to replenish the exchequer of Charles the First; "I'm surprised how well these old boys do themselves," he added with respect. Theodore thought Richard one of the most terrifying persons he had ever been unfortunate enough to encounter, hadn't a word to say to him, found that his eyes watered when he looked at him. In vain attempts to feel at his ease with Richard, he would cast his mind back to old ignominious scenes —Richard being given a good shake by his nurse or forcibly expelled from the schoolroom by Miss Minns.

"Funny how one bumps into people in this war," said Richard one evening. "I told you, didn't I, how a fellow filled a cup for me at a drinking fountain during the Retreat, and when he turned round and handed it to me, blest if it wasn't old John? Well, there's a fellow more or less from the village here just now. His father was at the Home Farm for some time, a most knowing chap in the matter of ferrets. Gipsy blood, I believe. The name's Twigg."

"Twigg?"

"Yes. We've a funny lot of names, haven't we?" said Richard feudally. "Heritage and Innocent and

Forrester and so on. Twigg is Anglo-Saxon, I should
think." He began to talk a slap-dash kind of etymo-
logy. Theodore didn't listen. It may be a younger
brother, he was telling himself. The Twiggs were a
large family and probably Jim, or Fred, or whatever
his name was, had had a large one too. "What sort
of aged man is Twigg?" he asked Richard, but his
question was drowned by Richard's louder voice asking
was "hog" an Anglo-Saxon word? The opportunity having passed, he found it impossible to reopen
the subject in cold blood; often he framed phrases:
"About this man, Twigg . . ." "By the way, you
spoke of a fellow from Widdingfold . . ." but he never
spoke them. The desire to see his son grew and grew
on him, however; as he went about, he searched for
some resemblance to himself or Hester, peering intently
into the faces of the cadets as they passed him. This
caused them endless amusement. On account of his
scurrying walk they had nicknamed him "Flying
Fletcher," but he now became known as "Peering
Pop," and their attempts to keep straight faces under
his scrutiny must have wiped away any resemblance
he might have observed. Despairing as the precious
days went by, he stopped a cadet in the cloisters and
asked: "How would it be possible for me to find a
man named Twigg?" The cadet, a kindly boy with
a grandfather of his own, said, "Twigg . . . Twigg
. . . I believe he's in Company B. Should I find
him and send him to you, sir?" "Yes, yes. Thank
you. But when had I better see him?" "When
would it be most convenient?" asked the sensible
youth. "Tea on Sunday," said Theodore, and with
his maladroit courtesy, "You come, too." He scurried
away and the cadet went round to Founder's Building
and hunted out Lennie, who roared with derisive
laughter and said did Cartwright think it was April

Fool's Day? It took the wretched Cartwright a week
to persuade Lennie that "Peering Pop" had really
asked him to tea.

Lennie was enjoying himself at Oxford. Within a
few hours of his arrival at St. Mary's, he had made
several friends. One of these, a man a few years his
junior, named Walter Logan, had relations living in
Oxford, in Staverton Road, and at the first opportunity he set off to call on them, taking Lennie with
him. "The girls—my cousins—are a cheery couple
of kids," said Logan. "You'll like Doreen." Lennie
knew where he was, then, and followed Logan into a
pink-and-white drawing-room, amiably prepared to
pair off with Doreen.

The Logans were not, as Mrs. Logan used to put it,
"in University circles"; her husband was a partner
in an auctioneer's business, which was chiefly concerned with the selling of farm stock. He was a small,
faded man, who worked hard all the week, and, during
the week-end, sat at fretwork in a tiny room looking
north, which was known to the household as "the
den." Mrs. Logan was an absurd, smart woman of
unbelievable snobbishness and colossal vanity; she
was, however, almost idiotically kind-hearted, and was
deeply loved by her exasperated family. She had had,
as she would be sure to tell you, an expensive education;
she could play the piano well; both her daughters had
small, true voices; "and in these dark days," said
Mrs. Logan, "a little cheery music is such a tonic for
the boys." Vain, vulgar, pompous and ridiculous, she
understood and sympathised with men as few women
do; and many a war-worn boy found new strength
and sanity joining in some nonsensical chorus in
her drawing-room. Her daughters had inherited
her kind heart and her love of clothes, but not
her boastfulness; although they were as pretty

as paint—the blonde and the brunette of the chocolate carton or the handkerchief gift-box—they were rather humble girls.

Lennie, presented in the pink-and-white drawing-room to "my cousin, Joan," said, "How do you do, Miss Logan?" and, being the last man in the world to poach on another chap's preserve, noticed, with chaste indifference, that the girl was a peach, golden-haired, blue-eyed, long-legged and slim. "And this is Doreen." Fair himself, he had always fancied that when he fell it would be for a brunette; and though a few minutes' conversation was generally enough to undeceive him, it made things much more exciting to be able to say to yourself, this may be the girl! Doreen was shorter than her sister, but not less slimly built. Her thick black hair curled entrancingly about her heart-shaped face, and a pair of dreamy eyes, set rather wide apart, looked out with absent-minded friendliness at soldier, sailor, tinker, tailor, rate collector or lost dog. Her complexion was not as good as it might have been if she had eaten fewer chocolates or walked up and down the Woodstock Road instead of "bussing it." Her work at her father's office, where she had replaced a male clerk since the beginning of the war, was deplorable, and grew worse and worse as she grew more and more tired of it.

Joan said, "Mother's having a nap upstairs. She'll be down in a minute and then we'll have tea." A table, covered with a cloth of drawn-thread work, was set with cups and saucers, and a wicker cake-stand bore a great variety of fancy cakes. Lennie, not long from Flanders, glanced with rapture round the room, at the pink carpet and chintzes, the white walls and overmantel, at the shining fire-irons, at the bright little fire in the neat little grate, at the washy water-colours, at the tea-knives, at the ebony china-cabinet, at the girls in their pale frocks and silk stockings. Never chary of expressing himself, he said, " By Jove, if I stopped here long, I should forget there was a war."

" You tell Mother that," said Joan, " and she'll love you for ever. She says that's her war work—cheering you boys up. I bet she does more good than a lot of those old Judys who pop on uniform and run round winning the war."

" Sure thing ! " grunted Walter, sinking into the depths of the pink sofa. " I say that when the war's over, they ought to make George Robey a peer."

Lennie turned to Doreen.

" Have you seen *The Bing Boys on Broadway* ? "

" No, I haven't. Joan has. She's lucky. She's been nursing in London. But we've got the music. We'll make Mother play it over after tea."

" I like that number, *First Love, Last Love, Best Love*."

" It's lovely, isn't it ? "

" Isn't it ?   Did you see *The Bing Boys* ? "

" No.   Joan did.   It was lovely, wasn't it ? "

" Tophole. *If You Were the Only Girl in the World and I Were the Only Boy*—that's a great song too, isn't it ? "

" It is, isn't it ? Violet Lorraine's tophole, isn't she ? "

" Tophole.   You ought to see this new show . . ." Lennie rose as Mrs. Logan, resplendent in a pink brocade blouse with a Medici collar, as advertised by Messrs. Debenham & Freebody, entered the room.

" Walter !   My dear boy ! "

" Hullo, Auntie ! "

Walter kissed the purple cheek with real affection, and turned to Lennard.

" This is my friend, Mr. Twigg, Auntie."

" I am very glad to see you, Mr. Twigg," announced Mrs. Logan, extending to Lennie a plump, pink hand, prickly with rings. " Any friend of Walter's is always welcome at ' Innisfree.' "

Lennie was impressed and affected.

" Most kind of you to let me come, Mrs. Logan," he murmured.

" Not at all, Mr. Twigg," she replied graciously, and then, " Press the bell, Joan, dear. I'm sure these boys are dying for their tea."

Scarcely had the bell sounded than a nervous little maid darted in with a tray which bore a silver teapot and a hot-water jug and a plate of hot scones. Mrs. Logan took her place at the table and began to pour out, casting into the general conversation clear enquiries about sugar and milk and the strength of the tea. " Now tell me how you like being at Oxford," she commanded Lennie, when her duties were finished. " You're at St. Mary's, aren't you ? That's one of our loveliest colleges."

" It's all right to look at," said Lennie. " But you couldn't call it homey, Mrs. Logan. It's awfully quiet, tucked away inside there, too. You might be miles from anywhere. I shouldn't like to be one of those old dons."

" They like it quiet, mouldy old things," said Doreen. " They're awful old kill-joys, you can't think."

" They're very wise and learned men," said Mrs. Logan. " The Warden of St. Mary's . . . let me see . . . that's Fletcher, isn't it ? "

Lennie and Walter hooted with laughter.

" ' Flying Fletcher ? ' He's a caution ! You should see him scoot across the quad ! "

" I think you're both very disrespectful young

men," said Mrs. Logan. "However, I'll forgive you. I'd forgive most things to the boys in khaki or blue. Now, Joan, are you going to take Dad's tea in to him?" Pouring out a cup of tea, she told Lennie, "We can't coax Dad out of the den."

"Is he a great reader?" asked Lennie.

"Fretwork's his hobby," explained Mrs. Logan, while Joan carried out a cup of tea and Walter a scone. "He gets quite absorbed in it. I don't like to drag him out to be sociable because he works hard with his brain all the week, and he says it's a rest for his brain to use his hands. Another cup, Mr. Twigg?"

Lennie said, "Yes, please, if it's not greedy, Mrs. Logan," allowed Doreen to pass his cup, and accepted another scone. He felt very happy. Mrs. Logan had a way of drawing you into the family circle, she told you that she couldn't coax Dad from the den or what it had cost to decorate the drawing-room or how pure were the ingredients of the cake that she was cutting for you, and you began to feel at home; it wouldn't matter, you felt, if you stayed on till seven or asked her the way to the bathroom. Oh, Belle Logan, Belle Logan, you were a silly, vain, and vulgar woman; sitting in your villa by your doll's-house fireplace, uttering platitudes, jerking your head because the supports in your Medici collar kept catching in your back hair, you were unbelievably ridiculous; but, long after the young men of other social circles forgot the brilliant or aristocratic gatherings they had attended, the boys you entertained at "Innisfree" remembered and sighed for cosy tea-times and jolly evenings in the pink-and-white drawing-room out of which, while retaining the glories, you had so firmly shut the miseries of war! "You'll play to us, Auntie, won't you?" said Walter presently, and his aunt replied, "Well, if

Mr. Twigg doesn't mind my strumming. I had the advantage of a very expensive education, Mr. Twigg," she explained as she crossed the room to the piano. "What my parents spent on my music alone must have run into three figures. But I'm afraid I was a lazy girl and often cut short my practices. If youth but knew! or *see junness savey*, I ought to say—I've often been complimented on my French accent. When my husband and I stayed in gay Paree before the war, the head-waiter at the hotel mistook me for a Frenchwoman." Joan and Walter had their heads together over a pile of music, and Mrs. Logan sat down at the piano and stroked out a few saccharine chords. "This dear old piano was my father's wedding present to me," she said. "He gave over three figures for it. The piano-tuner told me that it was one of the finest instruments in North Oxford."

"Play this, Mother," said Joan.

And Mrs. Logan played *They'll Never Believe Me*, and Joan and Walter at the piano and Lennie and Doreen on the sofa joined softly in the refrain. *And when I tell them How won-der-ful you are, They'll never be-lieve me, They'll never be-lieve me*, sang Lennie, comfortable in the big, soft sofa, warm at the bright fire, replete with buttered scones and fancy cakes, cheerful among these friendly people, three months of life in front of him, only one thing needed to complete his happiness—to find the substance of the shadowy You he sang of, not a girl just to take to shows and dance with because you had to go around with someone, but, since he had quite three months to count on, the Real Thing. *They'll never be-lieve me That from this great, big world you've cho-sen me*, sang Lennie, blowing the smoke of his cigarette through his nose, thinking how wonderful it must be to be chosen out of all the men in the great, big world by a lovely and innocent girl—*Your eyes, your lips, your cheeks, your hair, Are a class be-yond compare. You're the loveliest thing a man could wish to see*—who'd love you and trust you so incredibly that she'd accept an engagement ring, and marry you as soon as the course was over and you were an officer, and go away with you in a first-class compartment, and give herself to you in a handsomely furnished bedroom on the first floor of the Grand Hotel, Eastbourne. Mrs. Logan's nimble fat fingers pounced down on the final chord; Lennie glanced round the room—straight into Doreen's grey eyes. Perhaps her thoughts had been something like his, for she often thought about love and how wonderful it would be to have someone, not just to take you to the Cinema and to tea (with éclairs) at the George Café, but the Real Thing—someone who'd love you, and want you, and give you an engagement ring (a marquise one) and a wedding ring (a platinum one) and a honeymoon at a really smart hotel, and then a little white house and a darling baby, like the one in *Mighty Like a Rose*. Anyhow, as their eyes met, she coloured slightly, and Lennie felt a thrill run through him, from the back of his neck right down into his shoes. Good lord! he thought, is this the Real Thing? and he didn't feel comfortable, warm, replete, cheerful, any longer, but tremendously excited, never so alive! The pink-and-white drawing-room wasn't big enough now. Oh, lord! the little place was stifling! *If you were the on-lee girl in the world, and I were the on-lee boy, Nothing else would matter in the world all day, We would go on loving in the same old way. A gar-den of E-den just made for two With noth-ing to mar our joy. There would be such won-der-ful things to do, I would say such won-der-ful things to you, If you were the on-lee girl in the world, and I were the on-lee boy,*

sang the group round the piano, and never had a song
more accurately expressed a man's mood. But we're
not the only people in the world, thought Lennie;
we're two of this unlucky lot that's young while the
war's on. We've got to cram life and love into three
months, so let's get on with it. He looked at Doreen
and said, " Would you and your sister care to come
to the pictures one evening with Walter and me ? "

" Love to," said Doreen.

" Either George Street or Queen's Street," said
Lennie. " And we could have something to eat at
the George Café first."

" Hi ! What are you two arranging ? " asked Joan.

" I wonder if Walter and I might take Miss Joan
and Miss Doreen to the pictures to-morrow evening,
Mrs. Logan ? "

" I'm afraid they'd be only too delighted, Mr.
Twigg. I'm sorry to say that my frivolous little
daughters prefer any silly film to a really good concert. However, I forgive them," said Mrs. Logan,
getting up from the piano and putting her arm round
Joan's supple shoulders. " In many ways they are
very good little girls."

" Thank you for those few kind words, Mother,"
said Joan, and kissed her.

" That's fixed then," said Walter.

" We'll have dinner at seven at the George Café,"
said Lennard.

Doreen gave a shriek of protest. " I don't get out
of the mouldy old office till after six."

" My dear ! If you bus it both ways . . . " said
her sister.

" We'll make it a quarter past seven," said Lennie
readily, " if that will be better for Miss Doreen."

" And you'll be sure to see the girls home, right to
the door, won't you, Walter ? " said Mrs. Logan.

" Of course, Auntie. And I'll see that they behave themselves too. . . ."

Lennie's party was an unqualified success. His experience of hotels and restaurants had given him an easy, man-of-the-world manner in such places: he had reserved a table and ordered dinner beforehand: his way with waiters was impressive; he caused the orchestra to render Doreen's favourite, *First Love, Last Love, Best Love*, by request: he offered Turkish cigarettes and liqueurs with the coffee: and conveyed his guests to Queen's Street Cinema in a taxi, with boxes of Fuller's chocolates on their knees. In the cinema he sat next to Doreen. Joan and Walter held hands throughout the performance, but Lennie didn't touch Doreen, not even her foot with his foot; he was afraid that she would think he was just flirting—that it wasn't the Real Thing. He told her in an undertone about his mother and sisters and the fine position he had held with Messrs. Pugh & Roadnight; and, child of his generation, could watch, at the same time, right triumph over wrong, love cast out hate, journeys end in lovers' meetings on the sanguine screen. " Enjoying yourself ? " " Awf'ly ! " " Come again ? " " Love to ! " And so out into darkened Queen's Street to summon another taxi : " My show this time," said Walter at the gate of " Innisfree."

And, " They're a cheery couple of kids, aren't they ? " he said, stepping out down the Woodstock Road. " Uncle Ernest is a bit of a wash-out socially, but Auntie makes up for it." Lennie said, " I must thank you for introducing me there," with so much feeling in his light, expressive voice that it came into Walter's mind at once; he's struck—the Real Thing —on Doreen. Walter's regard for Joan was sincere and cousinly: music, lights and a couple of glasses of champagne could whip it into sentiment: had they been older, they might have considered settling down to a marriage based on so steady an affection. But they were magnificently young; both of them wanted the Real Thing, and would wait for it, for ever, thought Walter; and Joan, until jolly well the last moment before I go on the shelf. So Walter looked at Lennie's striding figure with envy; but he didn't say any more about his cousins. He had been prepared to discuss them, but now—well, hands off the Real Thing! He said, "This is a nice neighbourhood, isn't it?" and Lennard said, "Yes; nice and open after the old part of the town."

Happy days followed. Doreen, although she was so pretty, was not a capricious or an exacting girl; in spite of her youth she was ripe for love; dream waltzes and the picturesque heroes of *Home Chat* had done half Lennie's wooing for him before he came. Walter and Joan were sympathetic, the dumb, true friends that the young can be. Joan would suggest walking home from the cinema though her shoe pinched horribly and she and Walter had nothing to say: they would wait for half an hour, blue with cold, at the corner of Staverton Road, till Doreen and Lennie, warm as toast, voluble as starlings, came up with them. On Sunday afternoons, while Mrs. Logan was taking her nap and Mr. Logan tracing his tortuous brackets and pipe-racks in the den, Walter and Joan would retire to the dining-room and the poor company of an anthracite stove.

Lennie would not for a moment have considered missing a Sunday afternoon at "Innisfree," indeed he was only awaiting the time and the place to declare himself, when Cartwright managed to convince him that his invitation from the Warden of St. Mary's was a genuine one. But, as it happened, that after-

noon Joan and Doreen were taking part in a concert
at Wingfield Hospital, and Walter had week-end
leave. "Well, I'll go," said Lennie to Cartwright.
"Though goodness knows why the old buffer's fixed
on me." Cartwright, nearer the truth than he could,
in his wildest dreams, have imagined, suggested that
Twigg's features might bear some resemblance to
those of " Pop's " long-lost son. Expressing doubt
as to Theodore's capacity for fatherhood, Lennie took
himself off on parade.

And when Sunday afternoon came, Cartwright let
him down. He had a cold, he said, and he felt rotten,
his legs were like chewed string; and he was going
to bed and it might be 'flu, and if he wasn't better
to-morrow, he'd have in the M.O. He sneezed
horribly and emitted a resonant fit of coughing, but
as Lennie crossed the quad an hour later, he caught
sight of him, very spruce and apparently in the best
of health and spirits, swaggering out through the
lodge. Thinking of what he'd like to do to Cartwright, Lennie walked up to the door of the Warden's
Lodgings and rang the bell. He was admitted by
Parker's successor into the cedarn stillness of the hall,
and escorted up the staircase and along the corridor.
He thought, what a house for one old man ! and,
what it needs is a lot of kiddies chasing along these
passages ! He walked into the drawing-room, a very
large room, overlooking both the garden and the
quadrangle, which Theodore used solely for the reception of his rare guests. It was empty, and icy
cold. As the door shut behind him, Lennie walked
across the parquet to the lovely Adam fireplace where
a bright fire was burning; but, as soon as he got
near it, his chilblains, persisting in the face of the
bottle of maltine which Mrs. Logan had pressed on
him, began to itch, and he was forced to retreat off

the hearthrug, back into the cold. He thought of rooms he knew and loved—the kitchen in the Whit-stable bungalow, smelling of warmth and dishcloths and oil and shell-fish, the merry, sloe-eyed sisters gathered round the fire, and of the pink-and-white drawing-room at Staverton Road with the piano going; and, instead of feeling impressed by this fine room, he felt sorry for the man who lived in the chill and the silence, all alone. When the door opened and Theodore came in, scurrying across the room, his hand held out but his head down, his eyes looking at his feet, Lennie didn't think him conceited or potty or misanthropic or any of the things people thought Theodore, but he saw, quite simply, that the man was desperately shy. Theodore said, " You're Mr. Twigg, I believe ? " and Lennie said, " That's right, sir," in a heartening voice.

" Sit down, sit down, Mr. Twigg," said Theodore.

Lennie sat down on a chair which felt as though no one had ever sat in it, so convex it was, and shiny and cold and hard. Theodore sat down opposite him, his hand in his straggling brown moustache, his eyes still downcast. Lennie, wishing to make him-self agreeable, ventured, " You've a fine house here, sir."

" Yes, yes, yes," said Theodore. " If you're inter-ested in history, you'd like to look round it, perhaps. Archbishop Laud slept in my . . . er . . . bedroom in the year 1668."

" Good lord ! " exclaimed Lennie, trying to sound appreciative, though he loathed history and couldn't remember ever having heard of this Archbishop. "These old buildings are very instructive," he added.

" This is your first visit to Oxford, I suppose ? " said Theodore, and raised his eyes at last.

What did he see ? A young man, in the inevitable

khaki, sitting on the edge of his chair, leaning forward
a little, looking polite and alert and interested like
someone sitting by a sick-bed; a very fair young
man (khaki suiting his fairness) with large blue eyes,
a straight nose and a small mouth—a girlish face,
thought Theodore, but one couldn't complain of
that: one had called his whole generation effeminate
before it went to war. What else? Well, he had
a good body, tall, too slight about the shoulders for
perfection; in his fairness he resembled his mother,
and his small mouth was like hers, but he didn't
look quiet, almost depressed, as she had done, but
cheerful and voluble; something about his collar
and tie and the brown and yellow Liberty handkerchief, the corners of which were protruding from his
sleeve, suggested to Theodore a phrase he'd heard
once—" a summer number young man." Yes, Theodore could imagine him punting up the river, not at
Oxford, but at Staines or Maidenhead, with a gramophone in the punt and a girl, a girl with a Japanese
parasol over her head and a box of chocolate creams
on her knees. A couple of years ago he must have
cried out with horror that this bounder—there wasn't
another word—should be his son; but he knew better
now. He had learned to look for no heroic mould;
but in whisky-hardened men like Richard, in the
brutish farm hands of Widdingfold, in flapper-minded
flibbertigibbets like Lennie, to salute the heroes of
the war.

Lennie was saying something, leaning forward,
asking some conscientiously intelligent question about
the relative ages of Oxford and Cambridge; and
Theodore couldn't look at him any longer, was obliged
to answer. " Yes, Oxford is the older University,"
he said, not wishing to talk about Oxford at all. " You
come from Kent, I understand ? "

"Yes. I'm a Man of Kent," agreed Lennie. But
he must have had some vague notion that a scholar's
interest could only be in the past, for he continued
perseveringly, "I think Canterbury is our oldest
town." Theodore would not talk about Canterbury.
He hated history almost as much as Lennie did. He
said with the abruptness that undergraduates found
it so entertaining to imitate, "I should have amplified
my message to you."

Lennie, at a loss, raised his neat eyebrows and
emitted a questioning sound.

"I wanted you to come and see me because your
mother was a native of Widdingfold. My father was
Rector of the parish."

"Good lord!" cried Lennie, and, as you might
have expected, "Isn't it a small world, sir?"

"It is. It is."

"Colonel Oliver spoke to me a few days ago. He's
the big pot there, it seems."

"Yes. His late father, Sir Gilbert, was at the Hall
when I remembered it."

"I was never there. But I've heard Mother speak
of it. She didn't care for Kent—was always cracking
up Surrey. And Father came from the same village."

A certain doubt, somehow, all the more unwelcome
since he had seen the young man, and sat there, talking to him, came back to Theodore.

"Are you the eldest child?"

"The eldest? Yes, I am! And didn't I know
it, pushing the others around in the go-cart, as they
came along? If ever I have kiddies of my own, my
wife won't need a nurse!" Lennie laughed heartily.

Theodore laughed too, took his hand away from his
mouth, and asked Lennie a few question about his
family and his home. Lennie replied at amiable
length. Tea was brought in by the butler. Theo-

dore poured out. Lennie, eating a great deal of anchovy toast, told him about his fine position with Messrs. Pugh & Roadnight. " And Mr. Roadnight's a real gentleman. He's treated me very generously. And he's keeping my position open for me until after the war."

" Quite right, quite right," said Theodore.

As soon as he could do so with politeness, Lennie took his leave. Theodore escorted him downstairs, closed the door behind him, and stood at the hall window, watching him cross the quadrangle. An extraordinary feeling of happiness pervaded him, body and mind: some stream of gladness seemed to spring from his heart, run in his veins, at the thought that he had given to this straight-limbed, cheerful creature the life that he so patently enjoyed. I've missed life, thought Theodore. I was conceived as a duty, born a weakling, and they sat me at High Table when they lifted me into my first high chair. Because I'm weak, I've been a coward; I've been afraid of things ever since I can remember, and moral cowardice grows on you until it's almost madness. Though I'm Warden of St. Mary's, my days are full of petty evasions: I'm as shy as a child: I'm afraid of meeting acquaintances in the street, and of going into shops and of asking my servants to do anything for me. But, because blessed Nature was once too strong for me, now, in this my son, I go to war, wind up gramophones, shout at platoons, kiss without shame, call at drapers' shops and insist on seeing the buyers. He's ignorant and vulgar, thought Theodore, remembering how Lennie had spoken of " a real gentleman," and used horrible phrases—" the domain of the Sultan " for Turkey, and " denizens of the deep " for fish—but he's all I've never been; he's a man living his life, not evading it because it's painful or common or carnal. Into Theodore's head came an absurd metaphor: life's a plateful, pushed in front of you: eat it; the nice bits and the nasty bits, delicately, if you like, but eat it: don't leave scraps at the side of the plate; that's bad manners and you'll suffer for it; and don't make faces when you get a nasty mouthful—that's bad manners too. Eat it up gallantly, laughing with the company, and say Grace, and go. But I've left most of my dinner and I'm hungry, thought Theodore.

CHAPTER XI

THE REAL THING

Now! Lennie told himself. Now!

He opened his mouth, but, before a sound came out of it, Doreen said, " Throw the chocs over, Angel-Face! " and then " Ooo, I've got a pinky! What's yours? " Lennie had taken one from pure nervousness, and, just like his luck, it had turned out to be a caramel. " I've got a jaw-sticker," he mumbled ruefully. Doreen laughed and poked in the box with her manicured forefinger. " I'll look out a pinky for you, too."

It was Sunday afternoon, and it was raining, raining so hard that you could scarcely see across the pocket-handkerchief garden to the polite screen of lilac and laburnum. Up in the mauve bedroom above the drawing-room, Mrs. Logan, lying on her shiny brass bedstead, under her shiny silk eiderdown, with her things loosened, was absorbed in a novel from Boots which she hoped the girls wouldn't get hold of. From the " den " came the brisk hiss of a fret-saw. Joan and Walter were in the dining-room, playing all the records in the house over on the gramophone, stale old tunes like *Dreaming* and *The Girl in the Train* and *Nights of Gladness* and *Septembre*. Doreen and Lennie had pulled the pink sofa right up to the hearthrug, poked the fire, and placed between them the box of chocolates which Lennie had brought. The rain outside, the fact (he had mentioned it, trying to make a beginning) that

he had only another four Sundays in Oxford, enhanced the cosy intimacy of the bright little room:
the pink carpet was all the pinker, the fire warmer,
because Lennie had remembered for a moment the
grey slime of the trenches, the bitter cold of some
faint-spirited zero hour: Doreen, cuddled down in
the corner of the sofa, wearing a pale blue frock with
pale pink rosebuds on it, seemed all the sweeter, cleaner,
daintier for his memory of the muck and the blood
and the coarseness and the discomfort he would be
back in, perhaps only half a dozen Sundays from to-day.

Lennie chawed up his caramel, swallowed the
wretched thing and said, " Cease fire ! " because
Doreen was offering him another. " Look here, little
girl, I want to ask you something," he got out, and
didn't know that his voice sounded strange and trembly
so that Doreen, although she continued to poke coolly
in the chocolate box, knew exactly what he was going
to ask her, and felt as though her body must be
shaken to pieces by the frantic hammering of her
heart.

" Say on, Macduff ! " she observed with apparent
nonchalance.

" You're so sweet," said Lennie desperately. " I
love you ! But it's no use asking. You couldn't
be engaged to me ! "

" Oh, Lennie ! "

" Could you ? Oh, Doreen, the first time I saw
you, I knew you were my girl."

" Me, too. I felt that funny feeling—all through
me—the first time you looked at me."

" Really and truly ? "

" Yes, honestly."

" Oh, Doreen, marry me soon ! " cried Lennie,
burying his face in her lap, in the folds of pale blue
and the pink rosebuds, crying the prayer of his doomed

generation, resigned to death, only asking for a taste of life before he died.

"Of course," said Doreen, patting his head. "Before you go back to France." She had (you could not doubt it now) her absurd mother's beautiful understanding.

Lennie looked up.

"You angel. I do adore you."

They kissed.

"Oh, Lennie!"

"My dream girl!"

"Supposing we'd never met?"

"We had to. We were made for one another."

"*For ever to have and to hold, Till the end of the story is told . . .*"

Look on, Cynic, your dozen years, to the time when such words as these will be explained away as wartime hysteria, when such a marriage as is planned now, in this brief, pink-and-white haven, will be dissolved on the cold grounds of incompatibility—we didn't realise what we were doing—it was a mad wartime affair. Yet can you be sure that these children of calamity, with their music and their dancing and their Cliquot and their loving, and death not screened and unlikely behind his wreaths and crosses but as everyday a thing as going out and shutting the door, did not see clearer then than now, when the curtain has rung down on their melodrama and risen on a comedy in which they never thought to play? "Nothing can take our love from us," said Lennie, and aimed his remark at honest and rude death, no need to think of time or change or satiety in those straightforward days.

Doreen said presently, "Whatever will Mother say?"

"She won't mind, will she? I must say, I shouldn't blame her if she did."

" Why not ? "

" Well, if anyone tried to take you away from me . . ."

" Ooo ! You do look fierce ! I'm glad I'm not a German."

" And anyhow, I'm not good enough for you." He felt a passionate unworthiness, searched his blameless life for sin, but couldn't remember anything worse than getting drunk when he was trying to click with a Glasgow buyer and winking at a cinema attendant in Northallerton. So he could only add, " Nobody could be."

" Well, you are. And I know Mother's ever so keen on you."

" But will she be when she knows I want you ? Of course, it's not as if it were peace-time and you'd be going away altogether."

" Only wish I was ! I've been ever so happy at home, but now that I've found you . . ."

" You darling ! Anyhow, after the war, we shan't be far away. I expect we shall live in London or one of the suburbs. I've always rather fancied Beckenham."

" Sounds lovely."

" You'll like London. Lots of shops to buy hats in." Doreen pursed up her mouth and shook her head.

" Shan't buy hats," she said virtuously. " I shall buy brushes and brooms and . . . and cakes of soap."

" You must buy hats. And all sorts of pretty things. That's what I shall work for. Listen, shall we spend our honeymoon in London ? I'm sure to get a week."

" Oh, Lennie ! Just think of it ! A whole week with you—not even those darlings, Joan and Walter."

" *There will be such won-der-ful things to do. I will say such won-der-ful things to you . . .*"

When Joan and Walter came into the room, Doreen said, " Listen, you two ! I've got an announcement to make."

" I believe I can guess what it is," said Joan.

" Oh, rot," said Lennie. " We've only just got to know it ourselves."

" It's been coming on, though, hasn't it ? Slowly but surely. And not being *quite* deaf or *quite* blind or *altogether* devoid of grey matter, I've just got an inkling . . ."

" Well," said Lennie, " will I do ? "

" Certainly not ! You're much too young and frivolous. I'd like to see my little sister married to an aged man, a professor for choice, who'd have a sobering influence."

" Here, I say ! " cried Walter. " You don't mean to tell me that while Joan and I have been innocently playing classical music in the dining-room, you two have been and gone and got engaged ? "

" Yes, we've been and gone and done it," confessed Doreen. " Isn't it awful ? "

" No, it's splendid. Heartiest congratulations, both of you. Doreen—he's a jolly good fellow ! Twigg —she's a peach. And here comes Auntie. But, Auntie, you come too late."

" Too late for what, Walter, dear ? " enquired Mrs. Logan. She was wearing, for the first time, one of the new jumpers—mauve to match the floral toque upstairs in the handsome mahogany wardrobe—and now that she had it on, she wasn't really certain that the length at the back was a becoming one. Her manner was, therefore, a little distrait : she was thinking, I'll keep facing them.

" To stop the awful goings on," said Walter.

" Walter's in one of his naughty moods, I see," said Mrs. Logan, thinking, I wish I'd had the blue.

"However, I'll forgive him if he'll press the bell—on such a dull, wet day, I long for the cup that cheers."

"And does not inebriate," said Walter, reaching towards the bell.

Doreen checked him. "Half a sec., Walter. Mother, we've an awful confession to make. While you were innocently sleeping upstairs, Lennie and I got engaged."

"Oh, Mrs. Logan, may we?" cried Lennie. "I'll take such care of her!"

"This is no place for innocent young people," said Joan to Walter. "Let's go back to the dining-room and play *The Storm from William Tell*."

Lennie and Doreen were standing hand in hand gazing at Mrs. Logan, seeing first a start and a joyful look, then tears well into the pale, protruding eyes. This purple-faced woman, in the jumper that worried her, had thought first, my girl's loved; and then, my baby married! "Oh," she said, "I can't get hold of it for a minute. She's the first to want to leave me," and, forgetting the unbecoming length of her jumper, she pushed past Doreen and Lennie and plumped down on the sofa.

Doreen was beside her in a moment, flinging her young arms round the monumental figure. "I'm not going to leave you, Mumsie . . ."

"You won't lose her, Mrs. Logan," said Lennie. "The awful thing for you is that you'll have me around."

"I'm a selfish old woman," declared Mrs. Logan, wiping her eyes with a costly lace handkerchief. "Of course I want Doreen to have her happiness, and I must say, Lennie, though I hope it won't make you conceited, that there's no one I'd sooner trust her to than you. That naughty little girl you want to marry," she continued, cheering up, thinking, the mother of the bride wore a handsome dress of oyster satin, " has often teased me about having a soft place in my heart for you."

" Well, I'm sure I've one for you, Mrs. Logan. You don't know what your home life has meant to me."

" Here, I say, where do I come in ? " asked Doreen. " I'm getting jealous with all these declarations going on."

" You've no need to be jealous, dear," said her mother. " I can see how Lennie feels about you and I think you're a very lucky little girl."

Joan and Walter appeared at the door.

" Have you thrown him out, Mother ? Oh, Lord, he's still there. Surely you're not going to give me *that* for a brother-in-law."

" Can I ring the bell now, Doreen ? " asked Walter plaintively. " Not being in love and above all that sort of thing, I'm dying for my tea."

It was not until Mrs. Logan was pouring out her husband's cup that it occurred to her: " Of course, there's still Father."

" Father's not going to do me out of being a brides-maid," said Joan. " If he doesn't like the idea of Lennie—and I shan't blame him—he'll have to pro-duce a substitute." " Suppose," said Lennie man-fully, " that I take in Mr. Logan's tea ? " " Here's your tea, and I crave the hand of your youngest daughter," teased Joan, but Mrs. Logan thought it a good idea. " My future cousin's a brave chap," said Walter, as Lennie shut the door behind him. " As a matter of fact, I've heard that before, from a fellow who was in France with him. I've never thought there was much in *there*," he said, tapping Doreen's dark head. " But when it comes to choosing a husband—full marks, good girl; go to the top of the form ! "

Lennie walked across the hall, trying not to slop the tea into the saucer, thinking: this time, instead of a drapery line, it's yourself you've got to sell. And if you're anything of a salesman . . . " Come in," said Mr. Logan, and, without looking up, " Ah, thank you, Walter, my boy."

Lennie had met his future father-in-law about half a dozen times at Sunday supper but had scarcely exchanged a word with him. He was a man with whom it was impossible to sustain a conversation, for his hobby had become almost a vice with him: while you were talking to him, he was thinking of it, planning to get back to it like a drug-fiend to his dope. But Lennie's profession had taught him to make himself agreeable to all types, and not to mistake them; to laugh with the light-hearted, to grouse with the pessimist, to drink with the drunkard, to joke about sex with the Nonconformist buyers of the Midlands, to offer cigars, drinks, funny stories, scandal, *sub rosa* commission, on the strength of his summing-up of a man. In his time he had made his mistakes, had had his goods turned down by buyers who wanted commission while he plied them with double whiskies: once he'd offered commission to a high-principled inebriate who had only wanted a gin and bitters; and the mistake had nearly cost him his job. Now he laughed pleasantly and said, " I'm on duty to-day, sir, but I don't know if I make as good a waiter as Walter."

Mr. Logan looked up. " Ah, yes," he said. " Walter's friend, Mr. Twigg. Good afternoon, Mr. Twigg." And his glance dropped to his work.

" What a beautiful bracket, sir ! " Lennie exclaimed quickly. " It would be an ornament to any room ! "

He did not think so. Going about, in and out of

shops, up and down streets, he had learned what
was high-class stuff and what wasn't, in other lines
than his own. Brackets were dead, he knew, and
so was the sort of design that it had taken Mr. Logan
three week-ends to work out and trace; however,
where was the harm of giving the old fellow pleasure,
and doing himself a bit of good at the same time?
Like many angelically fair people, Lennie could look
you straight in the face while he told his blatant,
innocuous lies.

Mr. Logan beamed.

" It's handsome, isn't it? I don't think I've ever
worked from a design I liked better. I've used three-
ply wood, you see, because of its intricacy. I daresay this bracket would fetch a lot if I cared to sell
it."

" I'm sure it would. It's a wonderful piece of
work." Lennie moistened his lips. " I brought your
tea in to-day because I particularly wanted to speak
to you. Doreen and I . . ."

" Satin walnut would have been effective, but it's
brittle stuff," observed Mr. Logan.

" That's awfully interesting," said Lennie. " The
ordinary person knows nothing about wood. As I
was saying, I wanted to speak to you about myself
and Doreen."

" I thought of giving Doreen this bracket for her
birthday. But she happened to say that she particularly disliked it. There's no accounting for
tastes."

" That's quite true," Lennie agreed earnestly. Then
he raised his voice. " I want to speak to you about
Doreen, Mr. Logan. I want to marry her."

" Marry Doreen! " cried Mr. Logan, his attention
caught at last. " Good heavens! We scarcely know
you. What will my wife say? "

" We've spoken to her. And I think she's kind enough to approve. You see, I've been here a good deal since Walter first brought me, more than you've noticed perhaps while you've been making these beautiful brackets. And nowadays one has to get a move on."

Mr. Logan had remembered his duties. He placed his elbows on his fretwork table and pressed his finger-tips together.

" Can you support a wife and family ? "

" Oh, yes," cried optimistic Lennie. " I shall have a second lieutenant's pay and allowances. And my firm are keeping my position open for me. And, if I go west, there's the pension and all that."

" What are you in civil life ? "

Lennie explained. " Of course," he concluded frankly, " my father wasn't in the same position. He worked on a farm, but from all accounts he was very well thought of."

God knew that Mr. Logan was no snob.

" That's all that matters, my boy," he observed genially. " Now listen to me ! When I've finished cutting out this spray of oak-leaves, I'll be with you all in the drawing-room and we'll talk things over before supper; then perhaps at supper we'll open a bottle . . . we'll see . . . we'll see."

Lennie hurried from the room; and, in the course of an hour or so, Mr. Logan appeared in the drawing-room, pinched Doreen's cheek, and recalled his own courtship. It seemed impossible to Doreen and Lennie that they could ever have been lovers, this little man, old at five-and-fifty, who spent his home life fret-sawing in a " den," and his wife, who rested meanwhile on her bed or entertained acquaintances in her drawing-room, when (fortunate generation) they might have been sitting, year after year, day in, day out, on their pink sofa, arms entwined, her head on his shoulder, saying little but just being blissfully together. Well, they were Victorians, decided Doreen and Lennie, the most they had ever felt was affection and respect. However, Mr. Logan's sentimental recollections proved virile enough to prompt a promise that the wedding should take place as soon as Lennie's course was finished and that it should be, in spite of Kaiser Bill, a slap-up affair and no expense spared.

Lennie walked back to St. Mary's in a state of nervous elation. Having parted from Walter, who was quartered in the Garden quadrangle, he was making his way towards Founder's Buildings, when he almost collided with Theodore, who was scurrying to his Lodgings from the Senior Common Room.

" Sorry, sir ! I wasn't looking where I was going," Lennie apologised.

" Oh. . . . It's you . . ." said Theodore in a voice which must have puzzled Lennie if his head had not been among the stars. " Well, well. You've been out, I suppose ? That's right. That's right. I hope you had a pleasant evening."

" I should just think I did," cried Lennie. " It's been a red-letter day for me ! Guess what I've been doing ! "

Theodore remembered the young man's rather pathetic interest in history.

" You walked to Godstow ? "

" No."

" To Arnold's tree ? "

" I might as well tell you, for you'll never guess," said Lennie, bursting with his news. "I got engaged to be married ! "

" Engaged to be married ? That's right. That's right. Who is it ? "

" Her parents live in Staverton Road."

" Where's that ? "

" Well, you go up either the Banbury or the Wood-stock Road . . ."

" North Oxford. North Oxford. I don't know it. I've never been beyond St. Giles' Church. But people do live there."

" Yes. Doreen does."

" Bring her to see me," said Theodore. " Tea next Sunday. Or dinner. Yes, dinner. Why should one dine in Hall ? Eight o'clock at the Warden's Lodgings. Don't forget."

" I won't," vowed Lennie. " It's most awfully kind of you."

" No, no. I'm glad you're not making the mistake I made," said Theodore and rushed away—" as though the whole Germany Army was behind him," said Lennie, describing the incident to Doreen.

Doreen said, " The old josser must have lost his remaining senses," but Mrs. Logan said, " The dear old gentleman has evidently taken a fancy to Lennie, and *you* can't blame him for that, you naughty little Doreen." In the week, Doreen made herself a frock, a floral silk ninon, which she felt would brighten up the mouldy old college rooms. With her neat dark head, small mouth, touch of rouge added in the taxi, flowered frock and high-heeled shoes, against the sombre panelling and tapestries she looked like a Dresden china shepherdess; she was sheer femininity to Theodore's eyes. She had grumbled a little about coming—couldn't Lennie have found a more cheery way of spending an evening than having dinner with a mouldy old bird of . eighty at least ?—but as soon as she caught sight of Theodore, standing solitary in his enormous, cold drawing-room, coming towards her so queerly, with his hand extended, but looking

at his feet, her simple and kind heart went out to
an old man, who had lived so much alone that, learned
and famous though he was, he was all dithery over
having two young nobodies to dine. When Lennie
and I are old we shall have our children and our grandchildren, thought Belle Logan's daughter; and she
said, "How do you do?" very sweetly, and, "Ooo,
what a long walk to the dining-room!" Theodore
said, "I don't often use the drawing-room," and
Doreen said, "It's not very homey, is it?" "No,
it's not homey," agreed Theodore, and Doreen said,
"You can make a small house homey, if it's nothing
else. Lennie and I are going to have ever such a
teeny house after the war, but it's going to be most
awfully pretty, with cretonne curtains and pottery
like you see in Baker's window in Broad Street."
"Now which is Baker's?" asked Theodore. "In the
Broad, you say?" "Yes, that big, fairly new shop
at the Cornmarket end. Don't you ever shop-gaze,
Mr. Fletcher?" "Oh, yes, yes! I look into Blackwell's sometimes, and Chaundy's." Doreen laughed.
"Those are just the ones I never look into. Frocks
and hats are what I look at most." "That's right,
that's right," said Theodore.

He could not have told you why it was that he,
who was usually struck dumb at the approach of a
woman, felt so entirely at his ease with this girl, who
was everything that made him most nervous; young,
feminine and smart. He did not realise that in himself and Doreen, two very simple and child-like people
had met together, only, owing no doubt to some minute
difference in a gland they'd never heard of, one was
a brave child and the other a fearful one. Doreen was
not in the least conscious, while she talked to him,
of his position, erudition or circumstances ; in fact,
if anything, she was sorry for him because he spent

his days with his nose in mouldy old books, and must live, with depressing dignity, in this unhomelike house. She did not try, as Lennie had tried, to find some worthy subject of conversation, but chattered straight from her unaffected heart. Theodore, whose too sensitive mind reacted to the slightest embarrassment or nervousness on the part of anyone who conversed with him, now felt no such reaction; rather, Doreen's confidence was communicated to him. He was himself; simple, kind, considerate; the gentle, charming soul he might have been to all men could he have cast off his giant load of timidity, that probably physical heritage which his spiritually minded parents had neither recognised nor attempted to eradicate.

" And when is the wedding ? " asked Theodore.

" Wednesday week," Doreen told him. " You'll come, Mr. Fletcher, won't you ? It's going to be ever so pretty. Mother says it would be wrong to have quite so much of a show as we should have had in peace-time, but it's going to be a proper wedding, with flowers, chrysanthemums, not lilies, because of the coal to force them, you know; and no cake because of the sugar and the marge; but just a little champagne because Father says Lennie deserves it. You *will* come, won't you ? I'll look after you."

" I shall be delighted," said Theodore. " It's very kind of you to ask me, Miss Doreen. We old men in colleges begin to feel rather out of things. . . ."

" You shouldn't, sir," said Lennie. " You see, you're carrying on. We come back and see all this——" He indicated the table, agleam with radiant old glass and rich Crown Derby. " And it heartens us up to see it in the third year of the war."

Ah, they might be trivial and commonplace, these young people; ragtime might be music to them, Kirchner art, Kipling's dreadful " If " philosophy, but how comforting they were, how sane ! The world's commanders had gone mad and ordered them to war, and they went to war, but took their sane minds with them, hung Kirchner's girls in their dug-outs and sang ragtime along the roads of France.

" Doreen's mother says that's her war-work—keeping things cheery," said Lennie. " And, by Jove ! she does it too. I was lucky to have somewhere to go while I was in Oxford, quite apart from . . ." he looked across the table at Doreen and said softly, " . . . meeting you."

Yes, they were trivial and commonplace: in their love-making they probably resembled the manly young men and womanly young women for ever locked in juicy kisses on the posters outside their Cinemas: " meeting you," said Lennie, and surely in the next line skies must be blue and hearts true. But that was better than making the mess of love that Theodore had made. Knowledge doesn't help you to live, he discovered. How should it ? It's so little. And probably wrong. This girl stares into a shop window, buys a spring hat, puts it on, walks down the street; she's beaten you, Percy Shelley. This young man goes out to war, singing his revue songs, thinking his revue thoughts; John Milton, where's your epic now ? It's to live that we're here, thought Theodore, and I found that out too late; except to live in these, he thought, and blessed the bright faces at his table.

" How much leave will you get ? " he asked Lennie.

" I might get ten days," said Lennie, in the voice of one who sees a miracle wrought on his behalf: and Theodore, remembering his fifty-three years and no joy, observed, " It's not your time that matters but what you do with it."

"That's right, sir," exclaimed Lennie, "and you can bet we'll cram a lot into our ten days—as much music and dancing, as many shows as peace-time people get in the whole of their lives." He looked at Doreen and his eyes said: "and as much loving."

Theodore thought, I'll give him a cheque for his wedding present. Or will people think . . .? but I don't care what they think. I'll give it to him to-night—when the girl's putting her cloak on—and tell him to spend it on taking taxis to expensive restaurants—that's what they like. Would a hundred pounds seem excessive, he wondered? It was little enough for a man to give his son, but a good deal for the Warden of St. Mary's to give a cadet whom he had encountered exactly three times since chance had brought him to the college. Still, thought Theodore, one might decide to play godfather—ladies have their lonely soldiers in these times.

The dinner, in the preparation of which Theodore's underworked cook had been glad enough to display her ability, was a long one; and after a quarter of an hour's conversation in the chilly drawing-room, the young couple were obliged to take their leave: Lennie had to see Doreen home and be back in his quarters by eleven o'clock. "I'll go and get my cloak," said Doreen. Theodore, who had a vague idea that ladies had to be hooked into things, said, "I'll ring for Mrs. Carter," but Doreen said, "Oh, no, please don't. I'm not used to being waited on"; and she went out humming, *There's a Long, Long Trail*, and taking advantage of the admirably polished parquet to practise a dance step. Theodore approached Lennie, and muttered, looking at his feet: "I'd like to make you a wedding present."

"That's very kind of you, sir," said Lennie.

"No use buying you anything," said Theodore.

" Finger-bowls or the works of Marcus Aurelius are no use in this war. I'd prefer to write a cheque."

" I say, sir ! that's good of you."

" Come down to the library."

He led the way downstairs and ushered Lennie into that lovely solemn room. " Look round the shelves," he invited, and Lennie stared obediently at the New English Dictionary, while Theodore opened a locked drawer in his writing-table and took out his cheque-book. In spite of many furtive and ill-advised charities, he spent very little: he lived comfortably, but alone; and his servants were honest. His luxuries were wine, which he drank very slowly, and books. Year after year, he had been able to invest money in securities that his bank manager recommended to him; and he was now a comparatively wealthy man. He dated the cheque and wrote Lennie's name and his own signature; then his pen hovered uncertainly over the line where he should write the amount. He wanted suddenly to write Lennie a very large cheque, to make up for all the things he'd never bought him—teddy bears and toy railways and knives and cricket bats, four years at a public school, three years at Oxford. But I can't do that, he thought; they might display the cheque with the other presents . . . anyhow, they'd tell people . . . and everyone would guess . . . especially in North Oxford . . . What's the most that would seem reasonable? I *must* decide. The girl's not used to being waited on . . . she'll be down in a minute . . . besides, *he'll* notice that I can't make up my mind . . . I *must* decide . . . I *must* decide . . . Upstairs in the still house a door slammed. *Five hundred pounds*, wrote Theodore, and filled in the figures. " Here you are," he said, getting up, holding the cheque out at arm's length towards Lennie. " Thank you, sir," said Lennie, taking it, not sure whether it was good manners to look at the amount, but forgetting good manners when he saw it. "Good Lord!" he cried. "You don't mean this, sir? It's too . . . it's too generous!" "No," said Theodore, with his hand across his mouth. "It's not generous. You've got to spend it to please me—spend it on taxi-cabs and restaurants and theatres and dresses for your wife. Don't keep it. Never keep things. I made a mistake once, not with money but with something else. I hung on to it, was afraid of losing it. Don't mind losing things."

Lennie stared at him. Well, I never . . . fancy that old buffer thinking of restaurants and taxis and frocks! Standing there among his books in a dinner-jacket donkey's years old and a bundled-up tie, and telling you to blue five hundred! "I believe I'm dreaming, sir," said Lennie. "No, no, not a dream," said Theodore, almost crossly. "Nothing extraordinary about it. Nothing at all. You've got to go back to the trenches while I'm snug in my library—I'd like you to have what you want out of life first. And you don't want anything but silly worldly things, because it's the silly world you're afraid you're leaving. Nothing extraordinary." "No, but it's a thing everyone at home doesn't understand." "In the University of Oxford," observed Theodore, "we understand everything about young men, although we make no comment, not even to the *Daily Mail.*" As he spoke, the library door opened, and Doreen came in, wrapped in a rose-coloured velveteen cloak, the ruched collar of which framed, enchantingly, her little, dark head. "Oh, Doreen," said Lennie, "Mr. Fletcher has made us such a handsome wedding present." "Put it away! Put it away!" cried Theodore, grabbing Lennie's arm in an agony of embarrassment and considerate Lennie did so, placing it in his wallet among the snapshots of Doreen. " She'll thank you another time," said Lennie, and shook Theodore's agitated, moist hand.

Theodore saw his guests to the door, and then returned to the library and put away his cheque-book and shut the lid of his inkpot. He thought, well, that's my son, and that little girl who wants cretonne curtains and art pottery will be the mother of my grandson. And I'm glad of it, he thought, staring defiantly across the room at his exquisite mezzotint of the younger Pitt. And I'm glad I wrote him that cheque. And then—as always happens, he remembered, when one leaves the abstract plane—all the mean, little, practical thoughts that—God knows how—some people must live with, came crowding in, worrying his mind as vermin the body . . . what will the girl think about the cheque . . . ? Well, girls are innocent . . . she'll probably think no evil . . . but her astute tradespeople parents and the tea-tables of Summertown? And the clerks at the London County and Westminster Bank? And the bank manager? People who talk have to find something to talk about, reflected Theodore; I should have remembered how it leaked out that I'd paid that wretched Holloway boy's battels the term before the war: and he saw gossip, like a great, growing snake, curling out of Staverton Road, down Banbury Road, into St. Giles'. I wish I hadn't done it, I wish I hadn't done it, he inwardly cried, not hearing the same voice (despite his smart new philosophy of life) that cried wretchedly in a fir-wood beyond a September orchard, " I can't! I can't! Don't you see that I can't . . . They'd think I was mad . . .": not recognising the work (say) of the minute, minutely deficient gland. And the snake from Staverton Road crept down St. Giles', down the Broad into the Turl, through Brasenose Lane and past the Bodleian into

Cat's Street, down the High and into the very gates
of St. Mary's. "I heard a peculiar story . . . I can't
vouch for it. . . . But there's no smoke without a
fire, my dear Professor . . . I hear that the Warden
has an illegitimate son . . ."

CHAPTER XII

LOVERS' MEETINGS

" DOREEN, darling, you look lovely. I can't believe it's my baby."

" Now, Mother, don't get sloppy. One maternal tear on that oyster satin and it's done for," said Joan.

" The train hangs beautifully, doesn't it ? " asked Doreen.

She had chosen ivory velvet for her wedding dress, and had had it lavishly trimmed with a nameless but effective white fur. Her long lace veil was held by a pearl coronet which, closely fastened, revealed the charming shape of her little head. Pearl buckles secured her short velvet train to her slender shoulders. She picked up her bouquet of white chrysanthemums, and a fairy-tale figure smiled back at her from the long mirror. That's the real Me, she saw suddenly. The Me who sits grousing in that dingy office is simply what life has made me. " Oh, dear," she sighed, " I do feel lovely. I wish it was always my wedding day."

" Belle ! Belle ! " cried Mr. Logan from the hall. " Belle ! The motor-cars ! "

" Come on, Mother," said Joan, putting a few hasty last touches to her own toilette. " Doreen'll be all right. She's not a shrinking Victorian maiden. She's as hard-boiled as they boil 'em."

" You wait until you see a daughter of your own in her wedding dress, you heartless little modern girl,"

retorted Mrs. Logan, kissing Doreen, then dabbing her
eyes and peering into the mirror to straighten her
panne hat. " I must say," she observed with satis-
faction, " I have attended many Oxford weddings and
seldom seen the mother of the bride in a smarter *ensemble*."

" You look lovely, Mother," said Doreen.

" Cheerio, Dorrie," said Joan.

They left the room. Doreen heard her father's
voice sunk to a stage whisper, saying, " They've sent
Daimlers ! " and her mother answer, " Well, Ernest,
what do you expect ? I told them that no expense
was to be spared." Then the front door slammed and
the house seemed strangely, uncomfortably still.
Doreen glanced round her room, at her smart new
trunk, strapped down, and her smart new fitted
dressing-case, still open; at her bed, which looked
much flatter than usual because the sheets had been
taken out of it and the blankets just folded twice and
laid on it; at the pastel-blue December sky at the
window. Oh, Lennie, darling, she thought, I'm
coming to you, not as the ordinary girl who used to
wake up in that bed as cross as two sticks on Monday
mornings, but as this fairy-tale person who's all lovely,
outside and in. If life can be like it is to-day, why
can't it always be ? she asked, just touching her
cheeks with rouge now Mother had gone—thank goodness Father never noticed anything. " Doreen !
Doreen ! " called Mr. Logan, who had been instructed
to keep her cheery: and Doreen gathered her train
over her arm and slammed the door unregretfully on
her maidenhood.

Ernest Logan watched her come downstairs. She
was, he realised suddenly, an utter stranger to him:
he didn't know what she thought about marriage or
how much she cared for her young man: the most he
could do was to admire her dress and remember her

childhood's pretty ways. "You look very smart and
. . . bridal, my dear," he said, thinking, we beget
children and at the time it seems fearfully important,
but, when they're grown-up, for all we know of them,
they might just as well have come from among the
gooseberry bushes or out of the doctor's bag. "I
do, don't I?" said Doreen unrevealingly; and then,
"What about starting?" "Well, the car's at the
door," said Mr. Logan, comparing his watch with the
hall clock, the elaborate frame of which was his own
handiwork. "We're in good time—your mother said
not to start till twelve past—but we might get slowly
in."

They arrived exactly on time at the pale, precise
North Oxford church of Saint Philip and Saint James.
In spite of Kaiser Bill, as Mr. Logan had threatened,
a striped awning, a red carpet and a small crowd of
spectators awaited Doreen. The church was lavishly
decorated with white chrysanthemums and crowded
with Mrs. Logan's numerous friends: Doreen could
feel them rather than see them as she took her father's
arm and followed the choir—the full choir, no expense
spared—singing of her, Doreen Logan, *The King's
daughter is all glorious within* . . .

The Warden of St. Mary's, anxious not to be late,
had arrived very early at the church, and had been
given an excellent seat by one of the ushers, a poor
relation of the Logans, who, in peace-time, sold basket
chairs and punt cushions and tobacco jars to undergraduates, and knew him perfectly. He had got cold
and bored while he had waited, had picked the skin
at the side of one of his thumb-nails down so far that
it pained him horribly, and was disappointed by his
inability to distinguish Lennie from among the number
of blond young men in new uniforms, standing about
the church. When at last the procession did start,

he was looking elsewhere and did not see the bride,
and by the time that he realised that she had passed
him, Joan, very lovely in her bridesmaid's dress of
golden velvet with a bouquet of tawny chrysanthemums in her hands, was standing in the aisle just in
front of him, obscuring what view of the ceremony
escaped the brim of Mrs. Albert Logan's handsome
moiré hat. He heard Lennie's light, pleasant voice
repeat the vows: to a man who's going back to the
front in a fortnight they can't seem as serious as they
would have seemed in Widdingfold church in the placid
eighties, thought Theodore; and then, it shouldn't
be difficult to love and cherish, though I might have
found it so. I've never understood women, or perhaps
the women of my generation were different from this
amiable young creature *he's* marrying—certainly, they
hadn't her frankness. The trouble with my generation
was that we were beset by fear: if we had had to live
more dangerously, we shouldn't have been so careful.
We knew we had got to die, but not so soon as these
poor boys; death stood just far enough off for us to
ignore him: he didn't sit down at the table with us,
he stood at the door. So we took thought for the
morrow, in spite of our Sage. Will this material wear
well? What will she be like at forty? Is this a
lasting affection? I'd like to know something about
the foundations—questions that they don't ask to-day.
Regret, not searing remorse for something done, but
a wretched, despairing ache for a lost opportunity
came to him: if, thirty years ago, he hadn't taken
thought for the morrow, hadn't struggled, mad with
fear, from the trap that wise Nature had set for him,
he would have come to this ceremony, not as the Warden
of St. Mary's, who had taken an inexplicable, probably
senile fancy to play godfather to a man he scarcely
knew, but as the father of the bridegroom, puffed out

with the same absurd, fundamental, eradicable satis-
faction that was straightening Ernest Logan's insignificant little figure and swelling his wife's full bosom
under its expensive satin covering.

A hymn was sung—*O, Perfect Love*—and the pews
in front of Theodore's emptied in the direction of the
vestry, so that, now there was nothing to see, he could
see very well, a situation which, he thought miserably,
sinking into the corner of his pew, his legs stretched
this way and that, his thumb paining him, was significant of his whole career. He had not noticed, and
would not have recognised, Hester Twigg as she
followed the Logans; after your eye had been dazzled
by the mother of the bride in her oyster satin, and
the aunt of the bride—Mrs. Albert Logan—in her
purple velvet, and the cousin of the bride—Walter
Logan's mother—in her electric-blue face cloth, you
would not have noticed Hester, who wore a black coat
with a collar of skunk fur—prosperous Edna, who had
driven her mother into Canterbury in her Ford car, had
put her foot down on any of your dressed-up rabbit
skins—a plain, becoming black hat and easy *glacé* shoes.
" There's Mother, Doreen," said Lennie, who was on
the point of signing his name in the flowing copy-book
hand he was proud of, when he caught sight of his
mother: and Doreen struggled between the velvet
and satin bosoms of her own relations towards Hester
and, with some incoherent, kindly words, presented
her cheek, already sore from contact with the Logan
ladies' veils. Hester saw in a moment that Doreen
ate more chocolates than were good for her and wasn't
a patch, for real beauty, on Edna or young Daisy:
then she could allow that she was just the girl for
Lennie, pretty and dainty and full of life. She kissed
the too-pasty cheek.

Then, " Mrs. Twigg, you'll take my husband's arm

down the aisle, won't you?" arranged Mrs. Logan.
" And Walter will take Joan, of course, but who me?"
" My son-in-law—my Edna's husband—would have
come, only he's in Palestine," Hester meekly apologised. " Then we must forgive him," said Mrs. Logan.
" Ethel, you'll have to walk with me. Anyhow, it
will show our friends that the men of the family are
doing their bit." And behind Mr. Logan and Hester,
the oyster toilette and the purple one paced side by
side.

Theodore had been invited to the reception as well
as to the church. He had not meant to go. By
hurrying from the church, however, he defeated his
own ends, for he ran straight into Mrs. Logan, who
had seen Doreen and Lennie drive off and was now
engaged in packing Hester with her husband and herself and Auntie Ethel into the foremost of the Daimlers.
" Ah, there's the dear Warden!" she cried. " I'll
just make sure of him!" and she stepped towards
Theodore, saying, " You'll come in the next car, won't
you, Warden? Joan and Walter, take the Warden
in with you! You'll be quite comfortable," she
assured Theodore. " All the cars are Daimlers.
Mr. Logan grudged nothing on Doreen's wedding
day."

So Theodore made his first trip through North
Oxford, sitting in a Daimler that Mr. Logan had not
grudged, with Joan Logan on one side of him, and on
the other her cousin Babs and the pert little boy who
had held up Doreen's train; and opposite, Walter
Logan and two boys who looked as if they should have
been at school, although both wore uniform and one
(it appeared) an artificial arm which was referred to
by everyone as " Alice." No one spoke to Theodore
except to ask in a comradely fashion if he had room
and to apologise for knocking his knees with theirs:

they said how sweet she'd looked and how nice he'd
looked and who's turn would come next? Arrived
at "Innisfree," they swept him in with them—gentlemen's hats in the downstairs cloakroom, girls in
Mother's bedroom. "And the bride and bridegroom
are in the drawing-room, Mr. Fletcher," said Walter,
"and the food and whatnot in the dining-room and
the 'numerous and costly gifts' are in the den.
Come on, boys! Over the top!" invited Walter, and
led the way into the drawing-room.

Theodore hung his hat among the khaki caps and
followed. The room which he entered seemed to him
to be full already; he could not conceive how it could
hold one-quarter of the people he had seen in church;
but the car in which he had travelled had been hurried
away from the gate with instructions to "go back and
fetch some more along"; Staverton Road was a babel
of shrieking brakes, hooting horns and rasping gears;
and already people were pushing past him into the
room. He drew aside. But Belle Logan was looking
out for her lion; and she left the intimate group by
the window and hurried over to him. "Now, Warden,
you must congratulate the little bride." She led him
up to Doreen, who was standing with Lennie under a
hired palm, which had been placed on the piano.
Theodore took her hand and mumbled, "Congratulations."

"Thanks awfully," said Doreen. "Enjoying yourself?"

Theodore almost started at the question, but jerked
out, "Yes, thank you. Yes, yes."

"Oh, good afternoon, sir," said Lennie, finishing a
conversation with a stout lady wearing the tartan of
Macdonald of Clanranald. "Awful, isn't it? Look
here, I want to introduce you to my mother."

What could he say? What could he do? He

couldn't rush from the room or cry out the " No, for God's sake ! " that was on his tongue. " She . . . she'll have forgotten me," he murmured from dry lips; but Lennie, who had him by the arm and was guiding him across the room, replied in hearty tone, " I bet she hasn't ! " Then, " Mother," he said, " I told you how kind this gentleman had been to me— Mr. Fletcher."

For a moment Theodore couldn't see, couldn't hear. Then, the darkness and the soundlessness drawing away, he looked into a middle-aged face that meant nothing to him, heard a stranger's voice say comfortably, " and they were lucky at this time of year to get a fine day." " Yes, yes," said Theodore, and felt the sweat cool on his forehead. " December's a bad month in Oxford."

" It's a bad month anywhere."

" True. True."

" Except that you can look forward to Christmas."

" February, with the floods out, is our worst month here."

" It must be very unhealthy then," said Hester. " Lennie wrote as soon as he came here that he found the climate relaxing . . ."

Ah ! that's what endures ! Theodore realised again as the name stabbed him. Time buries passion ; heaps the sandy minutes up and up until what's underneath doesn't matter, until I can look into this woman's face and talk about the weather for the time of year. Love's nothing, thought Theodore, but the instrument with which we create our immortality: it's poets' work to make more of it. Jammed face to face with Hester, caught there as if Fate had meant it all along, had assembled for that sole purpose this innocent and festive crowd, he

felt a sudden, noble longing for truth at last, a longing
to say: I was a coward, but I lost by it: the only
way through life is to be blindly brave: but now that
that's over, dead as the sin of any Athenian youngster,
let me forget what's dead, and rejoice in my immortality. But who can speak the truth, he thought.
There's something between us all . . . and realising
that Hester's voice had ceased, he exclaimed (looking
very peculiar, thought Mrs. Albert Logan; but then
University people do get peculiar, she remembered,
and thanked goodness that Babs and Bertie were
gamey and not bookish) "Of course." "Of course,"
Hester had said, so the honeymoon was to be
spent in London, and the irrelevancy of Theodore's
rejoinder disconcerted her. Exiles of frankness, they
stood, racking their brains for something they might
say.

Mercifully then, in the packed room, there started
a movement towards the door. "Come along, Mrs.
Twigg," called Belle Logan. "We've got to go into
the dining-room to drink a toast! No cake, owing
to Mr. Logan's patriotism," she chattered to Hester.
"But we can't grudge a little ' bubbly,' as my naughty
girls call it, to a boy who's doing his bit . . ." Theodore dropped behind, but was, nevertheless, swept
into the dining-room, where Doreen herself thrust a
glass of champagne into his hand. Walter Logan
was making a speech, which ended, "And so I ask
you all on the word of command to raise your right
hands sharply from the elbow inwards and drink
to the health of Mr. and Mrs. Lennard Twigg!"
Everyone murmured, "Lennie and Doreen," and
sipped. Theodore sipped too. He disliked champagne, especially sweet champagne, and Mr. Logan's
champagne was very sweet indeed: but Theodore,
who had, when his anxious mind allowed it, admirable

manners, drank the full glass. "I noticed the dear Warden enjoying his little glass of 'bubbly,'" said Mrs. Logan, talking the wedding over for the twentieth time that night.

When the health had been drunk, Doreen, followed by her mother, struggled out of the room to change her dress. A party of girls took their leave, saying that they'd catch it from Matron if they didn't, and under cover of their vociferous exit Theodore left too. But he did not escape saying good-bye to Mrs. Logan, who popped out of Doreen's bedroom and leaned over the banisters to see who was going. "Good-bye, Maisie! Good-bye, Gwen! Yes, we'll forgive you for going—we know you're all brave little girls doing your bit." And then, "What, Warden, you're leaving us too? Aren't you going to see them off on their honeymoon——" she came a little farther downstairs and spoke in more discreet tones —"the honeymoon you're making so delightful for them with your generous gift?"

"I must go. I must go," said Theodore. "I've a meeting. I must get back to college. Thank you for your hospitality."

"No hospitality could repay what you've done for our young couple. When Lennie told me about your gift and how you wished it spent, I said, 'The Warden of St. Mary's is not only a very wise and very learned gentleman; he is a genius, or how else would he see into the minds of very ordinary young people like you, Lennie and Doreen.'"

"Good-bye," said Theodore.

"Good-bye, and thank you for giving us the pleasure of your company here to-day. If you ever feel like a little walk on a Sunday afternoon, I am always in at tea-time to receive and entertain my friends."

" Thank you.　Thank you."

Theodore dived into the cloak-room for his hat and scurried out into Staverton Road.

" Mother !　Mother !　Where　are　you ?　I　can't find the shoe-horn," cried Doreen.

CHAPTER XIII

DON'T SNIFF

THE ormolu clock on the marble mantelpiece was ticking away the minutes, not in the ominous fashion of grandfather clocks, nor in the omnipotent fashion of station clocks, but in gay, latin way which expressed the atmosphere, charming and rococo, of the "Empire style" hotel sitting-room. "It is with infinite regret that I announce the hour of Monsieur's departure for France," said the French clock and struck ten: and temporary Second Lieutenant Lennard Samuel Twigg withdrew his arms from around his wife's drooping figure, and rose from the gilt and brocade sofa, saying hoarsely, "Well, now I must go."

Doreen glanced at the French clock.

"Good gracious, so you must."

The peculiar, feminine horror of missing a train took hold of her. She hurried into the bedroom, powdered her nose, which had been rubbed clean on the shoulder of her husband's tunic, pulled on her favourite hat, and slipped into the moleskin coat which lay ready across the foot of the "Empire style" bed. Lennie followed her into the room. "Let's say good-bye, here," he suggested, and put his arms round her under her coat while they kissed. "You're such a comforting person," he said slowly. "No one who saw you could help seeing that you're the prettiest and the sweetest thing on earth, but they'd never guess how comforting you are." He went back into the sitting-room, and picked up his cap, and patted his pockets to make sure that he had got everything. Doreen, after powdering her nose again, joined him; and, without saying anything, they shut the door on their fourteen days of heaven on earth, and stepped out into the corridor.

The lifts were all going up. " Up, sir ? " " Up ? " questioned the lift-boys. ." No thanks," said Lennie. " Down." " Let's walk," said Doreen. " It's only one floor." Lennie groaned. " I shall have enough walking to do between here and Berlin."

At last the lift came down. Doreen entered it. It seemed to her as though some giant magnet had found out Lennie and herself, and had pulled them from their bedroom, through their sitting-room, into the corridor and into the lift; and would pull them from the hotel, through the streets, to Victoria station; for she felt that she walked forward by no will nor wish of her own. And at Victoria, she thought, it'll stop pulling me, but it'll go on pulling Lennie, pulling him out to France. But here, it's no use getting mouldy, she thought; that won't win the war; besides, it's ungrateful after the big slice of luck I've had. " There's your luggage, Len ! " she said brightly, as she pulled her coat round her and stepped from the lift. " Talk about a girl taking a lot of luggage ! " The hall porter helped Lennie into his British warm. The hall boy called a taxi.

They had had so many taxi drives in their fourteen days: taxis to the Army and Navy Stores, to Cox's Bank, to Fortnum & Mason's and to Harrods'; taxis to Scott's and Hatchett's and Stewarts and Rumpel-meyer's; taxis to Princes' and the Gobelins and the " Pic " and the " Troc " and the " Cri "; taxis to the Palladium and the Coliseum and the Empire and the Alhambra; last and best, taxis back to their hotel: and it seemed ironical that a taxi should turn traitor and take them to Victoria now. For the first time in fourteen days, they didn't hold hands in a taxi; and, for the first time in fourteen days, they made conversation: " Place looks full for this time in the morning," said Lennie, and, " This taxi dates from the year one "; and Doreen read out advertisements and the names of streets: " *Dear Brutus*," by J. M. Barrie . . . " *What did you do in the Great War, Daddy?* " and " *Buckingham Palace Road* . . ."

Mrs. Logan and Hester had promised to be at the station—" Oh well," Lennie had sighed, " we could only have had a peck on the platform, anyway " —and there they were, waiting together, under the clock. Hester, the smaller figure, betrayed her country origin: she stood stock-still, very firmly, her feet planted far apart, looking straight before her; Belle Logan fidgeted, looked about her, settled her smart furs. Doreen went up to them while Lennie saw to his baggage. " Hullo, Mother! Hullo, Lennie's Mother! Oh, Mother, we've had such a heavenly time." " You naughty little thing," said Mrs. Logan. " You only wrote to me once in spite of all your promises! But I'll forgive you," she added hastily, " because you're looking so well and happy, and Lennie too, because I can see how well he's looked after you." " Lennie's an angel," said Doreen, and Hester, who knew he wasn't, smiled at her, the charming smile that, at rare moments, would light up her face and contradict your impression of a comfortable country-woman.

Lennie came to them.

" Hullo, Mother! Hullo, Mrs. Logan! Doreen been taking my character away? "

" Quite the contrary," said Mrs. Logan. " From

what she says, I understand that she's spent the last
fortnight in the seventh heaven."

" A jolly strenuous heaven," said Lennie. " I shall
find the front-line trenches with a strafe on a haven
of peace and quiet after my honeymoon. I've forgotten what it's like to sit still since I've been married."

" Well, don't try to blame it on Doreen," said
Hester. " You was always one to like a bit of life."

" Now, Mother's giving me away ! It's time I was
off. That's true, as a matter of fact. There's my
train."

The magnet drew Doreen across the station, down
the platform where the leave train waited, " looking
just as if it was going to take you for a nice little
holiday to gay Paree," said Belle Logan, regarding
with animosity the crimson lampshades in the Pullman car. But Doreen hadn't been grown-up in a
world where you went for nice little holidays to gay
Paree, and she didn't feel the same animosity: this
was life and love as she expected it—fourteen days
of marriage and your husband going back to the
Front, probably to be killed; please God to get a
blighty one; but what was the use of worrying ? you'd
had a huge slice of luck anyhow, think of all the
poor girls whose boys had been killed before they'd
met them, before they'd had that wonderful time
together or known what married life was—that
rapturous whirl of " Pic " and " Troc " and " Cri "
and sacred nights in a first-floor suite in a really smart
hotel.

Lennie found a place in a Pullman and suggested
a walk down the platform. It was beginning to
rain, and the rain was blowing in under the roof of
the station, and Mrs. Logan, who had her floral toque
on, said that she would stay where she was. Hester
said that she would walk so far, and she walked to

where the roof ended, giving Lennie news of Edna and Beattie and Daisy and young Albert. Lennie and Doreen went on out into the rain; and behind a truck of milk-cans they kissed—"just a last, tiny one," they agreed, "to remember." Then they walked briskly and silently back, and, since there was less than a minute now and doors were slamming, Lennie said that he'd better get in, and he kissed his mother and Mrs. Logan and said, "Cheerio," and disappeared into the Pullman. A second later they saw his fair head through the window, and as he sat down at a table with one of the crimson-shaded lamps that Mrs. Logan had objected to, he smiled and waved to them. Then the whistle shrilled and the train drew slowly and grimly out of the station.

"He'll be better off as an officer," said Hester.

Belle Logan took a nice white handkerchief, scented with Zenobia Sweet Pea, out of her handbag, and wiped her eyes.

"Now we've got to 'keep the home fires burning,'" she said with a resolute sniff.

And Doreen, who had not said a word since Lennie had kissed her behind the milk-cans, managed at last to swallow away the sharp ache in her throat. In three months . . . thirty days hath September, April, June and November, all the rest have thirty-one . . . that's ninety-three days . . . I may be standing here waiting for him . . . It'll be spring then . . . he's never seen me in spring things . . . If yellow's in I'll have a yellow hat . . . and amber. . . .

"For goodness' sake, Mother," she said, "don't sniff."

CHAPTER XIV

PILGRIMS OF ER

WHEN Theodore had said, " Thank you, thank you," in reply to Mrs. Logan's invitation for any Sunday afternoon at " Innisfree," he had not had the slightest intention of ever setting foot in the house again. It was his invariable custom on Sunday afternoons to walk round Christ Church Meadow and return to tea in college. " At North Oxford tea-tables," he would remark sarcastically, " the college is efficiently represented by Quears." On Christmas Day, however, he was surprised, and, to tell the truth, delighted, to receive a Christmas card, gaily ornamented with a wreath of evergreen surrounding a sketchy map of northern France, out of which was bursting the droll face of a tin-hatted soldier, from whose mouth issued the inevitable " Cheerio ! " Inside the card was another picture—a fat and frightened German soldier chased across snowy No Man's Land by a slim and exuberant British soldier, who carried on his back a pack plastered with labels of the engagements in which Lennie's battalion had taken part—Mons, Aisne, Mancre, Arras, Ypres. *A Merry Christmas and a Happy New Year to You and Yours* was the unshaken wish of Lennard S. Twigg.

Theodore stuck the card up on his library mantelpiece, and after several days of indecision—would the young man be bored by a letter . . .? was it usual to return thanks for a Christmas card . . . ? —he made up his mind to write. On a very wet

Sunday afternoon, he trudged up the Banbury Road under his umbrella. He had hoped to catch a bus; had waited for a long time in the wrong place; had been too embarrassed, when he had realised his stupidity, to notice where the buses did stop; and had hurried on. That was in St. Giles'. A party of young townspeople, passing, had nudged each other to point out with perfect respect, " There's the Warden of St. Mary's "; and, unfortunately, Theodore noticed the nudges and imagined that they were drawing amused attention to his mistake. It did not occur to him that, even if they were, a man of his ability and position could very well afford to ignore the criticisms of a couple of grocer's assistants and their best girls; always to himself he was only Theodore, who could not see very well, and was bad at recognising people, and always had to wait so long in restaurants, and couldn't think of anything to say to strangers, and was fair game (he knew) for undergraduate mimicry, the same little oddity, in fact, whom Richard and Anne and Cecilia and John and even " Baby " had laughed at in the woods of Widdingfold long and long ago. At one phase of his career, just after he had been elected Warden, he had caught a glimpse of the more dignified self, which, for a brief space—just time enough to buy the cut glasses and the Crown Derby—he had believed that the world saw. But the discovery of the history of his election had sent that vision flying; he had not thought of himself as Head of a House again. Human nature was a closed book to him. He had never discovered that the magnificent self-assurance of such men as Richard Oliver might cover a heart as simple as his own (though probably a healthier stomach). Richard, he imagined, was magnificent all through.

He arrived, therefore, at "Innisfree" in his most self-conscious mood. True to tradition, he had exaggerated the distance between St. Mary's and Staverton Road, and, although he had had to walk, he entered the house as the hands of the fretwork clock stood at half-past three. Mrs. Logan was lying on her bed, hopelessly loosened. Doreen's marriage had given a new impetus to her father's hobby; he was constructing a series of objects with which to beautify her home when this tiresome war was finished and she had one ; and was certainly not to be coaxed from the den. Doreen was in her bedroom, polishing (why neglect the feet, girls? enquired *Home Chat*) her toe-nails. The sound of the front-door bell on a Sunday afternoon, once so intriguing, now no longer interested her—the drawing-room might be thick with subalterns : she'd sooner be sitting upstairs with Lennie's photograph on the mantelpiece and his regimental badge pinned in her dressing-gown, beautifying herself against his return.

So when she heard her mother's voice calling in muffled accents across the landing, she shouted back, without troubling to open her bedroom door, " I can't. I'm busy."

That brought Belle Logan in.

" Doreen ! It's the Warden of St. Mary's calling ! And just look at me ! Nothing but a dressing-gown and my combs ! Fly down, dear, and keep him till I come. That's right, your little blue frock. Talk to him ever so nicely, won't you ? And those blue beads . . ."

" Well, don't be long if you want to see him, Mother. He's a shy bird."

Doreen found Theodore in the drawing-room, sitting on the sofa, clutching his wet umbrella (the inaudible little maid had attempted to take it from

him, but, not hearing her distinctly, he had said,
" What is it ?   What is it ? " in so ferocious a tone
that she had not dared to repeat herself). " Good
afternoon, good afternoon," said Theodore. " Excuse
my calling at so inconvenient an hour."

" It's not a bit inconvenient. Sit down and have
another cush—there, that looks more comfy. As
a matter of fact, it's just the time when people do
come, but we've been so quiet lately. Joan's gone
back to her hospital and Walter's in Egypt, so there's
not much doing nowadays at ' Innisfree.' "

" You must feel the need of some distraction."

" Oh, I don't know ! It's no fun doing things
without Lennie."

" It would relieve the strain, though." He peered
at her anxiously. " You're looking a little pale,
I think." What could he do for her ? he wondered.
Get her tickets for something . . . ? The Boar's
Head at Queen's had been discontinued . . . Magdalen and New College Carols were over . . . The
Encenia was a long way off . . . There was the theatre,
of course, but that was given over to revue, no doubt,
and the names of the pieces would convey nothing
to him . . . how awkward if he bought her tickets
for a show that turned out not to be in the best of
taste ! " Perhaps you would come to tea with me
next Sunday," he offered. " It could hardly be
described as a distraction, but we might, perhaps,
call it a change of scene."

" I'd love that. Sundays do get pretty mouldy,
what with church bells and cold beef and beetroot
and no posts."

" Ah ! " said Theodore. " Now that reminds me.
I came to ask you for . . . for *his* address. He very
kindly sent me a Christmas card—you shall see it
when you come to tea; it adorns my mantelpiece—

and I'd like to acknowledge it . . . or does he find letters a bore ? "

" My dear ! Of course he doesn't," cried Doreen. " All the boys out there simply shriek to be written to. He'd adore you to write."

She got up and took from a drawer a sheet of Mrs. Logan's smartly embossed mauve writing paper, on which she wrote Lennie's address in her atrocious schoolgirl hand. " There you are," she said. " Do write to-night."

Theodore thanked her and rose to go. " Oh, won't you stop to tea ? " she begged. " Mother will be down in a minute."

" No, no," said Theodore, taking fright. This girl—*his* wife, poor child—with her way of treating you as if you were just a young friend of hers— offering you a " cush " and calling you, " my dear ! " —was delightful; he'd never felt more at ease with anyone. But the mother was a different proposition. She'd call him, " my dear Warden," search her memory and bring forth, to lay upon the altar of his eminency, wretched bits of knowledge, stiff flowers culled from the painfully planted borders of her mind . . . Oh, why couldn't such people realise how he hated the cultured mind's bright calceolarias and bring their cottage flowers instead? " I must go, I must go," said Theodore. " I've a meeting. I must get back to college. I shall expect you on Sunday at four o'clock."

Belle Logan, half in and half out of a grey satin jumper—now that one had a married daughter, grey seemed so dignified—was chagrined to hear the front door slam and Doreen come running upstairs, humming *First Love, Last Love, Best Love,* a tune of which her mother was really growing a little tired. Jumpers had been all very well when they had opened down the front like the old blouses, but now that they had to be pulled on over the head, it was a different matter. Belle Logan must be excused if she snatched off, rather roughly, the garment she had got so hot and arm-weary hurrying to put on.

And quite unconscious that he had caused a rent in a two-and-a-half-guinea jumper, Theodore hurried along Staverton Road. In Banbury Road a bus overtook him and came mercifully to a standstill within a few yards of him; and, although the rain had ceased, he was glad to get into it, for he was in a pleasurable hurry to be back in his library, writing to . . . yes, to his son.

When at length he reached his Lodgings—and now the distance seemed quite as far as tradition had it—he found tea set for him as usual on the slender mahogany table by the library fire. Next week, he thought, pouring out his tea, helping himself to his usual square of anchovy toast, next week, when I tell Carter . . . on Friday . . . or perhaps Thursday—that would give them more time to prepare—that I've a young lady coming for tea, I'll suggest some pink cakes. I'll have tea here . . . perhaps Mrs. Carter will think of putting some flowers about . . . and then she'll see *his* card on the mantelpiece . . . and she'll brighten the place up, too, sitting in the big chair, there, in her pretty frock. He munched up his toast, gulped down his tea, and walked over to the writing-table. He took from his pocket-book the sheet of notepaper on which Doreen had written Lennie's address, and could not help contrasting it with his own notepaper, so fastidiously printed for him at the University Press. His self-satisfaction was short-lived. No sooner was his pen ready to be put to paper than the first prob-

lem presented itself—how should he begin his letter
. . . Dear Mr. Twigg . . . Dear Twigg . . . Dear
Lennard . . . ? Mrs. Logan might choose atrocious
notepaper, his truthful mind realised, but she hadn't
got herself into the atrocious position of having to
begin a letter to the child of her body, *My dear Mr.
Twigg* . . .

My dear Mr. Twigg, wrote Theodore on his fastidious notepaper in his fine, academic hand. *I
have your card; and your wife has very kindly given
me your address so that I may write and thank you for
your thought of me.* And now what shall I say?
wondered Theodore, looking round the library, seeing
the firelight a-flicker on the books, hearing nothing
but the comfortable shifting of coals in the exquisite
Adam grate; what can I say, an old man in an Oxford
library to a young man in the trenches? Oh, you
books, he apostrophised, you four thousand learned
volumes, you can't help me now. That ignorant
little girl in Staverton Road can dash off something
in three minutes that would be of more comfort to
a boy in France than I could write—for all the wisdom I've got from you—in fifty years. He had very
little imagination and no knowledge of military
technicalities, but newspaper photographs had made
him fairly cognisant of the look of front-line trenches
in a clayey area; and a vision of the blond young
man, who had sat in his drawing-room and politely
questioned him on the antiquity of the University,
standing-to in the same dark dawn that would find
him snugly asleep under eight blankets in Archbishop Laud's bedroom, drove his pen. But to
what? *I called on your wife this afternoon*, wrote
Theodore, and stuck again; got up; walked about
the room; put coals on the fire; stared at the Reverend E. Cogan; munched cold toast; but still had

nothing to write. Then, suddenly, he saw in his
failure the eye for an eye, the tooth for a tooth that
Nature will have, my lords, despite the protests of
your intelligentsia. He sat down at his table, thrust
aside his futile letter and buried his face in his hands.

And when Doreen came to tea and sat in the big
chair, in her pretty frock, brightening the room
(Mrs. Carter hadn't thought of flowers and Theodore
hadn't liked to ask for them, but the pink cakes
were there), her first question was, had he got his
letter off to Lennie? Theodore stammered, " No
. . . No . . . " and Doreen said, " Oh, you are
lazy." " It's not that," said Theodore, nettled
(wouldn't he have done anything ?). " As a matter
of fact, I began a letter. But what can one say to
interest a man at the Front—a useless old Warden
of an empty college . . . ? "

" Now, don't get morbid," said Doreen. " I could
say the same thing. A useless girl, adding up figures
all wrong in an office . . . And then Lennie wouldn't
get *any* letters."

" Ah, no," said Theodore. " You're different.
You're a woman." A line came to him, and he
spoke it. " *These women who were summer in men's
hearts . . .* "

" Well, anyhow," said Doreen, who always felt
awkward when anyone spouted poetry. " Anyhow,
I *know* Lennie would appreciate a letter from you."
As she spoke, it occurred to her, perhaps writing
to someone young when you're old is as difficult as
writing to someone old when you're young. " Well,
give me a message for him, then," she said. " I'll be
writing to-night."

" Thank you." Theodore thought for a moment.
" Thank him for his card and his remembrance of me.
And wish him the . . . best of luck."

" Right you are." Doreen searched in her hand-bag. " I've got a letter here which I had last night." She brought out a flimsy buff envelope and took from it many sheets of paper written over in indelible pencil. " Shall I read some bits to you ? "

She had understood that the Warden of St. Mary's was intensely interested in Lennie. The Logan family had discussed his wedding present *ad nauseam*, but had never guessed at another motive than the benevolent wish of an old man, who couldn't go to the Front, to make a generous gesture towards a young man who had to go; a young man, more-over, who hailed from the same countryside. " The Warden has no doubt many happy memories of his childhood in that dear old Rectory," said Belle Logan to Hester, from whom she had extracted a certain amount of information. But Doreen understood more than that. When she spoke to the Warden about Lennie, there was always in the atmosphere between them that queer wave which emanates, though the mouth be shut, from the embarrassed mind; the same sort of feeling that you get just before a man asks you to marry him, reflected Doreen, or when someone's screwing up courage to tell you a home truth. What did it mean ? she wondered ? Lennie didn't feel the same about the Warden; any mystery there was must date from the days when Lennie's mother had lived in that place in Surrey that the Warden came from. If Theodore had been a different kind of man, without a doubt she would have stumbled on the truth; but it was quite be-yond her powers to imagine him a lover : it was hard enough for her to believe that her own parents —Father, so dried up and matter of fact, never saying anything but it's fine or it's wet or pass this or that;

Mother with so many clothes on that she didn't really look like a woman, and her hair all dragged up to the top of her head—could ever have loved; and nothing in her life had shocked her so much as she had been shocked one morning, when, sitting between her parents at breakfast, there had come into her mind, for the first time, the thought of her origin. So the mystery had remained a mystery, and she, being only too glad to find someone who wanted to listen to " bits " from Lennie's letters instead of saying, " After lunch, dear," or, " In a moment, when I've seen Cook," was content to leave it so. Her handbag was choc-a-block with Lennie's letters; and, in the end, she read Theodore " bits " from them all. It was quite dark and the bright stars of January were blazing among the pinnacles of the chapel when Theodore walked with her across the quadrangle. " I wonder if it's as quiet as this out in France," said Doreen, and Theodore, instead of saying brightly, " I'm sure it is, dear. Father thinks the news most hopeful," observed with sudden and surprising savageness, " I hate the quiet of this place. I wish the colleges were made of something we could melt down into munitions." Then Doreen knew for certain that he wasn't just an old man trying to help, but one whose poor heart was, like hers, in France.

January went by. The floods were out and Theodore couldn't get the whole way round Christ Church Meadow: very tiresome, very tiresome, he thought, secretly delighted to find an excuse; I'd better take the opportunity of calling on those people in Staverton Road. But Dr. Quears was back from his internment camp (he'd been exchanged like any nobody) and he suggested a walk on Sunday—" You'd like to hear my experiences, Warden, I feel sure."

"I should, I should," said mendacious Theodore. "But we can't take a walk, Quears. The floods are out and the smell is nasty. . . . nasty." "We needn't walk near the river," said Quears, horribly efficient. "There's Elsfield." "Can't get at it," said Theodore. "Marston's flooded." "Well, up Headington, then," said Quears. "St. Clement's isn't flooded, now is it, Warden?" Theodore was obliged to concur ; and on Sunday afternoon set out with Quears. It was an irritating walk for both men. Quears's experiences not only bored Theodore ; they exasperated him : he felt all the inferiority of the stay-at-home. "Of course you can't realise . . ." said Quears and, "You in Oxford had no idea . . ." Theodore kept chipping into Quears's narrative—"A young man in France, in whom I happened to be interested, tells me . . ." and, "That young man I told you of had an interesting experience . . ." but he had only to shut his mouth and Quears, without so much as a "Really?" or "Tch, tch," was off again. It was a muggy day, and Theodore, in his winter underclothing, felt hot and limp, while Quears, as a result of his deprivations, was in excellent training, and stepped briskly out. "In East Prussia . . ." said Quears, and Theodore rudely thought, I wish they'd kept you there!

Ultimately they fell out. Quears said something derogatory about the Philistine attitude of the cadets towards the University, sneered, "These temporary officers . . ." and Theodore was on him like a knife. "Our faith is in the trenches with these temporary officers, not in the Bodleian," he snapped. "Shut up in East Prussia, you've got deplorably out of touch . . ." "Out of touch!" cried Quears, striding over Magdalen Bridge, his white beard glossy with health, his pink cheeks shining. "Out of touch

when I've been interned for three years in the heart
of Germany!" "What Germany thinks or feels
doesn't matter," declared Theodore. "Whatever they
may think or feel, whatever is the situation in East
Prussia, we, with our temporary officers, will win
the war. Yes, we shall win the war!" he repeated,
waving his stick and humming something he had
heard the cadets sing with what breath was left to
him from keeping up with Quears.

Quears did not invite Theodore to walk with him
again, and the following Sunday afternoon he paid
his call on the Logans. Mrs. Logan was in the
drawing-room when he arrived, and pressed him to
stay to tea; and when he left Doreen said that she
wanted a walk and accompanied him back to St.
Mary's. He invited her in, and spent the hour before dinner in Hall showing her round the college:
the Hall, the Common Rooms, the Chapel, the But-
tery and the Library. "Ooo, what a lot of books,"
said Doreen on the threshold of the Library; and
his colleagues would no doubt have been surprised
to hear the Warden reply, "We've the finest college
library in the University, in any University, I may
say; but I'm not going to show it to you. You
. . . and *he* . . . have what I can only call a gift
for living; you don't need books to show you
the way through life. Perhaps," he continued,
half to himself, "you were wise enough not to
drink too deeply that night in the camp by the
river."

"Well," said Doreen, mightily relieved to see
that, true to his word, he was closing the door of
the Library, "we're certainly neither of us great
readers. But if there was any bubbly going that
night by your river . . ."

And while they walked back through the cloisters,

the February night with its faint, wild smell of spring beyond the grave, Gothic arches, Theodore related to Doreen, who decided that, as green was going to be *the* colour, she would have green instead of yellow, the legend of Er.

CHAPTER XV

BREAKING THROUGH

WHILE Theodore and Doreen were walking in the
cloisters of St. Mary's, Lennie was making an excellent supper of tinned soup and tinned salmon and
tinned peaches in a comfortable, concreted dug-
out in second-line trenches which had been evacuated
by the Germans less than a week before. He was
tired, wet and leg-weary. The thaw, which had just
set in over ground deeply frozen since a wet autumn,
had turned the valley of the Ancre into a sea of mud:
moving up from Albert had meant wading, mile after
mile, through a sucking slough, in the dark and a mist
of rain. But all the rain in France couldn't have damped
Lennie's spirits, which were but one instance of the
temper of the British troops in the soaking valley of
the Ancre that night. After more than two years of
trench warfare, they were on the move: wounded,
coming down from the counter-attacks round Serre
Hill, reported Jerry on the run: it'll be straight through,
non-stop to Berlin now, predicted Lennie and his
optimistic kind.

Being an officer had turned out very much what
Lennie had expected: good when it was a matter
of sitting in a dug-out drinking double whiskies and
censoring letters; bad—oh, very bad—when it was
a matter of going first over the top. Though his fair
head and girlish features (such an asset at the silk
counter in Margate) had, at first sight, prejudiced his
superior officers against him—" Good God ! " he'd

overheard. "They've sent us the Flapper's Dream this time ! "—the tact he had learned in buyers' offices, the easy comradeship he'd been accustomed to " on the road," soon reversed their first impression: he was not, obviously, a staff officer in embryo, but he made them an extremely cheery and willing subaltern. Among his men, he felt less secure. He was accustomed to responsibility but not to giving orders; it embarrassed him, for instance, to find fault with the rifles of older soldiers than himself. However, if he wasn't respected for his iron hand, he was loved for his unfailing cheeriness and imperturbable courage. In France, during those months of January and February, he was perfectly contented, often consciously happy: when he had nothing to do, he " yearned," as he expressed it to her, for Doreen; but, on the whole, he enjoyed " yearning," especially to the strains of a distant mouth-organ or an *estaminet* piano—much better than merely feeling bored was that slow half-ache, half-thrill which accompanied his rose-coloured memories and golden anticipations. After the war . . . dreamed Lennie, by the hour, in billets, and, if there isn't any " after " for me, well, I shan't know it, he'd think, moving up again towards the everlasting rumble of the guns.

But to-night he wasn't thinking of anything but tinned peaches and going through to Berlin. " If we once get them on the run, it'll be all up with them. We've always beaten them in the open, haven't we, Falkner ? " Lennie's company commander and oracle was a regular soldier, who took the war seriously and, while other people " yearned " or read the *Tatler*, pored over maps. " It's true the Boche isn't a soldier —but a row of soldiers," said Falkner. " However, you've got to remember that they'll be retreating over comparatively fresh country, while we'll be advancing over the infernal mud they've churned up." "You don't notice what you're advancing over," said Lennie. "It's when you're retreating . . . I've heard a rumour about cavalry, Falkner. Is it true?" "If we did break through, I suppose they'd get a look in, especially in this part of the country." Someone suggested that Lennie should join the cavalry in order to gratify his well-known ambition of being one of the first into Berlin.

The battalion had moved up in preparation for an attack, the objective of which was the high ground north of Thiepval, commanding the upper valley of the Ancre, and zero hour had been fixed at five-forty-five on the following morning. Lennie, after scribbling a short letter to Doreen—*we're going right through, this time, darling, and then, home at last to my Dream Girl*—turned in early, and, in spite of the fact that the thaw had made his chilblains particularly irritating, he slept soundly in a bunk which had been designed to outlast the resistance of British arms in France. He liked to go to bed early, and didn't mind how early he got up: both idiosyncrasies were, perhaps, a heritage from his rural forbears: and when, at the grim hour of five-fifteen, his batman brought a cup of tea, he woke instantly and amiably. It was a particularly unpleasant morning, dark, cold and damp, and a thick mist had penetrated even into the thirty-foot deep dug-out. Any slight hope of surprising the enemy was effectively disposed of by the sound of heavy firing. "It's been going on for nearly an hour. Brother Boche is up and about this morning," Falkner told Lennie as they left the dug-out together.

You couldn't see twenty yards in front of you, Lennie discovered, taking a peep over what had been the

German parados. If Fritz wasn't expecting us that might be construed into an advantage—it would have given us a sporting start, anyway. As it is, it'll mean a nice muck-up—no knowing where you are or what you're bumping into, some taking a trip round in the fog and coming back and throwing bombs into their own trenches, I daresay. After dinner on the previous evening, Falkner had given his subalterns a brief discourse on the lie of the land, and Lennie knew where the low, northward spur of the Thiepval Ridge was supposed to be, and a couple of villages that he couldn't remember the names of, and a Boche salient that to-day's show would wash out altogether. He had got an idea of what it looked like, too—the low, unimportant-looking ridge running up on the right, the little huddle of ruins that seemed scarcely worth the names he couldn't remember, the grey stretch of mud and shell craters and filthy water. But what's the use of worrying? thought Lennie. We've got to go over, so there you are! And he passed down the trench whispering jokes and encouragement, empty-headed, commonplace and brave.

Nothing went very deep with him, you'll say; or, he hadn't an imagination to worry him; or, it's all a matter of glands. Courage, like other virtues, is impossible to measure and compare—that deserter awaiting his firing party made a greater struggle, perhaps, than your hero proceeding to his investiture across the carpets of Buckingham Palace: nowadays we write a cycle of sonnets to the harlot and keep the finger of scorn for the suburban wife. Nevertheless, since the war had to be won, and it was won by the flapper-minded and the whisky-hardened and the brute-stupid, let us hand them their bouquets; call them brave men; and wait until they are history and fair game to analyse their bravery and prove it alcoholism, superficiality or brutishness.

Lennie, then, stood watching the hands of his wristwatch with no more of a sinking feeling in his stomach than you might feel before a tennis match, or, if you were Theodore, before a journey in the train. As automatically as the second hand touched the mark, he let out his yell of " come on, boys ! " and, being long-legged and of light build, was over the top in a twinkling. The ground, he discovered, was in an appalling state, huge shell-craters, the work of British artillery, were filled to the brim with water, blunder in and you'd have to swim for it; dodging them, you'd lose your sense of direction; God knew whether he was in front of the others or behind them now; but there were over a dozen men at his heels and he ran on. Suddenly, not twenty yards ahead of him, loomed up the broken outline of a ruined wall; and nearer, grimmer, than the crash of bursting shrapnel, the sharp stutter of a machine-gun and a storm of bullets revealed the presence and awareness of the enemy. Lennie saw his men go down—stop; crumple; and fall— the Sergeant, Corporal Haines, young Walker— " Come on, dash for it, boys," he shouted, only one idea—to get on—in his mind. Under cover of the wall—it was scarcely more than a pile of brick and mortar rubble—he threw himself down. There were half a dozen men with him, and another, who had been hit in the leg, crawled up to them. Lennie wiped the sweat from his face on his sleeve and said pleasantly, " Well, we're all right now."

Early in the war he had had some experience of village fighting and had found it much more to his taste than standing in a trench and being shelled. You could use your wits, anyway, and keep on the move, and you never knew what you'd come on round the next corner, which gave a sporty, hide-and-seek element to the affair. When he had got his breath, he crawled forward and peeped over the rubble. There was nothing to be seen but the ruined walls of houses looming up in the mist this way and that; and no sound now but an occasional shrapnel burst and the rumble of the guns to the south.

"I'd like to locate that machine-gun," he whispered to Corporal Fogden beside him. "Most likely it commands the whole village. A couple of bombs and we'd make things easy for the boys. Now listen: we'll make a rush for it to that wall where the door's hanging off its hinges. Now! before they start firing again!"

In a second Lennie and his men were dashing across what must once have been a neat little garden towards a wall, the angle of which would give them cover on two sides. The machine-gun promptly opened fire, and the last man to throw himself down on the wet mess of earth and brickbats was hit in the throat, and died as he fell. He was a bomber, and Lennie took a couple of Mills' bombs from the body. "Fogden, stop here, and don't move until you see them go up. I'll take Hendry and see if we can get near enough." Hendry was a doltish youth from a Thanet farm, famous as a slow bowler in the obscure village of his birth, and, with a grin at his comrades, he followed Lennie on hands and knees along the battered wall. "Now, Hendry, we're going to slip across this street, or whatever it is, into that building with the shutters, and round inside it. Stick to me, don't make more noise than you can help, and look lively," said Lennie, as though to a younger brother. Where the wall ended in

a collapsed heap of brickbats, he got to his feet and
ran lightly across a narrow space which might have
been a side street, into the shelter of the roofless house
opposite. The machine-gun was still firing, raising
a shower of earthy fragments from the ruined wall
behind which lay Fogden and his men, but it seemed
that Lennie and Hendry had crossed the street un-
observed. Keeping near the house wall, they passed
through the skeleton rooms and the yard behind
into a building so demolished that to keep under cover
they had to drop on their hands and knees again. After
a few yards, the wall of the building faded away
altogether, but, before reaching that point, Lennie
could peer through a window aperture into the
main street of the village, and there, to his joy,
not much more than thirty yards up the street,
was the machine-gun, mounted on a hastily con-
structed breastwork of sandbags. Hendry, on his
hands and knees in a puddle, had relapsed into a state
of bovine complacency: by signs, Lennie got him
up to the window: he peered cautiously through
and withdrew his head, grinning from ear to ear.
" Got to get across to that doorway," Lennie
hissed at him. " Then, from the top of those steps,
we can pitch 'em in." The back wall of the building
still stood to the height of a few feet. " There's our
cover. Wait till I'm across, then follow." Doubled
up, Lennie started, but hadn't taken three steps
when he felt a violent blow in the small of his back,
which flung him sprawling. Oh, hell ! I'm out of
it, he thought, and was conscious of an intense,
childish disappointment, before his brain registered
his body's atrocious pain. Then he realised that
he couldn't move; that his face was in the mud and
he couldn't roll over and get it out, or turn round
and see what was hurting him. Someone, however,

was hauling him up . . . out of the mud . . . dragging him . . . " Orl right, sir, you've got a blighty one," whispered Hendry, dragging him under the wall.

" All right, all right," said Lennie crossly. " Carry on."

He saw Hendry's brown, cow eyes looking doubtfully down at him; then the mist thickened and a stout lady in a tartan costume leaned her elbow on the counter and said, " That isn't quite what I wanted. Show me a better one, please." Lennie was reaching up to lift down the better-quality japs when an agonising pain tore across the small of his back. Must serve the old girl, thought Lennie, and the effort brought him back to consciousness—consciousness that he was lying propped up against a wall in a ruined village with a machine-gun stuttering thirty yards away from him, and that he'd been a fool to bring Hendry: though the fellow could throw a bomb more coolly and accurately than any man in the company, he'd no initiative: Fogden could have carried on on his own. But Lennie was mistaken. Josiah Hendry's brain didn't function as long as there was someone within hailing distance to think for him; but, long before he had come out to France for the purpose of keeping them there Germans on their own side of the Channel, without an officer to lead him he had taken cover under the hedgerows of Kentish apple orchards. While Lennie was still deploring his choice, he heard a sudden, loud explosion, quickly followed by another: a shower of earth spattered on the wall behind him: acrid fumes blew about him: and when the noise died away, he realised that the machine-gun had ceased firing. Good lad, good lad ! he thought, and tried to move, but the pain that the effort caused him

sent him faint again—he was back at Margate
. . . there was a fire in the Amusement Park . . .
how it smelled . . . everyone was running . . .
running. "Hullo, Twigg, got a blighty one, lucky
devil?" said Falkner, with a dirty face and a
trickle of blood from his forehead. "You've
put that machine-gun out of action—jolly good
work."

"Young Hendry did it," said Lennie. "On his
own. Didn't think he had it in him. He ought to
get something, Falkner."

"All right, I'll see to that," said Falkner. Then,
"The stretcher-bearers'll be along presently. Anything I can do?"

"Got a gasper?" asked Lennie. "Seems silly,
but I can't move to get at mine."

Falkner brought out his case, stuck a cigarette
between Lennie's lips and knelt down to light it.
"Well, cheerio," he said, rising.

"Cheerio," said Lennie.

"Give my regards to Leicester Square," called
Falkner as he hurried away.

Well, that's that, thought Lennie, puffing at his
cigarette and finding it extraordinarily tasteless.
And there's an end of *my* war—no marching up the
Wilhelmstrasse for me, after all. Still, he reflected,
every cloud has its silver lining; two days from
now I may be in dear old London . . . in hospital
. . . between clean sheets . . . warm, dry . . . and
Doreen coming in to see me, all fresh and lovely and
smelling of carnations. But I'm far from warm and
dry now, he began to notice: the mist can't have got
through; it's the mud I'm lying in—a puddle
probably—and the blood from my wound. Good
lor', what a mess, and very likely there's a worse one
inside of me—what is it down there . . .? liver or

kidneys . . . ? still, they'll straighten that out in hospital. He felt, for the first time in his life, the disassociation of body and mind, so obvious in moments of violent suffering: his body lay torn and shivering in the mud, but his mind could soar, ethereal and sane. I'll try to send a wire myself, he thought. I'd hate my poor little girl to get an official thing—*Regret to inform you Second Lieutenant L. S. Twigg wounded or seriously wounded.* I wish those fellows would turn up, he thought suddenly. Supposing I'm bleeding inside? He had a healthy person's usual ignorance of anatomy; but he'd heard of "internal hæmorrhage," and the horrid words occurred to him now. It would be a bit off, he thought, to lie here in this beastly fog and bleed to death alone, but still, it would be better than dying over the wire in No Man's Land like Ginger Harris and hanging there for the rest of the afternoon, spoiling everyone's appetite for tea. And it's no use getting the wind up, thought Lennie, and then finding yourself discharged from hospital in a fortnight, and the war all over, and your pension in your pocket, and your medals on your chest, and Mr. Roadnight shaking you by the hand, and nothing more to do but to get round to the house agents and hunt out that little house at Beckenham. Oh, Doreen, Doreen, thought Lennie, tired now, not regretting any longer Berlin and the march up the Wilhelmstrasse; I'm coming home, and when they've patched me up, I'll come back to you, and go to sleep as we used to, with you all warm and silky in my arms. He was beginning to feel drowsy, for he had not been far out in his guess at internal hæmorrhage, and, in a sleepy way, he fancied himself back in the Empire suite at the London hotel. "Let's have dinner at the Troc and go to the Bing Boys,"

said Doreen, but he said, " No, I'm too tired to. Isn't
it silly . . . ? too tired to have a good time now
we've won the war." Doreen said, " Never mind.
We'll have a good time when you're better. Go
to bed now," but as she spoke, he knew that he
couldn't go to bed and that the war wasn't over, for
the whole hotel was shaken by a deafening explosion . . .

Lennie opened his eyes. The mist was thicker
than ever and, oh lord ! he thought, how cold I am !
When are those fellows coming ? He heard the whine
of a shell in the air above him, and the shattering roar
of its explosion, and, without emotion, saw the wall of
the tall building on his right bulge out towards him
and fall over . . . over . . .

The German counter-attack was beginning.

CHAPTER XVI

O, ABSALOM

THE buds of the horse chestnuts were thickening, Theodore noticed, and the finest lawn in the world (Wadham, St. John's, New College, Worcester and Trinity said " no " to that) had taken a new sheen; a blackbird was singing in the bare may-tree by the gateway and a water wagtail was taking his quaint way across the grass (one had to allow Magdalen her kingfishers, but the ducks in Mesopotamia could be dismissed as importations, like her black swans); the ground under the cedar was white with snowdrops, fragile and clear against the strong dark tree, such perfect little forms that surely they must be more than flowers (but Theodore only noticed snowdrops); over the soaring pinnacles of the chapel the sky was a fleeting, rain-washed blue. Spring, nineteen hundred and seventeen, thought Theodore, and still no sign of the end of the war.

He was coming back from Convocation and had let himself into his garden through the door in the wall. He loved his garden—all the better since the Bursar had started pulling about the college garden, lopping trees, cutting slices from the turf to make room for herbaceous borders, bringing in rocks—fantastic it was to see them carted across the front quad—and crazy paving—why pave crazily? asked Theodore's logical mind. " I don't like them, I don't like them," he said, when the Bursar suggested that a herbaceous border or a rockery would brighten up the Warden's garden too. "I don't want my garden to look like Anne Hathaway's garden. It isn't Anne Hathaway's garden. Nor like the moraine of the Aletsch glacier. It isn't the moraine of the Aletsch glacier. Leave it alone. Leave it alone." So the Warden's garden had remained the green and philosophic grove which a seventeenth-century scholar had planned and planted.

Carter met Theodore in the hall.

"There are two ladies to see you, sir," he said in a confidential tone which, though low, wasn't anything so suggestive as a whisper. "Mrs. Twigg and Mrs. Lennard Twigg. I showed them into the library."

Theodore was taking off his gown. His hands began to fumble. He did not look at the man but said, merely for something to say, "Have they been waiting long?"

"About half an hour, sir."

Theodore didn't hear that. He was thinking fearfully: what can they want? If it were something unimportant, Doreen would have come alone. Why should *she* come? . . . into my house? Has she told them? After all these years has she been mad enough to tell them? In the presence of the servant he couldn't hesitate or stop to calm himself. He opened the library door and walked in.

Doreen was sitting in the big arm-chair with her feet on the fender, and Hester on the edge of the chair which Theodore used at the writing-table. Hester looked pale and miserable, and Doreen looked pale and obstinate, her pointed chin thrust out defiantly, her soft young mouth tightly set. Theodore did not observe their looks. He advanced towards them with his hand extended, looking at his feet.

"Good morning, Mr. Fletcher, we're sorry to trouble you," said Hester.

Doreen interrupted, without any good morning, "Lennie's wounded and missing."

Theodore stood where he was and his hand fell to his side.

"Oh, dear," he said piteously. "Oh, dear, dear."

"He's sure to turn up," said Doreen in a harsh voice. "Lots do."

"Yes, yes," said Theodore. "I've known several cases—St. Mary's men. Let me see—there's been an advance down near the Somme area."

"We don't know where he was," said Hester in an aggrieved, maternal tone. "Nor nothing more but what they said in the telegram. I'd come over to spend a few days with Mrs. Logan. I'd just arrived. That was last night. This morning I suggested to Doreen that seeing how good you'd been to Lennie . . ."

"No, no," mumbled Theodore.

". . . it wouldn't be too much to ask . . ."

"If you could *do* something," Doreen burst out. "It's so awful just sitting and waiting."

Theodore's heart bled for her. He didn't know much about how these children loved: he certainly credited Doreen with a more inconsolable sorrow than she was capable of: and he would have given anything to speak out his bleeding heart. But he couldn't do that. At most, he could have stepped to his shelves, and taken out a volume, and handed it to her, and let Milton speak for him or Shelley. But a girl would think that cold-blooded; wouldn't dream, at such a time, of opening a book. "I'd like to help you . . . I don't know what I could do . . ." he stammered. Then, as it occurred to him, "I'll write to someone . . . at the War Office. There must be St. Mary's men . . . Of course, of course . . . young Wycherley . . . up in '97. He's Lord

Risborough now. I'll write to-night. No, I'll go up and see him. They'll be working late at the War Office. Or he'll see me at his house, of course. Yes, I'll do that."

" There now," said Doreen. " As soon as Mrs. Twigg suggested it, I knew that you'd be able to do something." She smiled cheerfully at Hester. " That *was* a brain-wave."

And across the library, the grave, quiet room to which life with its shifts and its muddles had brought him, Theodore's eyes met Hester's.

It should have been an awkward moment—Theodore, at any rate, had been at pains to avoid it—but, although the girl's words compelled both minds back to the same surely shameful memory, Theodore had known moments made far more awkward by a broken suspender or a high wind at the corner of the Turl. Is there anything that the years can't belittle ? he asked himself; and saw Time, a huge rough-hewn colossus, a giant in seven-league boots, against whom, in some titanic contest, ran the lissom torch-bearers of the human race. And the hand into which I thrust my torch may be lifeless already, thought Theodore, ringing the bell in a fuss, asking for a railway guide, hurrying out Hester and Doreen, changing his suit, swallowing a hasty luncheon, speeding down Queen's Street in a taxi; no time to think until he was alone in a first-class compartment, drawing out between the cemetery and the gas works: what I told them's true— I've known cases where the wounded and missing have been found in German hospitals and prison camps or even hidden behind the German lines. And more will be found when the war's over—the insane, the dumb, the shell-shocked. But that's only a small proportion. Most of the wounded and missing remain wounded and missing. I ought to know that, he thought, remembering St. Mary's Roll of Honour. If we were retreating, he reasoned, there'd be more hope that he was a prisoner, but, if he were in this advance, it's not likely. There are so many weapons in this horrible modern warfare that leave no trace . . . and his inward vision showed him Lennie, fair and long-legged, in the inevitable khaki that suited his fairness, sitting on the edge of a Chippendale drawing-room chair, a brown and yellow Liberty silk handkerchief showing at his sleeve, something a little " summer-numberish " about his collar and tie, trying with all his amiable young heart to make himself pleasant —Oh, God ! groaned Theodore, picking at his thumb, staring at a photograph of the Suspension Bridge, Clifton. Oh, God ! why should I, having made such a poor thing of life, go on living, while he, so able for life, so at home in the world, has gone from it ? The Suspension Bridge, Clifton, dissolved slowly in mist: he realised that his eyes were full of tears. Thank God, I'm alone in the compartment, he thought, taking off his spectacles and wiping them, and wiping his eyes. What would Quears think . . .? He's got no child . . . he's got no need for tears . . .

Short of going out to France to look for Lennie himself, Lord Risborough did everything humanly possible to help the Warden of St. Mary's: and, in the course of a few days, there came for Doreen a letter from Captain Falkner, who, wounded himself at the close of that day's fighting, had had no reason to imagine his subaltern anywhere but in hospital. *He said, " Cheerio,"* wrote Billy Falkner in his round, illiterate hand, *and I left him there, thinking the stretcher-bearers would be along presently and having to get on myself. A bit later in the morning the enemy tried a counter-attack and dropped a few shells round the village,*

*but we must keep up hope. Your husband is a splendid
fellow*—in the fourth year of the war this came rather
glibly from the pen of a company commander—*nothing
ever seemed to put him out and we all admired his courage
and his cheeriness in troublesome times.* . . .

Doreen kept up hope: corresponded with neutral
philanthropists and French and British associations;
travelled to Colchester to see Lennie's batman in hospital and to St. Nicholas-at-Wade to see Private Hendry,
D.C.M., on leave. Mrs. Logan made up her mind
quite soon that Lennie had, as she expressed it, " given
all for King and Country," and with the best intentions
in the world—" anything better for the poor child
than this awful suspense "—she set out to persuade
Doreen into the same belief. Her transparent and
tender discouragement of what small hope could be
entertained exasperated Doreen into hysteria. " I
I don't get away from Mother, I shall go potty," she
exclaimed, bursting in on Theodore in his library one
fine May morning. " She tried to persuade me that
Lennie's dead and then wants me to get interested in
things so that I shall forget him," she stormed, crying
into the cushions. " Dear me, dear me," said Theodore; inadequate, perhaps, no human sympathy, you'd
say, in his dried-up scholar's heart: and in the same
abrupt way that he had turned to young Holloway,
desperate in that same chair the term before the war,
and jerked out, " I'll pay your battels. I'll pay your
battels. Don't tell anyone. Good morning," he
turned to Doreen and said, " I'll help you. I'll get you
a post in London."

Doreen blew her nose in a small jade-green handkerchief, and sat up, and said, " I can type a bit, but not
fast, and I'm fairly quick at figures but Father says
not accurate. I've done some filing, but I can't do
shorthand. . . ."

" Never mind, never mind," said Theodore, quite
certain of her inefficiency. " That doesn't matter.
There must be St. Mary's men . . ."

" Wanting a clerk ? "

" Well, let us say, able to find a post for one. I
should suggest a Government office. There's Risborough, I could write to him again. Or Whit-
head at the Censor's Office. Or Ronaldson at the
Admiralty . . ."

" You *are* kind. And you don't think Lennie's dead,
do you ? "

" I hope not. I still hope not."

" Even if you did, you wouldn't be like Mother.
You'd allow one to be miserable."

" I should be very miserable myself," said Theodore.

CHAPTER XVII

IGNORING CLAMOURS

DOREEN wanted to stay a little longer in the church.

The village people were going home in twos and threes along the path which leads from the churchyard to the white gate and the high road; and Theodore elected to wait for her between the yews outside the porch. It was cool there, and he knew how hot it could be along the path before the shadows of the elms slipped round to lengthen down the pastures; moreover, after that harrowing service, he needed a few moments of solitude in which to collect himself. He had never been more deeply moved than during that last half-hour in Widdingfold church; Doreen's kneeling figure; the serene blue of the midsummer sky at the windows; peace after war; the cold beauty of the bronze he had commissioned; the little sounds of life and summer stealing in through the doorway from the meadows; his pride; his grief; his memories of this place had exhausted him: waiting there, in the shade of the yews, he was near to tears—let anyone say, "That poor boy . . ." and he'd lose his self-control . . .

The choirboys came clumping and scuffling round from the vestry door; and then came the Rector, a muscular Keble man, who was sorry that the Warden of St. Mary's had declined his invitation to lunch at the Rectory. "A very beautiful little service," he remarked to Theodore. "Very affecting." The Warden of St. Mary's said nothing, nothing at all, just stood there with his hand over his mouth, not easy to read his eyes behind those thick lenses. The Rector couldn't (he felt) simply turn and go away, so he ventured, " Binyon's beautiful lines always occur to me: *They shall not grow old as we who are left grow old. Age shall not weary them nor the years condemn . . .*"

" Nonsense. Nonsense. Age is no tragedy, sir," snapped Theodore.

At the end of an astonished pause, the Rector muttered, " Perhaps not. Good morning, sir," and made off, stepping down the road, stretching his excellent muscles, facing the facts of life, thanking God that he had married, and come out into the world to labour usefully, and remained normal, instead of embracing an academic career, and staying at Oxford, and not marrying, and becoming strange in his manner.

Theodore watched the dark figure descend between the bright pastures, lost it where the trees stood about the mosquito-haunted ponds, caught another glimpse of it at the gate of the Rectory drive. He knew every step of that way, the sound the gate would make when the Rector opened it, the shadow of what branch would lie across the path's whiteness, how soon the scent of the azaleas would reach his nostrils; and in fancy he followed him up the steps, into the pitch-pine hall, past Lassie curled up in her basket, into the shabby dining-room. " A beautiful little service," he'd say to his wife, carving the sirloin, helping himself to green peas and boiled potatoes, chewing and swallowing with appetite and enjoyment justified by Binyon's beautiful lines. How Theodore, standing up in the churchyard, sick with emotion, hated this scramble to make things bearable, to console the inconsolable: how well he understood Doreen's sad cry, " You'd let me be miserable ! "

" Lennie wouldn't have wished us to grieve," stated

Mrs. Logan, weary of keeping her mind off the fascinating new fashions, and the Rector, *They shall not grow old* . . . You weak fools! thought Theodore, who had been afraid of railway journeys, giving orders, meeting strangers, rather than admit your desolation, you'd give thanks for barren corn.

The gate of the churchyard groaned on its hinges —the Rector had shut it behind him—and Theodore made out that it was Hester who was coming slowly up the path. Since Lennie's identification bracelet had been found under a pile of masonry by French labourers engaged in reconstruction work, she seemed to have changed from a middle-aged into an elderly woman; and in spite of the good clothes which her affectionate daughters insisted on choosing for her, she had reverted, unmistakably, to her peasant type. Until to-day, Theodore had not seen her since the May morning, two years ago, when he had come back from Convocation and found her with Doreen in his library.

"Mrs. Logan asked me to wait for Doreen," said Hester, as she came up to Theodore. "She felt faint and she has gone to sit in the car."

"Just as well. Just as well," said Theodore. "I'm afraid she finds her mother's attempts to brighten her up a little trying."

Hester nodded. "I've asked her to come and spend her summer holiday with me. My youngest daughter's husband has just got demobilised, and they're setting up a tea-shop at Herne Bay with me. It won't be quite what she's used to, p'r'aps, but it'll give her a change and a good blow by the sea."

"An excellent idea. I hope your tea-shop will prove successful."

"It should do. Daisy and Harold are very ambitious."

" That's right.   That's right."

They were silent for a moment.

" Lennie was ambitious too," said Hester, staring out across the meadows.

" Yes," said Theodore.   " Yes."

" The . . . *bas-relief*, you call it, don't you ? . . . is very like him.   It's beautifully done."

" I'm glad."

Doreen came from the church.

" Where's Mother ? " she asked suspiciously.

" She's gone to sit in the car, dearie," said Hester.

" I expect her feet hurt," said Doreen with an hysterical giggle.   " She would put on her new shoes out of respect to Lennie's memory."

" A curious instinct . . . wholly uncivilised," commented Theodore.

The three began to walk slowly from the churchyard. When they had passed through the gate, they could see, above the hedgerow which separated the high road from the glebe land, the red roof of the Goat and Compasses, and the doves perched on it, and the dark firs beyond.

" That's where you used to live, isn't it ? " Doreen asked Hester.

" Only for a short time," said Hester.   " My mother was separated from my father and, until she died, I lived with her at Manchester."

" I'd sooner live there than in Manchester.   I think it's just too twee.   Didn't you love it ? "

" It's all so long ago," said Hester.

Yes, it's long ago, thought Theodore.   The place is the same from that little cloud up there above the church tower to the stones in the road ; from the sound of the midday train chugging up the valley to the chirp of the grasshoppers ; and it smells the same ; and feels

the same, he felt beneath his feet. And I know quite
well that a young man walked up that road between
the fields one hot afternoon with *Paradise Regained*
weighing heavy in the pocket of his jacket, but what I
can't believe is that it was me—except for the bronze
in the chancel there, and this heavy heart, and, at the
end of it all, my thankfulness that my life wasn't the
useless, empty thing I once feared. The torch has
burned out, he thought, but that's my sorrow—and
he certainly found life worth living and was grateful
for it, however he died. Doreen and Hester had been
talking over the dates of Doreen's summer holiday,
and now the three were half-way between the high
road and the church. Beyond the kissing-gate they
could see the flash of the sun on the radiator of Mrs.
Logan's hired Daimler—once again Mr. Logan had not
grudged anything to Doreen. Doreen opened her
handbag and looked at herself in the mirror. " Oh,
dear, how awful ! " She took out a powder box and
fell behind the others.

Hester said at once, " I daresay I shan't have another
opportunity of thanking you for your kindness, Mr.
Fletcher . . . not only for this but for what you
gave Lennie when he was married. He liked a
bit of life, did Lennie, and, thanks to you,— he
got it before . . . he went west, as the young
ones say."

" Please don't. Please don't," muttered Theodore.

" If I didn't thank you now, I'd have to write," said
Hester. " And I'm a poor hand at letter-writing
nowadays. You see, Mr. Fletcher, though it all
seems such a long time ago and as if it didn't matter,
I've never forgiven myself for the things I said to you
—perhaps you don't remember, but I know at the
time it upset you. Girls don't think that boys feel
the same as they do, especially girls in a fright like

I was. And when it all turned out to be nothing, I should have let you know ; but I was spiteful. I thought, well, let him learn what it is to lie awake and worry till you're half crazy, let him suffer a bit too."

" What's that ? What's that ? " said Theodore.

" I thought, let him suffer a bit too. And I daresay you believed what I told you right up until you heard I was marrying Sam."

Theodore made no answer. He hadn't realised yet how it had happened, only that, on some trivial and chance error (error, that " inseparable shadow of knowledge ") he had built up an illusion which had denied the failure and repaired the omissions of his life that the clear values of a universal tragedy had taught him to despise. In this desolate moment, he could not estimate his loss, felt himself utterly denuded, hurried, with the master instinct of such softshelled creatures, first to hide his predicament. The woman had spoken again; was saying " . . . and considering the upset I must have caused you for what was as much my fault as yours—don't you doubt it —I've felt that mean ever since I heard of your kindness to Lennie. At first I couldn't credit it . . . though, of course, he'd a way with him . . ."

She was looking at Theodore . . . his straggly brown moustache, streaked with grey now, hid his mouth . . . not easy to read his eyes behind those thick lenses . . . But he didn't realise that, and, with an effort of will, composed his face and forced words from his aching throat.

" Of course, of course," said Theodore.

They were near the gate now; could see the hedge which sheltered the inn garden, and the highest branches of the walnut tree; could hear the coo of the doves on the red roof; could smell the firs. But on the road

between them and the inn stood not old Tom, a-dream
between the shafts of the Rectory governess cart, but
the mammoth Daimler with Mrs. Logan resting inside,
leaning back, eyes closed, a silver-topped bottle of
smelling salts and a nice white handkerchief in her
smartly gloved hands.

" Well, thank you, Mr. Fletcher," said Hester.

" It was nothing . . . nothing," said Theodore.

Doreen came up with them.

" Do I look all right now ? "

" Quite all right," said Hester.

Their voices roused Mrs. Logan.

" Ah, there you are ! " Dozing in the sunshine,
her lips had got dry and she moistened them with
her tongue and moved her mouth to increase the flow
of saliva. " Here you are ! Now, how shall we
sit ? "

" I'm going to have dinner with my husband's relations in the village, Mrs. Logan," said Hester. " So
I'll say good-bye here. I'll be seeing Doreen again
the first fortnight in August."

" I'm going to sit by the driver," said Doreen.

" Let me. Let me," begged Theodore.

" There's no need for either of you . . ." began
Mrs. Logan.

But Doreen, without another word, took the seat
she wanted, and Theodore had to get in and sit down
beside Mrs. Logan. The driver started up the car
and it slid away, past the porch where Adams used
to sit and smoke a pipe with Jimmy Marks, the carrier,
past the ground-glass window through which in
summer could be seen the broad red necks and lounging
shoulders, and heard the storms of laughter, and smelt
the fumes of beer.

Mrs. Logan thought, well, that's over. And now
perhaps we can expect Doreen to realise that it's her

duty to cheer up. Of course it's been a terribly sad
time for her, but God doesn't mean us to grieve for
ever. To be left a widow after a fortnight's marriage
is very tragic, but it's not so bad as it would be for
me to lose Ernest after twenty-five years. And I
hope I should remember what I owed to others better
than Doreen does . . . she doesn't try to forget—
wearing that wretched identification bracelet night
and day and making her room like a mausoleum with
photographs of poor dear Lennie . . . one on the
dressing-table or mantelpiece would be quite enough.
Even now the war is over, we can't enjoy ourselves.
Belle Logan had never asked very much of life: a dress
from Elliston, the drawing-room redecorated, a lion
at her tea party, and, provided all in the home were
cheerful and good-humoured, there was Paradise enow.
But Doreen, drifting about the house looking miserable,
with Lennie's identification bracelet jingling on her
wrist and the neck of her frock pinned with his regimental badge in enamel, cast her drooping shadow
over everything: when your daughter was crying in
the next room for her dead husband, how could you
enjoy unpacking your new hat? Like most people
who ask very little of life, she was, quite reasonably,
aggrieved that she didn't get it. I don't say that Doreen
should be her old bright self, she thought, only that she
should behave like an ordinary member of society,
rouse herself to talk to visitors and not appear at breakfast with swollen eyes.

Mrs. Logan's busy mind kept her mouth shut half-
way to Dorking. Theodore, who, dreading the drive,
had felt like pulling Doreen from the seat of which
she had so adroitly possessed herself, was supremely
thankful: he could neither have talked of Lennie nor
chattered, as people do on such occasions, of this
and that. His one desire was for solitude and home.

Oxford . . . he thought, Oxford . . . and the name
was shelter in the hurricane, a rock in the whirlpool . . .

For this error has sustained me for five years, he
acknowledged, seeing the hedgerows fly backwards,
noticing that wild roses climbed in them, hearing cuckoos
call, faint and faërie in the hills, and all of it nothing
to him: for five years the like of which no man will
see again. Without it, how could I have endured
that lengthy proof that what I had lived for was useless,
that I was useless? I thanked heaven, he remembered, that, in spite of my nature and upbringing,
the torch was forced into my hand. And now I've got
to realise that it was all in error—that I never had a son.
Life's made a fool of me, he thought bitterly, just as
the Olivers and the Harbutts used to, just as the Fellows
did when they elected me. I was mad to suppose
that " the poor little oddity " could share the common
lot . . .

Mrs. Logan, thinking, the Warden of St. Mary's
will think me as hopeless and helpless as Doreen if I
sit here saying nothing, remarked, " How sweet the
country smells ! "

Theodore made no answer.

" Are you a nature lover, Mr. Fletcher ? " she per-
severed.

" No. No."

" I wonder at that. A child among these lovely
surroundings . . . But no doubt, from the first, your
tastes were bookish ? "

" I can't tell you. It's too long ago."

" Time does fly," discovered Mrs. Logan. " And
sometimes I'm sure it's a blessing that it does. Such
a healer. I feel that with poor little Doreen."

Theodore said nothing.

" Youth's got such recuperative powers," chatted

Mrs. Logan. "You and I know that. We can look forward to the day when all this will seem far away and dream-like. That's because we're getting on. We've acquired the philosophic mind."

Theodore was silent.

"I've always felt that I should like to make a study of philosophy."

"Stick to housekeeping. Stick to housekeeping," said Theodore.

He spoke bitterly, his thought being simply that the housewife lives while the philosopher searches, and that when life's over and can't be had again, the riddle will be solved for one and all. But Belle Logan believed that he had snubbed her, considering her only fit for housekeeping (hadn't he opposed every concession granted to the women's colleges?) and she fell into a chagrined silence. And although she never related the incident to anyone—she would have hated to confess that her lion had snapped at her— she never forgot it, and in her heart she never felt quite the same liking for Theodore.

They lunched at an hotel in Dorking. Theodore, as usual, was badly served, and Mrs. Logan, faint with hunger, took matters into her own hands. "I am accustomed to travelling abroad," she told the waiter, "and there, at any little wayside inn, one can count on an omelette and common courtesy." "Abroad's abroad, and England's England, ain't it, m'am?" retorted the waiter pertly, and the Warden of St. Mary's, the only gentleman in the party, did nothing but sit there, for all the world like a school-boy, picking at his thumb.

And dinner, when it came, was just what you would have expected, hot roast beef and Yorkshire pudding, and hot cherry tart, although the month was flaming June; and you couldn't any longer say, "No wonder

we don't win the war ! " nor, for a few years, " What
a hopeless nation we are ! " Mrs. Logan, already so
hot that she couldn't think why dress preservers had
gone out of fashion, ate the hot food and watched
Doreen and the Warden pick theirs over. Well . . .
the service had been beautiful and the memorial must
have cost the Warden three figures, but, on the whole,
it had been a dreadful day . . .

Driving back to Oxford, Doreen sat with her
mother; and Theodore on one of the occasional seats
which faced towards the front of the car. After the
first few miles the ladies spoke little; Theodore could
see their reflections in the glass screen between himself and the driver, and he saw that, for the greater
part of the time, their eyes were shut. Accustomed
to a brisk walk on Sunday afternoons, he could not
doze: his sad mind brooded on his loss, not Lennie's
death—that was a human sorrow, something that
came with life and would go with life—but the loss
of what had proved to-day to be an illusion: eternity
itself couldn't repair that, he knew. On the long
road home, memory gave him its relentless shadow
show: the first scene in the Common Room, wine
and dessert on the table, the well-known faces,
Hamilton saying, " You've got nothing to worry over
—no one out there." Then his encounter with the
polite boy in the cloisters, and Lennie coming to tea,
sitting on the edge of his chair trying to talk about
history, walking away across the quadrangle in the
October dusk, tall and young and glad to be alive.
Then the chance meeting, almost a collision, in the
dark, and the excited voice saying, " Guess what I've
been doing ! " and the dinner-party, the cut glass
and the Crown Derby justified at last, the girl like
a Dresden china shepherdess, the unfamiliar chatter
of shops and hats, the young man's profile staring at

the New English Dictionary. Then the wedding, his human little regret that he wasn't puffed out with pride like the absurd Logan parents, and his meeting with Hester and the discovery that he could look her in the face and talk about the weather. Then Lennie's Christmas card, the English soldier chasing the German soldier across No Man's Land, and his calls at Staverton Road, and Doreen coming to tea with him, and his quarrel on Magdalen Bridge with Quears. And then coming back from Convocation and hearing that Lennie was wounded and missing, and his interview with obliging Lord Risborough, and all the days and the months of hope and fear until hope ended and one could only epitomise that commonplace and heroic life in bronze. And in all that happened I was an interloper, thought Theodore; my consolation, my affection, my benevolence, my grief were false from beginning to end, a house built on sand. All these years of war, I was just what I couldn't bear to be, what Hamilton and Quears and the rest of them thought me—a man who'd nothing to worry over because he had sat himself down at High Table and let common life go by, a pretender to the knowledge that had not spared the human race its Great War, living in a place that was a shell. If it should be true that one is born again, he thought, let me be born a farm-hand, to turn the clods and drive the beasts and giggle obscenely at the corner of the green on Sunday afternoons, but, at least, while I'm alive to live the life of earth . . .

Mrs. Logan did not wish to stop anywhere for tea. " We'll have some when we get back, Doreen," she suggested. " And I daresay the Warden, like many gentlemen, is independent of the cup that cheers." They reached Magdalen Bridge as the clocks were striking six. Men and girls were coming up from the river carrying punt cushions and picnic baskets, and the low summer sun shone down on the street into their eyes. The summer term . . . thought Theodore stupidly; the first summer term after the war. . . . The car slowed down and came to a standstill outside the gates of St. Mary's; and he got out, and said, " Good-bye. Good-bye," and turned away, although Mrs. Logan was speaking to him, and scurried into the college. Through the lodge he went: " Good afternoon, sir," said Jordan, but you didn't need to answer him: walk into the lodge clean or dirty, drunk or sober, on your hands or on your feet, he wouldn't criticise you; you were just the present Warden passing by: then across the quadrangle, with the noise of the street giving place to the familiar sounds of college. . . . Homeric laughter from groups gathered here and there, clear young voices bawling from mullioned windows, footsteps in a hurry on stone staircases, a bell tolling over by New College. For the war was over, Theodore realised suddenly; that which had seemed endless had ended, that which had seemed unendurable had been endured; and, through it all, Oxford had chosen " to await . . . ignoring clamours," to wait for a new summer and a new generation. And here, though he himself hadn't foreseen it, hadn't been strong enough, or brutal enough, or wise enough to foresee it, was the new generation, coming up from the river, bright-eyed in the sunshine with Hellenic limbs, boys and girls with their three score years and ten in front of them, no need for them to scramble into taxis and hurry off to " Pic " and " Troc " to fill themselves with meat and wine and get a taste of life before they died. I should have waited too, he told himself; I should have realised that the cup would pass, that there would be youth again and summer, though

Crete, Egypt, Sparta, England had their wars. A dark and to a stranger's eye a queer figure, he took out his key and let himself into his Lodgings, into the cool and cedarn fragrance of the hall and the long, dim library. There was sunshine in the room when he entered, the soft light of summer evening slanting across the bookcase. And the war's over, he thought, taking off his hat, supposing that he ought to wash before going into Hall (but to his bird's-eye view what did it matter if, on one of the twentieth century's six thousand and five hundred evenings the then Warden of an Oxford college went into Hall clean or dirty?), the war's over and it's taken its distorted outlook with it: but still, he thought, deciding not to wash, going over to the bookcase, taking down his own *History of Logic*, wondering if, after all, he *had* been rather rash in that chapter on the Peripatetics, still, "ignoring clamours," we seek the good and the true. . . .

OXFORD

MORE TWENTIETH-CENTURY CLASSICS

Details of a selection of Twentieth-Century Classics follow. A complete list of Oxford Paperbacks, including The World's Classics, OPUS, Past Masters, Oxford Authors, Oxford Shakespeare, and Oxford Paperback Reference, as well as Twentieth-Century Classics, is available from the General Publicity Department, Oxford University Press (JH), Walton Street, Oxford, OX2 6DP.

In the USA, complete lists are available from the Paperbacks Marketing Manager, Oxford University Press, 200 Madison Avenue, New York, NY 10016.

Oxford Paperbacks are available from all good bookshops. In case of difficulty, please order direct from Oxford University Press Bookshop, Freepost, 116 High Street, Oxford, OX1 4BR, enclosing full payment. Please add 10 per cent of published price for postage and packing.

THE ESSENTIAL G. K. CHESTERTON
G. K. Chesterton

Introduced by P. J. Kavanagh

The extent to which G. K. Chesterton is still quoted by modern writers testifies to his outstanding importance in twentieth-century literature. In this selection from his work, P. J. Kavanagh fully explores the many sides to Chesterton's personality and writing. Chesterton the novelist is represented by a complete work, *The Man Who was Thursday,* and his poetic gift is displayed in a fine selection of verse. But the lion's share of the volume goes to Chesterton as essayist and journalist. Here we can enjoy his lively writings on the issues and debates of his day.

'Mr Kavanagh's selection is extremely rewarding.' John Gross, *Observer*

AN ERROR OF JUDGEMENT
Pamela Hansford Johnson

Introduced by A. S. Byatt

Dr William Setter exchanges his plush Harley Street consultancy for a job, unofficial and unpaid, as rehabilitator of social misfits. One such misfit is a juvenile delinquent whom he suspects of having kicked an old woman to death. Slowly becoming convinced that the boy is a callous murderer, Setter finds himself obliged to make a moral judgement, not only on the boy but on himself.

THE SMALL BACK ROOM
Nigel Balchin

Introduced by Benny Green

Sammy Rice is one of the 'back-room boys' of the Second World War. The small back room of the title may also be Sammy's own living quarters, where he tries to control a drinking habit, and lives with a woman he loves but won't marry for fear of imprisoning her in a life he sees being slowly eroded by the unreality of war.

As an account of the war experience, the book is realistic and unsettling, and as a study of a personality under stress, it reveals perennial truths. As Benny Green says, 'to the battle which Sammy Rice wages against himself no precise date can be attached. The struggle goes on.'

'His theme is of intense and irresistible interest.' *New Statesman*

C
Maurice Baring

Introduced by Emma Letley

' "In this parcel," he said, "you will find a bundle of unsorted papers. You are not to open it till I die. They contain not the story but the materials for the story of C . . . I want you to write it as a novel, not as a biography, but write it you must." '

It is from C's personal effects, passed on by his dying friend, that C the novel is finally written; no ordinary novel, as Maurice Baring says, but one in which the truth of events and personalities is rigorously observed.

Throughout his short, unhappy life C is accustomed to hiding his true feelings. Belittled by his parents, misunderstood at Eton and Oxford, and out of place at the high society functions he is obliged to attend, C acquires a reputation for secrecy. It is only after his death that the details of his private life are discovered.

IN ANOTHER COUNTRY

John Bayley

Introduced by A. N. Wilson

John Bayley's only novel explores the effect of 'the first cold winter of peace' on a group of British servicemen stationed in a small town on the Rhine. Some, like the ruthless Duncan Holt, use army life to further their own ends; while others, like the naïve Oliver Childers, must fight against their own personal defeat in the wake of national victory.

'now that you can't get "books from Boots" any more, and country lanes and democracy seem to be going the same way as "proper drains", there is every reason to savour an intelligence as extraordinary as John Bayley's, and a novel as good as this' A. N. Wilson

RICEYMAN STEPS

Arnold Bennett

Introduced by Frank Kermode

Bennett's reputation as a novelist waned after the publication of his great pre-war novels, *Anna of the Five Towns, The Old Wives' Tale,* and *Clayhanger,* but it was emphatically restored by the appearance in 1923 of *Riceyman Steps,* the story of a miserly bookseller who not only starves himself to death, but infects his wife with a passion for economy that brings her also to an untimely end.

THE DEATH OF VIRGIL

Hermann Broch

Translated by Jean Starr Untermeyer

Introduced by Bernard Levin

Broch's magnificent novel describes the poet Virgil's last hours as he questions the nature of art, and mourns the death of a civilization.

'One of the most representative and advanced works of our time . . . an astonishing performance.' Thomas Mann

'Broch is the greatest novelist European literature has produced since Joyce.' George Steiner

'One of our century's great novels.' *Sunday Times*

HIS MONKEY WIFE

John Collier

Introduced by Paul Theroux

The work of this British poet and novelist who lived for many years in Hollywood has always attracted a devoted following. This, his first novel, concerns a chimpanzee called Emily who falls in love with her owner—an English schoolmaster—and embarks on a process of self-education which includes the reading of Darwin's *Origin of Species*.

'John Collier welds the strongest force with the strangest subtlety . . . It is a tremendous and terrifying satire, only made possible by the suavity of its wit.' Osbert Sitwell

'Read as either a parody of thirties' fiction or just crazy comedy, it deserves its place as a 20th-century classic.' David Holloway, *Sunday Telegraph*

ACADEMIC YEAR

D. J. Enright

Introduced by Anthony Thwaite

Three expatriate Englishmen teaching in Egypt towards the end of King Farouk's splendid and shabby reign live through the academic year of this novel. Apostles of an alien culture, they stand somewhere between the refined English aesthetics of Shelley and T. S. Eliot and the chaotic squalor of the Alexandrian slums, trying to balance the unattainable against the irredeemable, the demands of scholarship against the dictates of reality, while making a modest living for themselves. Their consequent adventures and misadventures are either hilarious or tragic, and sometimes both. And, we suspect, as near the truth as makes no difference.

'This first novel is funny, extremely funny; it is an Alexandrian *Lucky Jim* with much more humanity and much less smart lacquer.' *Daily Telegraph*

THE VIOLINS OF SAINT-JACQUES

Patrick Leigh Fermor

Epilogue by Simon Winchester

The Violins of Saint-Jacques, originally published in 1953, is set in the Caribbean on an island of tropical luxury, European decadence, and romantic passion, and its story captures both the delicacy of high society entanglements and the unforeseen drama of forces beyond human control. Throughout, the writing is as beautiful and haunting as the sound of the violins which rises from the water and conceals the story's mystery.

'Beautiful is the adjective which comes uppermost . . . outstanding descriptive powers.' John Betjeman

FACIAL JUSTICE

L. P. Hartley

Introduced by Peter Quennell

The world is recovering from its third great conflict when Jael 97 is obliged to present herself to the Ministry of Facial Justice. She is too physically attractive to pass unnoticed in a society that denies not only beauty, but individuality of any kind. She must exchange her 'alpha' face for a 'beta' one. But Jael has a sense of pride that won't be extinguished and in this fine novel Hartley explores how she becomes both instigator and victim of a new conflict.

'That Hartley was a fine writer with a strong moral sense had already been confirmed by his *Eustace and Hilda* trilogy . . . I hesitated to prefer *Facial Justice* to the trilogy, but, on points of imagination and originality of theme, it seems to win.' Anthony Burgess

NEVER COME BACK

John Mair

Introduced by Julian Symons

Desmond Thane, hero of *Never Come Back*, is a cynical, heartless, vain, cowardly smart-alec with a flair for seductive charm, an inexhaustible capacity for deceit, and a knack of bending pokers in half. He is also a very desperate man, who finds himself pursued by the agents of a shadowy political organization bent on turning wartime uncertainty to their own advantage. Unwittingly, he becomes the prime obstacle to the success of their operations.

John Mair was one of the most promising literary figures of the 1930s, and a man whose charisma is still remembered. When first published in 1941, *Never Come Back* was immediately recognized as worthy of his promise. George Orwell saw in it the beginnings of a new kind of thriller: a powerful, politically astute burlesque. This is the first reissue for over forty years.

'Don't on any account miss *Never Come Back*—lively, exciting, and intelligent.' Maurice Richardson, *Observer*

'vigour and imagination, and humour as well as nastiness: a drink with a kick in it' *Sunday Times*

THE ROOT AND THE FLOWER

L. H. Myers

Introduced by Penelope Fitzgerald

Myers's great trilogy, is set in exotic sixteenth-century India and records a succession of dynastic struggles during the ruinous reign of Akbar the Great Mogul. It is an absorbing story of war, betrayal, intrigue, and political power, but Myers's ultimate interests lie with the spiritual strengths and weaknesses of his major characters. The book explores a multitude of discrepancies—for example between the vastness of the Indian plains and the intricacy of an ants' nest—and yet attempts subtly to balance them. Throughout the trilogy Myers persists in his aim to reconcile the near and the far. *The Root and the Flower* demonstrates both his determination and his elegance in doing so, and, it has been said, 'brought back the aspect of eternity to the English novel'.

THE DEFENCE

Vladimir Nabokov

With a Foreword by the author

This novel, by one of the twentieth century's most accomplished novelists, has attracted widespread critical acclaim but not the popular attention it deserves. All Nabokov's characteristic power and grace are much in evidence in this sad but sympathetic story of a Russian Grandmaster of chess who comes to perceive life as a great game of chess being played against him.

'Nabokov treats the theme of obsessive genius in a light comic vein with superb results.' *Birmingham Post*

'Endlessly fertile, overflowing with an energy and intelligence that converts whatever it touches to literary gold.' *Observer*

'marvellously executed, with wit and precision and a shining newness of vocabulary' *New Statesman*

'The style is dense and allusive, the intelligence vast. *Lolita* was a best seller because of its theme—a perverseness which lubricious readers gloated over while missing the beauty and intricacy of the writing. *The Defence*, less regarded, is more metaphysical and more typical of Nabokov's large talent.' Anthony Burgess

BIRD ALONE

Séan O'Faoláin

Introduced by Benedict Kiely

In late nineteenth-century Ireland Corney Crone grows up in a family marked by poverty, pride, and spoiled aspirations. The recurring theme in his own life is the Faustian one of solitude, present in the private dreams of his boyhood and the insistent independence of his manhood. In old age the note of loneliness is more dominant: he is the 'bird alone', reliving the experiences of his youth, above all the secret love for his childhood sweetheart, which began in innocence and happiness, and ended in tragedy and shame.

Everywhere the book shows a poetic mastery of its material and a deep understanding of human nature. Corney Crone's private joys and sufferings belong to a common humanity, and as we read, his experiences become ours.

TURBOTT WOLFE

William Plomer

Introduced by Laurens van der Post

When this novel first appeared in 1925 the wide critical appreciation it attracted in England was matched by the political controversy it caused in South Africa. It remains acutely relevant, and if, as Turbott Wolfe declares, 'Character is the determination to get one's own way', then history bears the marks of this book and testifies to the depth of its perception.

Plomer records the struggle of a few against the forces of prejudice and fear. The book is full of images of exploitation and atrocity. Yet it is also the love story of a man who finds beauty where others have seen only ugliness. The narrative, which never shrinks from witnessing the unforgivable, is also characterized by sensitivity and self-control, and in the end manages perhaps the most we are capable of: continuing bravery, the voice of individual affirmation.

MR BELUNCLE

V. S. Pritchett

Introduced by Walter Allen

'At twelve o'clock Mr Beluncle's brown eyes looked up, moving together like a pair of love-birds—and who were they in love with but himself?'

The imposing figure of Mr Beluncle more than fills his world. Neither his home life in the London suburbs nor his failing furniture business can contain his fantasies. He speculates in imaginary businesses and prepares to move into smart new houses he cannot possibly afford. He spends profits he has not earned. His motto is 'Give Love'. Yet as Mr Beluncle's suits become more fashionable and expensive, his wife's dresses grow shabbier, his sons are morbid or foolish, and his mistress and business partner, Mrs Truslove, desperately tries to shake off her infatuation with him. Throughout Mr Beluncle steps grandly towards financial ruin. This is his novel, and by the grace and consummate art of V. S. Pritchett, a novel not only of laughter, but also of tears, and often both at once.

THE DESIRE AND PURSUIT OF THE WHOLE

Frederick Rolfe

Introduction by A. J. A. Symons

New preface by Philip Healy

'The desire and pursuit of the whole is called love' Plato

Grahame Greene described Frederick Rolfe—better known under his *nom de plume* of 'Baron Corvo'—'a writer of genius'. *The Desire and Pursuit of the Whole* is one of Rolfe's most autobiographical novels and was written in Venice in 1909, a year of tremendous hardship when he came close to starvation. It is a masterpiece of invective—a bitter attack against almost all those around him—yet it also celebrates life and love. One of the first English novels to extol homosexuality, it was considered too subversive and libellous to publish until long after Rolfe's death, but is now ranked among the finest novels of the early twentieth century.

BEFORE THE BOMBARDMENT

Osbert Sitwell

Introduced by Victoria Glendinning

Written in 1926, *Before the Bombardment* was Osbert Sitwell's first novel, and also his favourite. It studies change, both social and psychological, when a world of obsolete values come under the bombardment of a new and harsher era. Set in an out-of-season seaside hotel, it portrays the loneliness of the few remaining guests with a masterly satiric humour.

'It is a book which you will never forget; a book which nobody else could have written; a book which will frighten you, yet hold you with the richness of its beauty and its wit.' Beverley Nichols, *Sketch*

'Few novels that I have read during the past year have given me so much pleasure . . . a nearly flawless piece of satirical writing.' Ralph Straus, *Bystander*

BELCHAMBER

Howard Sturgis

Introduced by Noel Annan

The hero of Howard Sturgis's best-known novel, *Belchamber*, published in 1904, is 'Sainty', heir to one of Britain's premier earldoms, but constitutionally unsuited to fulfil his exalted position and exploited by all around him. Both Sainty and the novel itself are, in many ways, products of their time: Victorian values are in decay as the ancient families fall before the *nouveaux riches*. Like Henry James, Sturgis maintains the outsider's perfect poise and yet writes with the insider's sense of intimacy.

'Belchamber is more than the study of a personal calamity. It is the indictment of a society.' Noel Annan

NOCTURNE

Frank Swinnerton

Introduced by Benny Green

Frank Swinnerton (1884–1982), critic and prolific novelist, was a familiar figure in the literary life of the first half of this century.

In *Nocturne*, a masterly portrayal of relationships and the way they work, Frank Swinnerton takes a romantic theme and casts it in a realistic mode. As a result his lyrical evocation of the night's changing moods is matched by its powerful insights into his characters' anxieties and jealousies as two sisters struggle to make sense of their feelings for their father, the men they love, and each other. One of the novel's admirers was H. G. Wells, who wrote of it: 'this fine work . . . ends a brilliant apprenticeship and ranks Swinnerton as Master. This is a book that will not die. It is perfect, authentic, and alive.'

KIPPS

H. G. Wells

Introduced by Benny Green

The story of Arthur Kipps, a poor, uneducated draper's assistant who inherits not only a fortune, but all the problems that a sudden elevation in social status can bring, recalls Wells's early life in the drapery trade.

'*Kipps* is the finest of H. G. Wells's deeply personal novels using his early experience in the draper's shop, an autobiographical theme explored by Benny Green in a fine introduction.'
Sunday Times